THE RAGE WAR BOOK 3

ALIEN™

— VS —

PREDATOR

ARMAGEDDON

THE RAGE WAR BOOK 3

ALIEN™
VS
PREDATOR

ARMAGEDDON

TIM LEBBON

TITAN BOOKS

ALIEN VS. PREDATOR™:
ARMAGEDDON

Print edition ISBN: 9781783296194
E-book edition ISBN: 9781783296200

Published by Titan Books
A division of Titan Publishing Group Ltd
144 Southwark Street, London SE1 0UP

First edition: September 2016
10 9 8 7 6 5 4 3 2 1

This is a work of fiction. Names, characters, places, and incidents either
are used fictitiously, and any resemblance to actual persons, living or dead,
business establishments, events, or locales is entirely coincidental.

A CIP catalogue record for this title is available from the British Library.

Printed and bound in the USA.

Did you enjoy this book?
We love to hear from our readers. Please email us at readerfeedback@
titanemail.com or write to us at Reader Feedback at the above address.

To receive advance information, news, competitions, and exclusive
offers online, please sign up for the Titan newsletter on our website
www.titanbooks.com

This one's for the NEWTs

PREDATOR : INCURSION

When Yautja attacks across the Human Sphere of space grow in frequency, Colonial Marine units are put on high alert. Soon, an invasion is feared.

Meanwhile Liliya—an android—escapes from the Rage. Originally known as the Founders, the Rage are humans who have fled beyond the Human Sphere over the course of centuries. Now led by Beatrix Maloney, they are on their way back, bearing alien-inspired technology and weapons far exceeding in their power those possessed by the Colonial Marines or Weyland-Yutani. Maloney's aim is the subjugation and control of the Human Sphere.

When Liliya flees, she carries with her a sample of their technology that might help humanity fight back. Maloney sends Alexander, one of her best generals, in pursuit.

Isa Palant is a research scientist fascinated with the Yautja. Slowly learning their language, she is almost killed in a terrorist attack on the base where she is stationed. It's one of many such attacks instigated by the Rage across the Human Sphere in preparation for their return.

Johnny Mains is leader of an Excursionist unit, a Colonial Marine outfit created to keep watch on a

Yautja habitat beyond the Sphere. When someone—or something—attacks the habitat, Mains and his crew crash-land there. What they discover is beyond belief.

The Yautja aren't invading the Human Sphere. They are fleeing an assault by weaponized Xenomorphs.

This is the army of the Rage.

At the end of Book One:

Isa Palant and Major Akoko Halley, the Colonial Marine sent to rescue her, confront the Yautja elder Kalakta and broker an unsteady peace between humans and Yautja.

Liliya, taken into custody on a Yautja ship and tortured at the hands of the warrior called Hashori, escapes with her captor when the Rage general Alexander closes in and attacks.

Lieutenant Johnny Mains and the surviving member of his crew, Lieder, are trapped on the Yautja habitat UMF 12. They have witnessed and fought the weaponized Xenomorphs, and a Rage general, Patton, is also aboard, seriously injured. Mains and Lieder have uncovered evidence of ancient human colony ships, returning from the dark depths of unexplored space. They theorize that these could be used as birthing grounds for tens of thousands more Xenomorph soldiers.

The Rage are coming...

ALIEN: INVASION

Johnny Mains and Lieder are rescued by another Excursionist unit, and they send a warning into the Human Sphere—someone or something is launching an attack with weaponized Xenomorphs, using ancient Fiennes ships as nurseries. The Rage invasion has begun.

As their forces start taking control of dropholes, their ships penetrate further and further into human space. The attacks are brutal, the Colonial Marine defenders stunned by a series of terrible defeats.

After forging an uneasy alliance with the Yautja, scientist Isa Palant is convalescing... but quickly finds herself drawn into the heart of the conflict.

Jiango and Yvette Tann, seasoned scientists with a grudge against Weyland-Yutani, find themselves hunted by indies—mercenaries hired by the Company. But the Rage War is bigger than all of them, and when Liliya lands on their space station chased by Rage general Alexander, enemies must join forces to protect her.

The Rage are sweeping through the Human Sphere, destroying all forces allied against them. Gerard Marshall, a W-Y Company man, proposes an unthinkable option— shut down all dropholes to avoid the Rage penetrating deeper into the Sphere. This will also isolate billions of humans across the frozen void of space.

It's a doomsday scenario, but as more time passes, the closer doomsday appears to be.

At the end of Book Two...

Isa Palant and the indies are taken on board a Yautja asteroid habitat, where they can study the captured Rage general together.

Mains and Lieder sacrifice themselves to destroy the *Othello*, a major blow to Beatrix Maloney and the Rage. But even this might not be enough...

Because Beatrix Maloney now plans to drop directly into Sol System and take the war to humanity's home.

1

LILIYA

Space Station Hell
November 2692 AD

I can't run forever.

Liliya sat on the bridge of the *Satan's Savior*, the large Yautja known as Hashori standing beside her, while on a holo screen in front of the viewing window she witnessed a space battle. It took place ten billion miles away, but was all because of her.

Alexander is coming for me. He follows, and follows, and always finds me again.

She had fled the Rage ship *Macbeth* on her own, leaving behind Beatrix Maloney and all her twisted, corrupted aims. Alexander had been sent in pursuit. He and his army had followed her to the edge of the Human Sphere, managing to find her small ship in the infinity of space. After she had submitted herself to the mercy of the Yautja, he had come again.

Being taken by Hashori, travelling through a drophole, even putting light years between them had not shaken him off.

Perhaps now really is the time to stand and fight.

"I need to speak with the Council," Jiango Tann said. Although not a member of Hell's governing council, he still had a responsibility to report what he knew.

"But we'll be ready to leave within the hour!" Captain Ware said. She was the leader of the small indie unit the Tanns had hired to transport Liliya to the nearest Weyland-Yutani representatives. While they were hard and brash, Liliya also sensed that the indies were very professional and good at their chosen careers.

They still did not make her feel safe.

"We can't leave now," Liliya said. "If we do, Alexander and his army will simply put a trace on us, and follow. They're too close for us to outrun them, and even if we could…" She trailed off.

"Even if we could?" Yvette Tann asked.

"I've outrun him before," Liliya said. "He always finds me again."

Jiango looked her up and down, as if searching for whatever the Rage general might be using to track her through trillions of miles of cold, empty space. But it was nothing visible. She suspected it had something to do with what she had stolen—injecting it into her veins had been the best way to carry the alien-inspired technology away from the Rage. In doing so, perhaps she had doomed herself.

She saw the Tanns' shoulders drooping as realization hit home.

"Here, then," Jiango said. "This is the best place to stand and fight."

"Yes," Liliya said. "Especially now that the Yautja have arrived."

"And who's to say those fuckers are here to help?" one of the crew said. It was Robo, the woman with the mechanical arm.

"Hashori does," Liliya said.

Robo looked back at the Yautja, dwarfing them all on the ship's bridge. The mistrust in her eyes was obvious.

"And how do any of us know what that thing really wants?" Robo asked.

The indie was right. The Yautja was unreadable. Liliya had suffered terribly beneath Hashori's hands, and her android skin still bore scars and wounds from that period of sustained, vicious torture.

Yet Hashori had also saved her, accompanying her to this space station when she knew very well what the reception would be like.

The Yautja watched Robo, eyes narrowed, tusks flexing slightly as she perceived what might be an enemy. She tightened the grip on her battle spear.

"We have to trust it," Jiango said. "You've allowed it onto your ship. Do you really want to pick a fight now?"

"The true fight's out there," Liliya said. Her voice was low, but it caught their attention. "The Rage are coming. They'll be unrelenting, unstoppable, and they perceive me as a threat. Otherwise they'd have never sent Alexander and his army to bring me back. That wasn't just wounded pride on Maloney's part. As for the Yautja, they're here to help. We have to trust that. It won't be long until Alexander is close enough to launch an attack."

"So those are your friend's companions out there, the Yautja, engaging the enemy in battle ten billion miles away?" Ware asked.

Liliya asked Hashori, speaking in her native tongue. They all looked at the Yautja warrior, and she nodded. It seemed like an unfamiliar gesture, her effort to use the most basic form of human communication.

"You'll be safer on the station," Jiango said.

"She's safer on the *Satan's Savior*!" Ware said. "Who

knows what this Alexander character is going to open up with? One direct hit from a big nuke or particle modulator, and the station's toast. At least on board with us, you'll stand a chance of getting away."

"I need to meet with the Council," Jiango said again. "Warn them."

"Then warn them," Ware said. She nodded toward Liliya. "You told us how precious she is. Seems to me she's the priority in all of this."

The priority, Liliya thought. She looked at the Tanns, man and wife, and their pain was obvious—because they knew it was true.

The space station Hell, the place they had called home for so long, might well be doomed, yet it was absolutely essential that Liliya avoid capture.

"Be back before they arrive," Ware said to Jiango. "Seriously. I won't wait for you."

"I don't expect you to," Jiango said. He stood, still clasping his wife's hand.

"Once they attack, there'll be chaos," Ware said. She was still watching the battle on the holo screen. Even from this vast distance, their sensors picked up nuclear blooms and dazzling arcs of laser fire. It was difficult to tell who was who—Rage, Yautja, or whoever else might have joined the fight—and impossible to make out any victors. The losers were obvious, however, flowering into brief, dazzling plumes of radioactive gas before fading into the darkness of space. "Confusion. The smoke of battle. That's when we'll get away."

"Running from a fight, boss?" another of the indies asked.

Ware glared at him, then smiled. "Probably toward a bigger one, Millard."

Probably, Liliya thought. *There's no probably about it.*

"I reckon you've got an hour," Yvette Tann said to her husband. "Make it count."

He kissed her cheek, then looked across the bridge at Liliya. His smile was supposed to convey hope, but she saw only pain. That was her fault. She'd come here and caused all of this.

The true pain hadn't even begun.

While Jiango was gone, Liliya watched the battle playing out on the holo screen. Hashori remained standing beside her, and Yvette Tann sat on her other side. The indie crew busied themselves preparing for flight and running diagnostics on their weapon systems.

There was a terrible inevitability to events. While each new explosion or slice of laser fire brought a gasp or comment from one of the crew, Liliya knew what it meant—Alexander was getting closer. Whatever force he had come up against along the way, it would be brushed aside, destroyed, blown to atoms, and then he would storm in closer and bring violence to Hell.

From the bridge's port window she could see part of the graceful superstructure of Hell and one of its long docking arms, several ships hanging there like seed pods on a giant stalk. There were so many people here, and all of them were in danger because of her.

Despite that, she was firm in the belief that she was doing this to save people. She carried knowledge that might combat the Rage. She already knew from Hashori that the Yautja had suffered great losses, and she and Hashori had witnessed first-hand what had become of one drophole and its attendant control station. Its fate must have been echoed across the Sphere, and perhaps even now she was too late.

In truth, *she* was not the priority. What she carried was the priority. That was all that mattered.

The traces of distant battle began to fade from the screen, and Ware and her crew seemed suddenly more anxious than ever.

Hashori shifted by her side. "I should be out there in my ship," she said. Five of her Yautja companions were circling Hell several hundred miles out. Their arrival had probably caused the space station to move to combat status, but their attention was aimed outward, not inward. They were readying themselves for the enemy's arrival. Fresh from battle, the general and his army would be ready for a fight.

"Thank you for staying with me," Liliya said.

"What's happening?" Yvette asked.

"Looks like your husband's got influence," Ware said. "Hell's defenses have all gone hot. Nuke drones have launched, several combat craft are firing up. Couple of ships have done a runner, but the bulk of the station is preparing for an attack."

"How close are they?" Yvette asked.

"They might be here within an hour," Ware said. "Computer's crunching data, should give us some indication of strength."

"One big ship, with associated attack craft," Liliya said. "Alexander's flagship is a construct of the Faze, powerful and fast, built for war. His attack ships will be sleeker than the Yautja craft, and more heavily armed."

"What's a Faze?" Yvette asked.

"It's…" Liliya trailed off. She had no idea how to explain the things they had found on that faraway alien habitat.

"Hubby's back," Hoot said. Another of the indie crew, he was a short, solid man oozing danger.

The bridge door whispered open and Jiango entered. Yvette stood, and for a few seconds silence hung heavy as the couple hugged each other. Maybe a part of them had believed they'd never see each other again.

"So?" Ware asked.

"They've been watching," Jiango said. "They're ready to fight."

"For me," Liliya said.

"No," Jiango said. "For themselves! They're defending Hell, and I've told them we'll do everything we can to help."

Ware sighed heavily. "Make up your fucking mind, Pops. You want us to run and save her? Stay behind and fight?"

"I've thought of a way we can do both," Jiango said. He glanced at the holo screen, dark and filled with infinity now that the distant battle was over. Then he looked directly at Hashori, and asked Liliya to translate. "Listen. We don't have long."

When the attack came, it was fast and furious.

General Alexander pulled his main ship out of warp just a million miles from Hell, powering in on sub-warp engines and unleashing a barrage of nukes at the ships circling the station. Seven craft had taken off to defend the large structure.

The nukes carved unseen lines through space and then exploded, glaring in bright, sparkling blooms before fading again. One of them took out a salvage ship too slow to pull away, but the other ships ducked and weaved through the fading glows of destruction.

"Where're his attack ships?" Liliya asked.

"I'm guessing they're the main surprise," Ware said.

Jiango had given her the access codes for Hell's mainframe, providing them a complex, in-depth picture of the assault. She shifted the views visible on the bridge's three main holo screens, and pointed one of them away into the void behind where the main attack had been centered.

Sure enough, within seconds several sparks of light pulsed, as a slew of small ships dropped out of warp.

"And there they are."

"Now?" Robo asked.

"Just a few more seconds," Ware said. "If what the old man said is true..."

"It's our best bet," Jiango said.

"He's not *that* old!" Yvette said. If it was a brave attempt at humor it fell flat.

"Holy shit, what *is* that thing?" Millard asked. Alexander's main attack ship filled one of the smaller holo screens, slowing as it approached Hell, sparkling as it spat countermeasures to lure away the missiles and laser cannon blasts being fired at it. Liliya tried to imagine what it was like, seeing a ship like this for the first time. Vast, glowing a soft pink like the insides of some huge creature, the ship rolled and spun as it came onward, deflecting laser blasts and firing off its own weapons like seeds flung to the night.

"The Faze made that," Liliya said. She frowned, trying to think of a way to explain so much in so little time. But there *was* no way, so she left it.

Another defending ship was struck and pulverized to nothing, and then Ware spoke into her throat mike.

"Hell, this is *Satan's Savior*, attack ships closing from sector six-six. We're engaging."

"What?" Yvette snapped.

Ware did not respond. Her crew didn't question her statement, and in a matter of seconds they dropped from their docking arm and Hell fell away below and behind them. Ahead seemed to be empty space.

It quickly filled up.

"Hoot?" Ware said.

"Already on it." The ship shuddered as an array of their weapons opened up. Laser blasts streamed into the night, three nukes burned through the darkness, and a pulsing purple light seemed to sparkle as it zigged and zagged ahead of the ship, like the probing fingers of a blind giant. A nuke exploded as it struck one opponent. Another ship caught fire and started spinning, rolling toward and then over them when Ware shifted their course slightly.

The other ordnance expended itself in empty space.

"Two down," Hoot said. "The other three craft bypassed us and are closing on Hell."

"Oh, no," Jiango said. Liliya saw him and his wife holding hands, and she wished for someone who might give her comfort. She glanced sidelong at Hashori. The Yautja had placed her helmet on her head—it was scarred by ancient battles. She was inscrutable.

"Okay, one more swing around and then we'll hit it," Ware said. "Hoot, you ready?"

"Yeah."

"You'll have maybe three seconds."

"More than enough."

"Liliya, you ready?"

"Of course." She grasped the communicator that had been handed to her earlier. She had no idea what she was going to say. It didn't really matter.

Ware swung the ship around in a tight arc until Hell became visible in the center of the main holo screen. Liliya was surprised at how far away they'd come. Her heart sank as she saw that the station was already taking hits.

Alexander's flagship was close, and she could see

countless specks flowing from the ship toward the station, like seed pods floating on an invisible wind. Explosions sparked all around as Hell's defenders struggled to fight off the terrible assault, but they were ineffective. Once the surviving attack ships arrived, the increase in weapons fire was brief and terrible.

"What are they?" Yvette asked. No one responded. Liliya had told them what soldiers Alexander would be bringing with him.

"We should have stayed," Jiango said. "We could fight them, all of us, every one of us would have made a difference."

"Only she can make a difference," Yvette said, but she didn't look back at Liliya, as if she could hardly face seeing her. Instead she buried her face against her husband's neck.

"Liliya," Ware said.

Liliya activated the communicator.

"Alexander," she said. "You call yourself a general? You've lost me again."

"Okay," Ware said. She stroked her control panel and Hell slipped down and to the left of the screen, quickly shrinking and then disappearing as their powerful engines pushed them away at a proportion of light speed. The warp drive cycled up but did not yet activate. They had all agreed that they would take any chance they could to halt Alexander's pursuit, for good.

"We've left them to their fate," Yvette said. "All of them, everyone on Hell."

"They can fight," Jiango said.

Liliya thought of saying something, but decided it was best to remain silent. She knew what the inhabitants of Hell would now be facing. She knew that they had no chance at all. Vocalizing that would help no one.

"They're coming," Millard said.

"How many?" Ware asked.

"All of them. The big ship and three remaining attack craft."

"They've abandoned their assault," Hoot said, glancing back at the Tanns as if offering some hope. Then he caught Liliya's eye and his face fell.

"Hope your friend's friends are still there," Ware said.

"They are," Liliya replied. "Alexander will see them before we do."

"Good, because he's closing fast. Millard, keep the warp engines cycling up, and get ready to jump to warp on my signal."

"We can't jump until—" Liliya began, but the captain cut in.

"If the Yautja don't appear in the next six seconds, we're jumping the fuck away from here."

A cool silence descended over the bridge, interrupted only by soft warning chimes and buzzes from various instruments, and the distant, constant hum of the *Satan's Savior*'s powerful engines.

If we jump, he'll keep looking until he finds me again, Liliya thought. *Hashori's ship... Hell how many more people will I doom?* In her centuries of existence she had worked hard at being as human as possible, but right then she would have traded humanity for the cool, calm, guilt-free mind of a committed android.

"There!" Hoot said. "There, look, beautiful, *beautiful*!"

The view behind them was projected onto the main holo screen, and they all gasped at what came next.

Alexander's pursuing flagship was suddenly set aflame by a dozen explosions, each one of them throwing out spears of light which seemed to curve around and punch into the ship again, and again. The explosions pulsed, flare after flare crawling across and around the vessel. The attack ships with it were destroyed, as well, and then flashing across the screen they saw the brief, wonderful trace of a Yautja ship.

Uncloaked, fully weaponized, it and its four companions swung around to unleash another volley against the Rage vessel.

"Direct hit!" Millard shouted.

"Don't celebrate just yet," Liliya said.

"The Yautja triumph," Hashori said in her own tongue, and Liliya did not reply.

Perhaps, she thought. *Maybe we really have beaten him at last.*

Born from the conflagration that Alexander's ship had become, a laser speared out and one of the Yautja craft disintegrated into nothing.

A gasp went around the bridge.

"Nothing could have survived that," Hoot said.

The Yautja attacked again, nukes and eon pulses brighter than any sun pounding into the spinning ball of flame and destruction, explosions bursting out, glaring, blooming large on the screen.

No more responding fire blasted outward, and eventually the flames and glow began to recede. They left behind a shattered, floating remnant. The corpse of Alexander's ship spun slowly, parts of it peeling off, some wreckage moving with it.

"Done," Ware said. "Rather them than me." She glanced over her shoulder at Hashori and nodded. The warrior did not acknowledge the gesture.

"Hell," Jiango said.

"You know we can't go back," Yvette said. "Whatever's happening on Hell, it's their story now. We can't risk Liliya, not after all this."

Liliya heard the conversation but did not respond. She was concentrating on the wreckage of Alexander's ship. The Yautja circled it, and two of their ships edged closer. Perhaps they sought a trophy of their kill. The huge ruined vessel still glowed from nuclear fires burning within, and she tried to grasp onto the knowledge that she was finally free.

Maloney, I have escaped you at last, she thought. She only wished she could have sent the idea as a transmission, directly into that madwoman's head.

2

GENERAL MASHIMA

Various Dropholes—Gamma Quadrant,
November 2692 AD

Before the start of each day, General Mashima took time to kneel and worship his god.

In his cabin on board the *Aaron-Percival*, he first took a silent moment to prepare himself for the transmission. Never a vain android, still he always insisted on ensuring that he was presentable, before his messages were sent back to Mistress Maloney. He was alive because of her, after all. He existed because she had allowed that existence, and deemed it necessary. She was the nearest thing he had to a mother, and if a mother could not be thought of as a god, then what could?

His cabin was small and sparse. It contained a comfortable chair, a comms point, and a full-length mirror on one wall. Mashima never slept, but from time to time he spent periods in his chair, contemplating his mission and ensuring that everything was going according to plan.

Now he stood before the mirror and checked his appearance.

His uniform was smooth and sharp, perfectly fitted and immaculately cut. His face was unblemished and plain. Mashima recognized himself in the mirror, but he was also aware that the face could have belonged to anyone. It was a functional visage, with little character.

I provide the character, Mashima thought. He smiled. The creases across his cheeks looked like deep cuts in his skin.

He had been in existence for almost fifty years. His birthing was clouded in his memory banks, a period of time when his physical self was settling and being serviced, and his mind was uploaded and expanded by Maloney and her Rage scientists. There was no one time that he could recall as his first memory, but rather a growing awareness that had expanded into everything he was to become.

In those cloudy, then clearing visions, Beatrix Maloney was always there.

He and his android companions—some of them generals, others lesser creations that were used around *Macbeth* or in some of its escorting attack craft—were all given choice and the ability to grow, and all of them regarded Maloney as their one and true superior. Mashima didn't know whether that was a programming function created by an insecure leader, or a natural conclusion of their free will.

If the former, then that same programming would never yield the truth. So he assumed the latter.

His greatest wish was to serve Maloney and the Rage to his best ability, or die in the attempt. Little else mattered. The Rage's aims were his own, although they were of secondary importance to pleasing and obeying his mistress.

Mashima had been sent on a mission of great

importance, and every moment of his existence was spent preparing for its success.

He signaled the bridge and spoke to their communications officer.

"Jacobs, I'm ready to compose."

"Thank you, General. Systems online, ready now."

Alone in his cabin, Mashima stood before the comms point and recorded a situation update.

"Mistress Maloney, I'm pleased to tell you that our progress is good," he said. "Seven days after leaving you, we passed through drophole Gamma 123. It had already been taken by General Rommel, so our passage was unhindered. Sixteen days after that, we approached Gamma 114. This drophole was controlled from a nearby moon and guarded by a contingent of Colonial Marines. I sent three of my six attack ships to neutralize the marines guarding the hole, while I took the *Aaron-Percival* into orbit about the moon.

"Resistance was heavy, but no match for our soldiers. We lost more than a hundred Xenomorphs, but no ships and no Rage personnel. Success was complete. We dropped a day later, and currently we are approaching Gamma 98. Sensors indicate that it's controlled from an orbiting station and also guarded by independent military contractors. With no Colonial Marines present, the engagement might take on a new, interesting perspective. I'm looking forward to another fight, and fully expect success within the next two hours.

"At current progress I anticipate two more drops and arrival at Weaver's World within eighteen days. Then my true mission will begin. We are preparing for our arrival, and following our taking of Gamma 98 I'll conduct a full inspection of troop preparation.

"For the glory of the Rage, I serve you, Mistress." He

paused, feeling the need to express some deeper form of love and devotion. But he knew that Mistress Maloney would not wish that. She'd see it as weakness in his android psyche. Duty and dedication to the mission were enough. Instead, he deactivated the recording device before saying, "My heart and soul to you, Mistress."

Mashima's room fell silent. A green glow from the comms point indicated that his message had been stored, and he knew that Jacobs would be preparing it for a sub-space transmission.

"Send it immediately," he said.

"Yes, General."

"And have Kilmister meet me on the bridge."

"He's already here."

"Good. I'm on my way."

Mashima disconnected the comms, checked himself one more time in the mirror, and then left his small, empty room.

It was time for another fight.

Kilmister was waiting for him on the large bridge. Several other shipborn Rage members were settled in front of the range of control points, although the *Aaron-Percival* essentially flew itself.

Jacobs kept track of comms between the ship and the six attack craft that accompanied it, and other persons assessed ship systems, navigation, and troop and weapons readiness. There really was little for them all to do. The Faze had taken this centuries-old human Fiennes ship and adjusted and adapted, reworked and rebuilt, forging it into an advanced weapon of war.

No one who had originally built or flown the craft would recognize it now. On the outside, functional sleekness had given way to strange shapes and protrusions that lent it the impression of being grown, rather than built. On the inside, most control systems had been removed or upgraded, and its warp drive and fuel systems were beyond Mashima's understanding.

He didn't *need* to understand. Self-maintaining, self-repairing, the ship was almost a living thing, and they were its passengers.

"General," Kilmister said, nodding. He was another shipborn, but older than most, approaching a century and as eager for war as ever. Scarred and marked by various combats down through the decades, Kilmister was the Rage's greatest human commander. Being human, he wasn't graced with an android's capability of controlling the Xenomorph army they carried in the *Aaron-Percival*'s vast holds. Instead he was a pilot, and commander of the six attack craft all flying within a thousand miles of Mashima's flagship.

"Captain. Are all preparations in place?"

"Of course. I'm ready to give the order, on your command. Gamma 98 doesn't appear to have noticed our approach. By the time they do the station's defenses will be out of action, and you can land your troops."

Mashima nodded and looked around the bridge.

"General…" Kilmister said, trailing off.

"Captain? If there's something on your mind, you should speak it."

"I'd like to lead the attack."

Mashima raised an eyebrow. "Of course you would." He smiled. "And of course, you should."

Kilmister nodded once. "Thank you."

"Make me proud, Captain."

Kilmister hurried from the bridge, and Mashima took his place on the large circular platform at its center.

From there he could see everything—the entire bridge, an array of viewing screens, and broadcast views from each of the six attack craft. A few minutes after Kilmister departed the bridge, three attack ships peeled off and accelerated away, skipping through skeins of hyperspace and disappearing from view.

Fifty minutes later the screens brightened again, and a magnified image brought drophole Gamma 98 in close. The familiar circle of the hole's material construct caught starlight and set it aflame, and a hundred miles away the orbiting space station—its point of control, and their target for the day—came alive. Several small, sleek craft launched from its docking bays, and a larger battleship parted from the base and began deploying an array of advanced weaponry.

It must have been ready for an attack. A number of dropholes had already been taken by the Rage, and before that there had been sporadic attacks from Yautja elements fleeing the Rage's approach to the Human Sphere. Kilmister and his pilots were prepared for some resistance, but there was no way of knowing just how fierce it would be.

Just for a moment, Mashima was worried.

The battle was brief, fierce, and confused. Views from each of the Rage attack ships danced and swung, stars smearing across the screens as explosions burst into brief, dazzling suns. Laser fire mirrored the star effect. Shuddering impacts blurred the images.

Mashima stood and squeezed the handrail that circled his observation platform. The threat of failure—the mere *idea* of it—rarely touched his mind, and perhaps blind confidence was one of his faults. But in his years serving the Rage, failure had never been considered a possibility. He believed that made him strong. Perhaps in truth it made him naive.

The view from one of the Rage attack ships brightened momentarily, holo screen crackling with the power of its illumination. Then it went blank, and the screen folded away.

"Is that a ship lost?" Mashima asked. No one on the bridge responded. They were checking, and it took a few moments for Jacobs to confirm ship-to-ship communications.

"One ship down," he confirmed. "General, there are Yautja ships defending that space station, as well as mercenaries."

"Yautja?" That didn't worry him, because they'd confronted and defeated Yautja elements several times over the past few decades. But it did surprise him.

The space station suddenly grew huge on one of the screens as Kilmister took his ship in close. A barrage of laser fire took out a docking arm, the sudden explosion and decompression setting the station into a complex spin.

The battle continued. Data streams ran above Jacobs' control point, but Mashima kept his eyes on the displays, frank and honest representations of the confusion and chaos of battle.

The large enemy battleship took a direct hit from a Rage eon blast, its superstructure immediately beginning to melt and flow as its subatomic structure was disrupted. The effect's spread was immediate and unstoppable. Some of its ordnance must have been detonated as a last-ditch attempt to take out more enemies, but it only resulted in a spectacular, almost beautiful blast that expanded over a dozen miles, bright yellow and white at its center, red and purple further out, like a rapidly developing bruise on the canvas of infinity.

Mashima's concern bled away after that, and for the rest of the battle he enjoyed watching the consummate skill and effectiveness of the Rage pilots, ships, and advanced weaponry.

It took fifteen minutes.

"Station is secure," Kilmister said from his remote position. "All mobile defenses destroyed, station's weapon arrays out of action. Sensors indicate over a hundred survivors on board. I'm about to match the station's spin, and then land troops."

"Good work, Captain," Mashima said. "Send those troops immediately. We don't want the drophole damaged in any way, or deactivated."

This was the moment Mashima had been waiting for. The moment when he watched his children work.

They floated through space. Fired by brief pulses of air that pushed them from the attack craft, more than a hundred Xenomorphs drifted quickly between the ships and the space station, unfurling themselves as soon as they landed, skittering across the surface, seeking entry. Some of them crept in through the destroyed portions of the docking arm and various blasted weapons arrays, while others sought hatches and windows and forced entry that way.

In several places trapped bubbles of atmosphere burst outward as seals were broken, and here and there struggling humans were visible as they were pushed away from the structure.

Even with the thousands of miles between them, Mashima could feel each and every Xenomorph linked to him, sense their fury and excitement, and he channeled his feelings to instruct and encourage them all. They knew their mission—to board the vessel, hunt, and kill. As he closed his eyes and allowed his senses to join more fully with their own, the scope of his surroundings began to fade, and his awareness opened up. Hot and cold no longer registered, movement and stillness became facets of the same state of being. He was no longer simply a faux human.

He was Xenomorph.

The slaughter ended quickly. Once they penetrated the station, there was little resistance. Most people on board had already died due to explosive decompression, and those who had managed to slip on suits were quickly overcome by the Xenomorph hordes. Suits were torn and tattered, oxygen escaping in clouds of diamond-ice. Blood sprayed, freezing into dark globes in the airless confines. Soon, the only living things left on the station were those deadly Rage soldiers.

"The station is secure," Kilmister said.

"Yes," Mashima said. "I know. We'll be there imminently. Withdraw the troops, take a defensive orbit." He drew back into himself and initiated an open channel. "All crews, prepare for a drop within the next fifteen hours."

Mashima looked around the bridge, pleased at another successful engagement. The loss of an attack ship was troubling, especially as they still had another drop to make after this one, and then the approach to Weaver's World might be heavily defended.

"General Mashima to Berlioz," he said. "I'm coming down to the birthing hold."

"Of course, General," the woman responded. Behind her soft voice he heard the sounds of soldiers being born.

Screams. Cracking, tearing. A cry.

Sometimes, Mashima needed nothing more than to welcome a new group of offspring into existence.

* * *

Berlioz met him in the entrance area leading to the birthing hold. This was one of three massive holds on board the *Aaron-Percival*, each of them filled with thousands of humans who had been kept in cryo-sleep for centuries. Their story was an incredible one and, if Mashima had been prone to periods of introspection, probably a sad one, too. However, although he could understand the tragedy in their fate, any sense of sadness was smothered beneath the glory of what they were enabling, what their sleeping bodies were hosting, and what they birthed.

These bodies had been sealed within cryo-pods many centuries before anyone now alive was born—even Mistress Maloney, ancient though she was in human terms. Without them, the Rage could not fulfil their destiny.

Sent out from home to inhabit the stars, these explorers were returning to Earth with death nestled beneath their ribs, among their organs. Glorious, wondrous death.

"General, I hear we're another step closer," Berlioz said. A strange woman, more comfortable alone with her sleeping charges than with anyone else. Mashima found communicating with her awkward. He'd once asked Jacobs whether it was because he was an android, and the response had surprised him—a laugh, and then an admission that she was like this with everyone.

"*She's less human than you, General.*"

"We're dropping soon," Mashima said. "I just came to look."

"To look," Berlioz said. Her constant, cool smile twitched just a little.

"Things are going well?" he asked.

"*Very* well," she said. "Better than… ever."

An awkward silence. Then Mashima said, "I'd like to see."

"Of course!" Berlioz stood aside from the doorway and gestured for him to enter, glancing away as her smile dropped. Mashima understood. It was obvious. These holds were Berlioz's domain, and anyone else paying a visit was an intruder. Even him.

"I never dreamed it could be so wonderful," she said. "I never expected to be birthing so many at once and… it's glorious. I haven't slept for three days. There's *so much* to do!"

Mashima stepped onto a floating platform that stood beside the door and urged it aloft. Berlioz stepped on with him, and when they were drifting closer to the ceiling than the floor, he looked out on her work. She was right. There was so much being done.

Their impending assault on Weaver's World would require every Xenomorph they could birth, and Berlioz was taking her task seriously. The hold had become a production line of birth and death, and until the start of this mission Mashima had never before witnessed it happening on such a scale.

To his left were the hosts, row upon row of pale, slick humans, naked and still gleaming with cryo-gel. Their pods were kept in one of the adjacent holds. When the occupants were removed, they were sent through on a suspension field, bobbing softly as they nudged against the pile of sleepers that lay ahead of them. All were still in cryo-sleep, though some were shifting slowly, limbs flexing, stomachs sucked in as their organs regained function and their brains slowly, slowly began to rise from the deepest, longest slumber any of them had ever experienced.

Few of them were given the chance to wake fully.

While in their pods, they had each been impregnated with a Xenomorph embryo. Now those were waking, too.

Below and in front of where Mashima and Berlioz

hovered lay the birthing zone. It was a wide area cleared long ago when the ship first was captured and its sleeping denizens harvested, its basement structures readjusted and molded by the Faze. As the pre-programmed suspension field drew individual sleepers into the space, hovering robot drones directed subtle charges down into their chest cavities. Each gentle hiss galvanized the sleepers closer to full wakefulness and, more importantly, urged the creatures they carried out toward the air, and the light.

Nine times out of ten, the birthing happened before the host was truly awake.

Just occasionally, some of them opened their eyes.

Mashima watched as several Xenomorphs were born each minute. The withered human bodies shook and shivered as ribs were smashed from the inside, chests stretching and then ripping open, bloody flowers splattering across the red-soaked floor. Some of them groaned, and one or two of them screamed before dying. The sound was a constant background symphony to the wonderful moment of birth.

Sighing, groaning, cracking, ripping, screaming, gasping, dying… and then the gentle squeals of the newborn, given to the world at last.

Mashima *felt* their arrival. Already impregnated with the controlling nanotechnology that linked every one of these Xenomorphs to him, they came into the world his servants, his soldiers. Some of them even seemed to turn his way as if sensing him, and perhaps that was the case.

"My children," he whispered, and he was not shocked when Berlioz echoed that sentiment.

The Xenomorph young were gathered by a larger floating drone and transported across the hold to the raising pens that lay beyond, hidden away in those dark, damp places where the beasts would rapidly grow to their full forms. These individual, bubble-shaped spaces were designed to grow with their occupants, constantly providing nutrients. Once they reached their full size, the Xenomorphs would receive the branding on their exoskeleton that marked them as belonging to him.

"How many so far?" he asked.

"Since leaving the *Macbeth*, I have birthed almost seven thousand," Berlioz said.

"Yes," Mashima said. "I feel the power of them. Strong. Healthy."

"Of course they are," she said. "I look after them, and feed them well."

Mashima could hear the food being made. After birthing, the dead humans were flushed down through vents in the floor and into great mixing vats below. There, grinders and then blenders did their work, crushing and mixing the remains into a stew that was supplemented with vitamins and then pumped through to the raising pens. Nothing was wasted.

"I want four thousand more by the time we arrive," Mashima said.

"General, I intend to complete all birthing within the next fifteen days."

Mashima raised an eyebrow.

"Another twelve thousand," she added. "An army sixteen thousand strong."

"All under my command," Mashima said. He closed his eyes and briefly considered the future, waves of Xenomorphs flowing across the surface of Weaver's World and killing anything, *everything* in their path.

It was glorious.

It was red.

3

ISA PALANT

Gamma Quadrant
December 2692 AD

The most surprising thing about the Yautja asteroid base was that so much of it was familiar.

We always believed they used other alien tech to create and expand their own, Isa Palant thought. *This pretty much proves us right.* Within the asteroid, with the massive landing bay doors closed, they could have been inside any large Colonial Marine base. Carved out of the body of the asteroid, the cavern was huge. Lighting systems hung from ceilings and walls, as well as monitoring equipment and grappling arms, and several ships were moored at various points around the large space.

This was where the similarity to a Marine base ended, because these were so obviously Yautja ships. While no two were exactly alike, there were common features and designs with which Isa had become more *au fait* over the years—the deep gray coloring, sleek, fish-like designs to aid cloaking, weapon blisters on the ships' hull instead of inside, always ready to be deployed.

There were databases in Weyland-Yutani quantum folds where any known examples of Yautja vessels were recorded and stored, from the basic appearance of those imaged from afar, to composite makeup and the macro and micro features of those few that had been captured or partly destroyed. Isa had never trusted the Company record to be complete, or fully open to outside inquiry, so years ago she had started her own fold.

Her fascination lay with their biology, society, and language, but these were inextricably bound to their technical and martial aspects. She suspected that she carried more Yautja information in her private quantum fold than anyone else in the Human Sphere.

If she so wished, she knew that fold could be expanded hugely in the coming days.

"Fuck me," Bestwick said.

"All things considered, I'd really rather not," Sprenkel responded.

"Yeah. I'm out of your league."

"Look over there," Huyck said. He was still in the *Pixie*'s pilot's seat, but their ship had been surrounded by a suspension field, and they were slowly being drawn toward one edge of the large cavern.

"Welcoming committee," Huyck said. "Don't like that, boss. Not one bit."

"I think it's too late to think about what we like," Major Akoko Halley said.

Palant's stomach performed somersaults while the gravity fluctuated. The *Pixie*'s artificial gravity had been slowly reduced on their approach to the asteroid, on the assumption that a body so large—forty miles across at its widest point—would maintain some degree of pull.

However, the Yautja base itself used gravitational augmentation, and upon passing through the hangar doors they shifted through the effects of this field. She closed her eyes and tried to swallow down the queasiness. She hadn't suffered from space sickness for a while. But then, until the recent destruction of her laboratory and the deaths of her friends, she'd hardly been away from solid ground in more than a decade.

As the *Pixie* approached a ledge in the rock, and the docking facility protruding from there, the ship's computer, Billy, chimed in.

"All my sensors have been blocked. Communications arrays disabled, life and movement detectors jammed. We're blind."

"For now," Palant said.

"Maybe they just want the ship," Sprenkel said. "Fuck, this is Gerard Marshall's personal craft, one of the most advanced in the fleet. Have we just delivered *Pixie* to the enemy?"

"We never even considered that," Huyck said. He glared back at Palant. "We let *her* steer us, and now we've gone AWOL. We're in the belly of the fucking beast and—"

"You're the one who stabbed Gerard Marshall's man to death," Palant said softly. The murder was still fresh and terrible in her mind. She'd believed McIlveen to be her friend, but he'd threatened them all, ready to take control of the ship and fly them back to the Company.

The tattered android they had on board was filled with knowledge and tech the Company would kill for, and McIlveen had threatened to do just that.

Instead, they'd killed him.

"This is a decision we *all* made," Halley said. Her troops called her Snow Dog, because sometimes she seemed cold. Not now, though. Now, she was fired up and angry. "We're all in the same mess here, whatever it is. Infighting won't help." She stared at Palant. "I trust Isa to see us through this. We *all* have to trust her. She's done it before."

Palant nodded.

The ship juddered slightly as it docked, and then the sense of rolling calmed as the gravitational field settled. Silence fell.

Palant unstrapped and walked back through to the rec room. It was here they'd kept the android, strapped securely to the wall. None of them wanted it on the bridge where it could observe them, but they needed it where they could keep an eye on it.

She'd stood over the thing many times during their twelve-day journey to the asteroid. Vacuum-wrapped in a clear plastic storage bag, the android's torn and broken body was curled in on itself, one arm almost detached and crushed across its chest, one leg shredded and pale like a fish's half-eaten corpse. White fluid seeped and bubbled against the tensioned surface of the tight bag. Its hair was flat, each filament clearly defined. When they'd originally packed it like this, one eye had been pressed against the bag, half-crushed yet still swiveling in its socket.

Watching, wet, sickeningly intelligent.

A day after McIlveen's death, Halley had pasted a med patch across the eye and shut it from view. Now, Palant grabbed the edge of the patch and tugged, ripping it away from the bag, standing back.

The eye stared directly at her, pupil shrinking beneath the sudden light.

She stared back.

"Time to find out what you know," she said.

Something happened to the eye. Crushed as it was, expression should have been impossible. Yet Palant was certain that somehow, in some way, the damaged android had found a way to smile.

* * *

There were three Yautja waiting for them out on the ledge beyond the docking structure. Palant recognized one of them as the creature that had handed them the android aboard the crippled Rage ship *Cooper-Jordan*. It did not acknowledge them in any way, even when Bestwick and Sprenkel pushed the android out on a suspension field.

One of the others was shorter, but thicker-set. The third was tall and thin, heavily armored, and carrying an old Marine pulse rifle, toy-like in its left hand. All three wore their helmets, marked and scarred with the traces of old battles.

They also wore trophies on belts and garlands. Polished skulls, mummified hands, teeth and claws, and leathery remains that were unidentifiable.

One of the skulls was human.

Halley and the others were looking to Palant, and she felt the awful weight of expectation. Her human companions depended on her to communicate with the Yautja. The Yautja seemed to be waiting for her to speak.

In her left hand she carried the old datapad that she and McIlveen had been using to build a translation program for the Yautja language. Now it was just her. Even after what he had done, she felt McIlveen's absence.

"So we're just going to stand here?" Bestwick asked.

Palant started typing. She kept the words and expression simple, in the hope that the translation would make sense to the Yautja standing before her.

"We were told to follow you here." The datapad clicked and groaned in its Yautja impersonation. "What happens next?"

The three Yautja shifted a little, heads tilted. The one

they'd met on *Cooper-Jordan* half-turned, and then looked back at them.

"I think it's waiting for us to follow," Palant said.

They followed. The other two Yautja brought up the rear, and it felt strange leaving the *Pixie* behind. The ship had brought them across many light years of space, and Palant had grown used to feeling its protective hull around her. Even the humorless ship's computer, Billy had made an impression upon her.

She had never felt so exposed.

They followed the Yautja into tunnels formed through the solid rock of the asteroid. They were lined with lights and service routes, the walls and floors rough, and soon there were other tunnels leading off left and right, up and down.

"Keep cool," Halley said behind Palant. "They've left us with our weapons. There's nothing threatening so far."

"We've come this far," Palant agreed. "The time comes when we just need to trust."

No one replied from behind her, but neither was there dissent.

They entered a long, sloping tunnel leading deep down into the asteroid, and after ten minutes' walking the lead Yautja paused in a large, open space. It looked like some sort of control center, although there were only two Yautja present. They both turned to observe the party's arrival. Then the aliens commenced talking among themselves.

While they did so, Palant glanced back at the marines and the thing they pushed between them. The android's eye was flexing, turning as it took everything in, and Palant was uncomfortable with its interest. The damage to it was immense—if it had been a human, it would have been dead—but she could not shake the idea that it was still working for the Rage.

The Yautja turned to them and gestured toward the datapad. Palant turned it on as the creature spoke, and ensured that the audio function was activated so that the rest of the crew could hear the translated words.

"I'll take you to a room." The device's speech was flat, but perfectly translated. "Tell us what equipment you need and we will bring it to you."

Without waiting for a response it crossed the control center and entered another tunnel, and they followed. This one was short and it ended with a heavy steel door. Behind the door was the room.

It was large, with a low ceiling, and at its center stood a containment cell, its blue, opaque walls glowing softly. A control point marked with Yautja text stood on a small pedestal a few steps away.

Without a word the Yautja stroked the panel and the blue faded. It grabbed the android and shoved it inside the containment field. The blue walls manifested again with a soft buzz, and it was safely locked away.

The Yautja gestured around, saying nothing. It pointed toward the far corner where another set of doors opened into a darker room. Palant guessed that would be their sleeping quarters.

Just before it left, it spoke one more time.

"Yaquita will be with you soon."

Then it passed through the door and was gone. It did not close the door behind it. They were not prisoners. Although Palant guessed that if they tried to make it back to the *Pixie*, their hosts might have something to say.

"Home sweet home," Bestwick said. "Right then, Yautja Woman. What's next?"

"Next is, we see who Yaquita is," she said. She pointed at the imprisoned android. "Then I get to work on *that*."

* * *

The room came to life around them.

Floor pedestals as high as Palant's hips were spaced around them, and at first she'd believed they were empty platforms for something that would be mounted on top. But when Bestwick approached one of the pedestals, it opened up to reveal its interior. She stumbled back into Sprenkel as the structure seemed to grow and expand into something amazing.

It unfolded to reveal an object suspended in some sort of examination pod. At first glance Palant thought it was a mechanical implement of some sort, but as the movement settled she saw that it was biological. A limb, perhaps, as long as one of her legs, coated in silvery skin that had the appearance of metal. One end consisted of a clubbed hand or foot, digits curled in upon themselves. The other end was torn and trailed veins, flesh, and muscle tissue. They hung suspended in the clear gel bubble that held the sample, veins like wires, a broken bone similar to a torn cable.

Arrayed around the object were tools of scientific study and research. A few she recognized—a hand-held bone scanner, some sort of magnascope screen—but most she did not. Blue lights glowed gently in some of the equipment, and the gel containing the limb pulsed like a living, breathing thing.

Other pedestals began to open.

"What the hell?" Huyck said loudly. He drew his sidearm, but Halley reached out and held his arm down by his side. Palant was pleased to see that. She would have hated to think these warriors were threatened by science and knowledge.

"It's a lab," Palant said. "The Yautja don't only destroy. They learn. We've known that for years—it's obvious, because much of their technology is far superior to ours."

"I guess we're seeing where some of their tech

comes from," Sprenkel said.

"We've long suspected it," Palant agreed. "I think this is confirmation. They borrow from other civilizations."

She walked closer to a nearby pedestal and examined what it contained.

There was a small silvery globe, speckled on the outside with precious stones that changed color and size in a constant, dazzling display. It was held in a containment field. She had no idea what it was or what its function might be, but she knew that it was alien.

Elsewhere, a hive of flying things, each as large as her thumb, buzzed and worked as if in ignorance that their every movement and moment was being observed. The structure they hovered around and within consisted of some sort of crystal. Images flowed back and forth across its surface. Palant couldn't quite see what they were, because they were moving too quickly, like fragments of a dream eluding capture. The Yautja had arranged a series of sensors around the hive, that might have been cameras, radiation gauges, and a variety of other measuring and evaluation devices.

One of the marines muttered something.

Another gasped.

"Look here, Palant," Halley said. She and her DevilDogs were gathered around another station, and Palant heard a curious note to her voice. When she approached and they parted, she was fully expecting to see something to do with the Xenomorphs.

On the platform, surrounded by an array of tubes and sampling devices, was a creature about the size of her fist. As with every other sample—and the android, even now glaring around from the center of the large room—it was restrained in a soft blue containment field. Wires and tubes penetrated its thin, opaque hide or skin. Its insides were visible. They throbbed rhythmically, most of its internal shapes soft and seemingly pliable. Then inside she caught a glimpse of something different.

Something *hot*.

"What the hell's that?" she asked breathlessly.

"Fire spite," Halley said.

"Never heard of it."

"Lucky you," Bestwick said. "Came up against a swarm of these bastards on a habitat in Delta quadrant a few years back."

"Where do they come from?" Palant asked. "Why have I never seen or heard about them?"

"They've only been encountered three times," Halley said. "Three times where there were survivors to report the contact, at least. Ours was one. Another was seventeen years ago, and the third was around the turn of the century. A Titan ship was infested, its crew mostly wiped out. It's thought that they're spaceborne."

"Nothing survives in space," Palant said. Halley only shrugged.

Palant stared at the strange creature. Her scientist's interest was piqued, but the true subject of her concern still lay behind her.

"Looks like the Yautja know them pretty well," Huyck said. "Maybe we can trade knowledge."

"We have no knowledge of these bastards," Sprenkel said. "Well, other than the fact that their teeth leak fire, and they can bite your head off with one snip."

Palant turned and looked around the rest of the room. There were a dozen more pedestals open and displaying their samples and experiments, and ten more that were still closed up and silent. Awaiting a subject, perhaps. Or maybe closed because whatever they contained was something secret.

In the center of the room, the largest containment field hummed and glowed, and the android's single wet eye stared directly at her.

"I'll know you," she said.

The room's main door darkened and a shape walked in. Palant's datapad clicked into life, and its mechanical voice translated the new arrival's first few words.

"I am Yaquita. Do not fear me."

"Easily said," Bestwick mumbled. "Shit, what do they feed these things?"

Palant glanced down at the datapad, terrified that she might have left it on voice recognition, and that Bestwick's words would have been translated and sent. In truth, perhaps looking away had been an unconscious ruse to grab her breath.

Yaquita was unlike any Yautja Palant had ever heard of or seen. Legless, the creature entered the room on a wheeled platform, eschewing hover technology for a more mechanical means. It must have been over nine feet tall. Long dreadlocks trailed across the floor, constantly at risk of being crushed by the wheels, yet always appearing to be missed. Its dark, leathery skin was marked by a network of tattoos, tusks worn and yellowed, one eye missing and replaced with a mechanical one that hummed and clicked as it swiveled in the creature's great skull.

Yaquita's hands were large, long-fingered, and almost delicate in appearance. Palant assumed it was a female, although that was difficult to tell.

She couldn't decide whether Yaquita was ancient and worn by time and experience, or young and wounded. Even her one remaining natural eye gave no real clue. Indeed, if eyes were windows onto the soul, then Yautja seemed soulless. Palant was an atheist, and had no interest in old religious beliefs, other than as a historical curiosity. Yet the idea of soullessness was still somehow disturbing.

She tapped at the datapad.

"Your samples are fascinating."

Yaquita seemed to laugh, swaying on her platform.

"I'm glad you like them," she replied. "They are my… fascination."

Palant wasn't sure whether the translator missed a word, or if the Yautja was hesitant about declaring a fascination. Perhaps she conceived it as weakness. Already, she was beginning to suspect that this Yautja was vastly different from any she had encountered before.

"Mine also," Palant said. "Especially this one." She turned and pointed at the android while the translation was played.

Yaquita's one good eye seemed to narrow, and her platform drew her closer. She came directly toward Palant and Halley, expecting the two humans to step out of her path. They didn't disappoint her.

"Its name?" she asked.

Palant frowned. *We don't know*, she thought, but instead of admitting a lack of knowledge, she thought of the puppy her grandparents had owned. It had been a bug-eyed beast, something she'd only ever seen in holo messages and never in the flesh. Once, it had pressed itself up against the camera while her grandparents were recording a broadcast to her and her parents. It had made her laugh, that one big eye and a spread of black and white fur looking so huge and lifelike in the holo frame.

"We won't grace it with its real name," she typed. "We can call it Oscar."

Yaquita nodded. "I have some questions for Oscar. As, I suspect, do you."

Palant nodded. Halley and the others milled around,

standing close before this huge Yautja.

"Then let's begin," Yaquita said.

By the end of that first day, the level of high tension so strained that it caused a buzz among the Colonial Marines had lessened somewhat to something manageable.

Halley and her crew retired to the far room just off the lab, discovering a sleep area and also several food and drink replicators. They had to borrow Palant's datapad to write a selection of orders. What the replicators presented wasn't quite what they had in mind—and sometimes, something very different from what they'd intended—but Sprenkel declared the food "eminently edible."

A well-fed Colonial Marine unit was a happy one. As the hours passed by, stresses lessened, and soon Palant even heard brief bursts of soft laughter coming from the room.

In the lab, she and Yaquita got to work on Oscar.

It was an interrogation that became a delicate dance.

The battered, torn android issued a series of mechanical clicks and sighs as they released him from the confines of the airless bag. A stink accompanied the noises. It was an inhuman smell, yet distinctly biological, with an acidic tinge that had Palant covering her nose and mouth. Oscar rolled his eye and what was left of his face twitched.

For the first time, she was able to assess the true extent of the damage the android had suffered. She felt safe in his presence now, trapped though she was within the blue containment cell. Yaquita was in there with her. One wrong move from the android and the Yautja would tear what was left of it into shreds. Of that Palant had no doubt.

The thing's limbs were broken and torn, body shredded across the ribcage to expose its mysterious innards. She had seen androids before, and once or twice she'd viewed their insides. None of them were quite like this. Oscar's organs seemed to replicate a human's, and at first glance she would have found it difficult to discern much difference. Perhaps these had been grown from the donor cells of humans. Or—more sinister and quite likely—they may have been complete donor organs, harvested from humans sacrificed to furnish this android.

Its blood was white. She was used to that. The fluid was nutrient heavy, lacking the red blood cells that many living things used to transport oxygen around the body. An android produced its own oxygen in a series of nano-factories.

Oscar's head was a mess. His brain was exposed, and this was where she observed the first glaring difference between human and Rage androids. Oscar's brain was entirely mechanical. It was a computer implanted within a flesh-and-blood body, although she didn't recognize many of the components. The technology employed was beyond her.

His eye watched every movement she and Yaquita made.

As they examined him, Oscar's mouth started moving.

"It's trying to talk," Palant said. She didn't need to translate. Yaquita wheeled forward and thrust her fingers into the android's mouth, working slowly and gently until she had cleared a mess of broken teeth from its airway. She prized the jaws apart and looked inside. Palant could see Oscar's tongue slipping and flopping wetly inside, white blood leaking from a dozen wounds reopened by the Yautja's fingers.

His mouth worked, fluid flowed, and though he made grunts and hisses, there were no real words.

"Too badly damaged," Yaquita said, the datapad translating. "I have something."

A wave of her hand brought a spherical shape up from the floor, forming and solidifying before Palant's eyes. Yaquita reached inside and withdrew something that resembled a limp sea creature of some kind. Tendrils and tentacles glimmered with moisture, but Palant saw the gleam of mechanical lights along their length. Its body changed shade as Yaquita approached the pedestal supporting Oscar.

"You will help," the Yautja said. Palant had no intention of saying no. While she held Oscar's head motionless, Yaquita fitted the object into his smashed skull. She connected tendrils here and there, pausing as if listening, then changing the connections again several times. When the room was filled with a wet, fluid sound, she finally wheeled back.

Palant glanced at the Yautja.

Yaquita raised her eyebrows. Her mechanical eye whirred.

"You and the Yautja bitch started munching on each other yet?"

Palant's breath caught in her throat. The voice was flat and artificial, but the hatred and venom came through well enough.

"Come on," Oscar said. "Don't tell me you don't want her, human. All that wet skin. Those long fingers."

Palant glanced sidelong at Yaquita. The datapad was translating Oscar's words, the clicks and rattles emanating from its small speakers. The Yautja didn't respond.

"Watch out for those tusks, though," he continued.

"If only you could see yourself," Palant said. She immediately regretted being baited by the android, and responding with something like that was playing right into his hands. But it had been a natural response, an automatic defense.

Oscar laughed. The sound came from his mouth as well as from the object the Yautja had wired into his brain. More fluid leaked from his torn nostrils. His eye rolled. The other eye was missing, socket ruptured, and a solid material had hardened over the hole. He likely had some method of self-repair, but hadn't been able to extend it much past the damage to his head. He had been protecting his brain, because for an android that was all that really mattered.

Yaquita nodded at the datapad, and Palant switched it to display-only mode. "Keep it talking," the Yautja said.

"Where do you come from?" Palant asked.

"Rage," Oscar said.

"How did you get the *Cooper-Jordan*?"

"The Rage found it. Filled with fresh fruit."

Palant remembered that fresh fruit—humans sent to sleep centuries before in the hope that, upon waking, they would be somewhere else they could call home. The original crew and passengers.

"You need to tell us everything," she said.

"Everything? No one knows everything. Not even me."

"Who's your leader?"

"Ah," Oscar said, and his eye seemed to glaze as if looking into a distance, and a future, she could not see. "Perhaps there's *someone* who knows everything."

"What's their name?"

"Rage."

"What is their purpose?"

Oscar looked around, as far as he could. He took in the blue containment field, the huge Yaquita motionless on her wheeled platform, and the wide room beyond.

"The Yautja know more than you," he said. Palant noted his use of the plural.

"We're now allies," Palant said. It was a bold

statement, and she glanced at Yaquita as the datapad translated. She seemed not to react. In fact, her attention seemed to be elsewhere.

Glancing at the sphere that Yaquita had conjured from the floor, she saw several displays across its upper surface, out of Oscar's line of sight.

"It'll do you no good," Oscar said. "Humans are weak and foolish. Yautja are beasts."

"And yet it's you lying there with your guts hanging out," Palant said.

"It's war. There are losses."

"You're happy being one of them?"

"I'm happy being Rage."

"Tell us what comes next."

Oscar looked from Palant to Yaquita, and back again.

"You want her, don't you?" he said. "Those fingers. That slick skin."

"You have no idea—"

Yaquita made a noise—a cross between a roar and a shriek of surprise. Palant hadn't heard its like before, certainly not from a Yautja.

The response was immediate. Across the room Halley and her crew came dashing out, sidearms drawn. Palant held up her hands, signaling that she was okay.

"With me," Yaquita said. She rolled forward and ripped the device from Oscar's head. He issued a wet, gurgling sound from his mouth. It might have been pain.

The Yautja deactivated and passed through the containment field. Palant followed. Yaquita kept moving toward the far end of the room, shifting past pedestals bearing things known and unknown, mundane and amazing. By the time they reached Halley and the others, Palant could hear Yaquita's breath coming in short, sharp bursts.

"What is it?" Palant asked, switching the datapad back to audio.

Yaquita answered. The datapad paused, as if processing the sounds for longer than usual. As if even it, too, was scared. Then it spoke one single word.

"Drukathi."

"What's that?" Palant asked.

Yaquita sighed, an incredibly human sound.

"This changes everything," she said.

4

GENERAL ALEXANDER

Close to Space Station Hell
December 2692 AD

In his dreams, the android calling himself General Alexander was burning. He watched his body melting away, flesh consumed by the blue-white flames and turned to heat and gases and ruin. His blood boiled and evaporated, sizzling into a thick haze. His skeletal structure stretched, hardened and began to snap, and his organs shriveled beneath the heat. Inside his chest cavity, the heart pumped its last.

Yet Alexander still lived. He would only die when his brain was fried, circuits and bio-junctions scorched to nothing.

He would not allow that.

Mistress Maloney also would not allow that. She stood before him, furious, reaching for him through the flames and smoke and blindingly hot gases, ready to grab and wring his purpose from his molten core.

I haven't finished yet, he thought. *I'm still moving, still chasing and following, and if you'll give me one more chance…*

Another white-hot agony burned in from afar. Mistress Maloney vanished into a darkness lit by occasional flowers of flame, fires curling and dancing in zero gravity. Alexander knew that, were he so inclined, he might have found such a sight beautiful. He understood the concept of beauty, because although he and his fellow generals were built with functionality in mind—strong, powerful, yet with few nods to aesthetics—their programming was full, wide, and inclusive.

But he had never found a cause or purpose for beauty. Now the flames that bloomed around him were heat, pain, and destruction. They were another hurdle between him and the successful accomplishment of his mission, and he could not allow them to triumph.

The general struggled to bring himself fully back online. All systems and contacts between him and his flagship had been interrupted. He reached, adjusted his broadcast frequencies, attempting to bypass any glitches in communications. He seemed to be broadcasting into nothing, and to be searching for return signals that no longer existed.

He accessed his immediate memory stores and replayed the past sixty minutes. The pursuit to the human space station, unleashing his army, Liliya's mocking tone when she broadcast from a ship powering away from the battle. The chase, and then the ambush.

He should have been more aware. Should have seen it coming. He would never have believed that Yautja and humans would work and fight together, yet clearly he should have considered the possibility. The attack by the Rage had changed many things around and within the Human Sphere, and many more changes were afoot.

The Yautja had uncloaked and launched a blistering assault on his flagship and its escorts. They had fought back, but the attack had been rapid and without pause or mercy. Alexander had automatically been sucked into a survival pod, once the ship's bridge was compromised and blasted into fragments by the roaring nuclear fire.

Around the protective chamber, his ship burned.

And now… Alexander thought.

The memories continued, bleeding into his current awareness, and as he made contact with some elements of his ship, the scope of his predicament became apparent.

His vessel was a ruin. Its hull was smashed in a dozen places, back broken, atmosphere vented, weapons holds open to space. His army was destroyed. His mighty, unstoppable army was gone, some of them even now fighting and killing back on the human space station, the rest mostly sucked out into space or burned to nothing in the nuclear fires that had consumed much of the ship. He felt the pain of their demise, a thousand deaths burning white hot… and then simmering into the deepest, darkest void beyond existence. His connection to them was forever, and even though most of them were dead and gone, the agonies would remain.

If he had been anything other than android, these experiences would have driven him mad.

The vessel rolled and spun, its structure in a constant state of flux as the disintegration continued. Soon it would come apart fully, and then Alexander would also be lost to space. Spat out of the wrecked craft like just another dead thing.

But I'm not dead yet! he thought. Defiance burned brighter than any flame. He might float in space forever, his mind still active and afire, his mission still bright.

Or he could take control and forge ahead.

There would be a way. There *had* to be.

Alexander went through a superficial diagnostic check

of his personal systems. He was a mess. His body was useless, smashed and burned, and much of what remained lost and still leaking. Where limbs had been lost, only phantom sensations remained. His head was mostly whole, although his skull plate had been pulverized on one side, leaving his brain and associated systems open to the void. At any other time he might consider his position useless.

His self-destruct mechanism was still whole. One signal, one wish, and he would take the remnants of the ship with him into the void.

No more pain, no more agonies shared with his decimated army.

But there was still hope.

The Watcher remained with him. It pulsed and exuded its strange energies, constant as ever. Events did not appear to have troubled its strange mind. Perhaps it had not even noticed the destruction and chaos, focused as it was on its one single purpose—find and follow Liliya.

Alexander reached out with his one good hand and almost touched this arcane fragment of the Faze. Almost. He had never laid hands on it before, and something told him that to do so would be to change himself irrevocably. It was an alien intelligence beyond the understanding even of Beatrix Maloney. What right did he have to touch it?

Instead, he returned to the immediate task of making himself whole again. Once that was done, he would concentrate on the next step. And the next...

Liliya was still close. Still within his reach.

Alexander flexed his one remaining hand and grabbed hold of a chunk of floating wreckage. He issued commands for the pod door to open. Nothing happened, and he was not surprised.

So he opened the door manually, turning the mechanism, metal grinding on warped metal until there was a gap large enough for him to wriggle through.

The Watcher followed. As ever, it knew his purpose and intention.

Outside, parts of his dead crew floated around the almost unrecognizable bridge. They were in pieces. Weak, human, flesh and blood shreds and dregs, they were no use to him. He moved on.

The passage of time was strange, and difficult to judge. His mind was damaged, after all, and he was glitching. Senses focused in and out, his awareness uncertain. He experienced blank spots, periods when his quest through the terrible ruin of his ship did not register, the moments lost forever to the void.

Yet he saw enough, and when he came across what he sought, his resurrection began.

The Xenomorph soldier had died from explosive decompression, its internal systems shocked and freezing. As such, its programmed instinct to melt down had not been realized. Alexander grabbed one of its heavily spiked limbs and pulled it close, then he set to work on its left forearm. It took a while to detach it, and longer to mold its tattered end so that it might fit well against his own shattered shoulder.

He knew the pain to come, but knew also that what he was attempting was possible. On his journey through the ship he'd visited the medical bay—he must have, though he had no memory of it. Even in that blackout zone he had been working hard toward success. Attached to a belt around his torn waist were a dozen vials, each of them containing a dose of the nanotech that might yet save his life.

He injected one into the Xenomorph limb, another into his wrecked shoulder, and then pressed them close together.

As the soldier's acid joined his own bloodstream, his systems burst alight, and his core processor shut him down.

When Alexander came online again, the limb was attached. The tech in his flesh and that which coursed through the donor limb were doing their job. The arm already felt a part of him. He couldn't yet clench and unclench, flex and point, but awareness of his own body had grown. No longer a phantom, it was real again, and soon it would be stronger and deadlier than the arm he had lost.

He moved quickly, harvesting parts where he could find them, transplanting, injecting, passing out and waking. The further he went, the less human-like and more Xenomorph he became, but he was still Alexander. His mission remained whole.

As he grafted a curve of carapace across the wound in his skull, he could not help finding humor in the moment. It hadn't been intentional, yet it fit perfectly. Across his head, part-human, part-Xenomorph, the word "Alexander" reminded him of who he was.

Feeling whole and strange, he pushed rapidly through the airless wreck toward the holds. If there was a vessel left intact—an attack ship or even one of the smaller emergency escape craft—that might be his only way out. The chance was remote, but he would not allow pessimism. However unlikely, this might yet be a step forward.

When he arrived at the main hold, and saw that it was blasted open to the void, he took pause to consider his next move.

But then fate dealt him a hand.

A ship approached, matched speed and attitude,

and then drifted slowly into the chaotic space, blasting large drifting chunks of wreckage with a laser cannon, knocking aside countless smaller pieces with its hull.

The ship was Yautja.

It paused and powered down, and moments later a door materialized in its hull. Light shone from inside. A shadow was cast across the vented hold.

Alexander's sharp, chitinous limbs flexed and pointed.

The Yautja had not seen him. Its targeting laser played around the hold, illuminating the shape and formation of the damaged structure and relaying it back to the alien's suit computer. Alexander had not fought a Yautja before, and this was the first time he'd seen one in the flesh. He had heard about them, though. He knew their capabilities and powers, their skills at fighting.

Looking forward to testing his new capabilities, he pushed off from the shadowy doorway. Powering down all but his repair systems, he drifted across the hold toward the ship.

The Yautja did not notice him. The heat he gave off was negligible compared to the residual radiation resulting from the attack. His ship still burned, and the expanding wreckage would be sizzling with radiation for centuries to come.

As he drew closer to his enemy, Alexander felt a growing sense of excitement.

The ship was long, sleek, and a deep gray, reminiscent of most Yautja vessels. Two weapons blisters were the only protuberances, the shiny black globes quiet and innocuous. Their firepower would be staggering, he knew. He was also aware that the Yautja could control the ship from its suit computer, and that they were often inclined to suicide, should the occasion arise.

That could not be permitted. His mission still burned

bright in his android heart, and he needed this vessel.

Drifting alongside a piece of melted and reformed wreckage, Alexander grasped it and rolled, keeping it between him and his opponent, his weight subtly changing its trajectory.

Closer... closer...

The Yautja sensed the altered movement. It pushed off from the doorway, floating and turning at the same time, its shoulder blaster unleashing a fusillade of shots that smashed into the wreckage. It was blown apart and Alexander shoved himself aside, impacting the Yautja's ship, pushing off again instantly.

Before the Yautja warrior could use its suit's small retros to turn and face him, he was on it.

The interface between his mind, damaged body, and the newly grafted Xenomorph parts was surprisingly effective. He had expected some lag time between his mind's signals and the new body's responses, but already his movements were lightning-fast.

One slash and the Yautja's suit was ripped open.

Another, and its helmet was smashed.

A jagged portion spun away, green blood spewing in flexing globules that spread around them.

Its shoulder blaster fired again and missed, impacting against a bulkhead far behind.

Its hand came around, a spike protruding from the wrist armor. Alexander hacked it off.

As the beast struggled, a slash from his new, better right arm parted its head from its body. He sent the body drifting away, to join his ruined ship for eternity.

Inside the Yautja vessel, with the door closed and atmosphere already adjusting to his android demands,

Alexander sat in a seat that extruded from the floor. It molded to him perfectly.

Thanks to the actions of the Watcher, the ship already recognized its new master.

As mysterious and unknowable as ever, the Watcher interfaced with the ship's computer and projected a new course.

Once again, and against all odds, Alexander was hunting Liliya.

5

GERARD MARSHALL

Charon Station, Sol System
December 2692 AD

For Gerard Marshall, his posting on Charon Station, the Colonial Marines' main base, was only supposed to be short term.

He hated being in space. Nothing artificial could replicate the feel of solid ground beneath his feet. He even imagined that artificial gravity felt different from the real thing, in the same way the manufactured foodstuffs on the station weren't quite the same as they would be on Earth. Same ingredients, same constituent parts, identical chemical makeup, yet different. Fake.

Gravity on the station was exactly that of Earth, yet Marshall sensed the difference every minute of the day.

Now everything was going to hell, and he figured he'd be there for a long, long time.

He'd once believed in God. It was a belief he'd kept secret from Weyland-Yutani, because a company so driven by the acquisition and use of science had no place for such superstitions, especially among its ruling Thirteen. He had nursed a private faith, though, comforted by it yet never allowing it to intrude on his work or disturb his growing influence. As he'd moved upward in the hierarchy, and eventually found himself as one of the ruling elite, his faith had become something less overt and more internalized.

Eventually his beliefs had withered and died, and sometimes he was sad that he hadn't even noticed it happening.

Now he was tempted to pray to God once more, although Marshall doubted that He would hear, much less listen.

General Paul Bassett had come to Marshall's cabin to issue his latest report. Usually Bassett summoned Marshall to his own main control center, but the center was abuzz with activity. So the General had seized this opportunity for a brief escape. To recharge his batteries, stretch his limbs.

Even so, the General had two Marine aides with him, both of them perpetually connected to datapads, frowning and listening to reports via their ear implants.

"So is there *any* good news?" Marshall asked. "Not a shred? Nothing?"

Bassett shrugged, his expression remaining impassive.

"What about the systems and sectors we haven't heard from yet?"

"There's no indication to suggest Rage incursions anywhere other than the Gamma quadrant," Bassett said. "But it's only a matter of time. With the number of dropholes they've taken, and the speed of their proliferation through Gamma, I don't think we're going to see them stopping."

Marshall shook his head and looked at the holo screen. It displayed a range of information uploaded directly from the General's own datapad—stats and imagery that sent a shiver down even his icy spine.

"It's all gone to hell," he whispered.

"We're mounting defenses," Bassett said. "I won't go into detail, but—"

"Why not, Paul?"

The question seemed to throw the General. He paused, frowning, then relaxed a little, leaning back into his seat.

"Because I can sit here telling you about every defeat as it happens, or I can be in my central control room overseeing our defense."

Marshall nodded. Sighed. Closed his eyes.

"You're the soldier."

"I'll leave the file with your holo frame. It's all there. Review it, message me if you've got any queries." He paused, and added, "I don't guarantee I'll respond instantly."

"And Charon Station?"

"As of four P.M., we're on a war footing, level one alert."

"But we're safe here, aren't we?" Marshall asked.

"As safe as anywhere." The General stood, turning to leave.

"Paul," Marshall said. He stood as well, swaying slightly, space sickness always threatening, teasing. "The inhabited worlds. Addison Prime, Weaver's World, all those other planets…"

"No reports of problems as yet," Bassett said. "We're reinforcing defenses wherever we can. It's all on there." He nodded at the holo screen.

"Because if these things get down there—"

"Yes, Gerard."

"I mean, there are millions of people on those planets."

"Yes."

The two men—Company man, Marine commander—

stared at each other for a moment, and for that brief time they were equals. Men, humans, vulnerable and scared. They held a grudging respect for each other, even trust.

"We're doing everything we can," the General said. "You need to see if there's more you can do." It was a loaded comment, directed not at Marshall, but at the Company, and the cabal of the Thirteen who controlled it.

Without another word, Bassett left the cabin and returned to the war.

Marshall sighed heavily, poured a drink, and sat back down. However hard he stared at the holo screen, he could not wish things better, and the information it conveyed remained the same.

News from Gamma quadrant was grave. Seven dropholes were confirmed lost, their control points— on orbiting space stations or habitats, nearby moons or planets, or asteroids—either destroyed or overrun by the Rage. Contact had been lost with another seventeen, and it was safe to assume that those had also been taken. That was a comprehensive network of dropholes covering a substantial area of Gamma quadrant.

All of the seven confirmed lost subsequently had been activated, and it was impossible to tell where the enemy ships had gone.

Reports of attacks on Marine bases and drophole infrastructure were staggering. Losses were terrible, and the weaponized Xenomorphs were virtually unstoppable. They had even been used in deep-space attacks, sent across between ships like pollen flying on the air, equipped with some form of breathing apparatus or life support system that enabled them to withstand the cold, airless vacuum.

Some attacks involved hundreds of the beasts. In other instances, thousands. And they were being controlled, tasked like traditional troops and sent on their missions.

No one had been able to capture one alive. Whatever tech was being used, it was mysterious, almost arcane.

For his entire career with the company, Marshall had been striving to discover the ways and means to control a Xenomorph. As director of ArmoTech, he considered it the ultimate prize. The Xenomorph was an almost unstoppable force—vicious, violent, fast, unpredictable. Its defense mechanisms were second to none. Its reproductive process was sublime. There were even those who suggested that the Xenomorphs were a bio-weapon, manufactured by an unknown alien intelligence. Creatures of war.

Whatever their provenance or history, a human intelligence had now harvested and nurtured those creatures, and created their own war.

Shortly Marshall would contact the Thirteen, and he knew he should prepare, but he was struggling to find anything positive to relay to them. He was the man closest to the war, and as such he was best placed to provide the directors of Weyland-Yutani with the latest data. But he didn't fool himself, and never had—more than likely, every member of the Thirteen would be up to date already.

No, this contact would be more about the Company than the war. What it could gain, how it could benefit.

With a chill, he realized that he must also ask them how Weyland-Yutani could help.

Nevertheless, he reviewed the information Bassett had left behind. As he finished his whiskey, a chime told him that the time had come. A dozen more holo screens drifted down from the ceiling, and each screen turned opaque. The rest of the Thirteen appeared, their instant communication a marvel of technology. The images of these distant people flickered and danced with the strange sub-space ghosting he could never grow used to. Some of them seemed to age and then grow younger, others faded in and out of existence. It took massive computing power, and a mind-boggling energy expenditure, to settle the shifting images and secure the open communication channels.

Weyland-Yutani possessed a thousand marvels. Marshall only wished they could find one to win this war.

James Barclay, their notional leader, was the first to speak.

"Let's not waste time here," he said. "We all know how dire the situation is in Gamma quadrant. Perhaps Gerard could fill us in on what he knows, just in case some of our own sources are misinformed, or behind the times. Gerard?"

Marshall stood to make his presentation. He told them everything that Bassett had told him, skimming over details where they weren't required.

"Where do we stand with obtaining a sample?" one of the Thirteen asked. She was a harsh woman, older than she looked, and Marshall had never met her in person. The holo screen projection made her eyes look like deep, soulless pits.

"So far we've been unsuccessful," Marshall said.

"Didn't you send one of the Marines' best majors? With Bassett's own personal Arrow-class ship?"

He sensed a mocking tone. Bit his lip. Maintained composure.

"Major Akoko Halley and the *Pixie* have vanished without trace," he replied. "In this time of war, it's still a great and noticeable loss. Before that, however, they succeeded in rescuing the Yautja expert Isa Palant, and as you know, it was she who secured a peace treaty with the Yautja."

"For all the good it did us," the woman replied.

Marshall offered a humorless smile. "Obviously your information isn't as up to date as you believe."

The Thirteen shimmered, as if their emotions could affect their sub-space transmissions.

"Please, fill us in," Barclay said.

"There are reports of Yautja ships fighting alongside Colonial Marine units," Marshall said. "At least seven confirmed instances of this happening. In four of those engagements, the Yautja involvement changed the course of the battle.

"Remember, the Yautja traveled into the Human Sphere from beyond, ahead of the first wave of Rage aggressors. There's no saying how many times they'd met contingents of Rage warships before. Many of them are more battle-hardened than most of the Colonial Marine regiments. One of the engagements occurred on LV-1657, close to drophole Gamma 116, and resulted in the *Pixie* and crew making their escape."

"Their escape to where?" Barclay asked.

"That, we still don't know."

"The Yautja are unpredictable beasts," the woman said, "and the last thing we should do is involve ourselves with them."

Such ignorance, Marshall thought. *And she calls herself a leader*.

Maxwell, another of the Thirteen, interrupted. His voice was low and deep, and quite scathing.

"Is that really what you think of them?" he asked. "Fool."

"Unpredictable, true," Marshall said, "but in these engagements, their technical superiority has proven decisive. Pitch a Rage ship against a Colonial Marine destroyer, and the result will inevitably go in the Rage's favor. But the Yautja ships we've seen have all possessed advanced cloaking tech, as well as weapon systems we've never before encountered, even in our own battles with them.

"Without them, our losses would have been far greater."

"So what do they want for helping us?" the woman asked.

"Want? I'm not sure they want anything," Marshall said. "Elder Kalakta, the Yautja with whom Palant made peace, has informed us that he's ready to share intelligence. There's been no official attempt to create a joint force, but the informal situation seems to be holding well. Perhaps it's a case of 'the enemy of your enemy is your friend.'"

"I'll never call the Yautja our friends," the woman said.

"There are those among the Thirteen I'd never call friends," Maxwell said, his voice causing a ripple of reaction—some smiles, some frowns. "That doesn't prevent us from being a formidable organization. Am I right?"

The woman said nothing. It was answer enough.

A flicker in the corner of his vision, and Marshall glanced at his main holo screen. A flow of new information came through in lines of statistics, graphics, and imagery laden with dread. He felt a thud in his chest, a hollowness growing inside him.

"Marshall?" Barclay asked. "Anything else?"

Marshall took a few moments to read and absorb the new information. It must have been fresh, unfiltered, and gathered from multiple sources, because much of it was confusing. But he was used to identifying the truth embedded in such a mass of data. It was part of what made him good at his job.

"Nothing good," he whispered. There was a wash of expectation from the Thirteen, and an impatient cough from James Barclay.

"Well?" Weyland-Yutani's leader asked.

"Attacks in Beta and Delta quadrants," Marshall said. A deathly silence from the other Thirteen members indicated their shock. "Two dropholes taken in Beta. Five in Delta, with more gone silent."

"They're spreading too fast," another of the Thirteen said. "They have to be stopped. What's Bassett doing there, Marshall? What the fuck are the *Colonial Marines* doing?"

"Everything they can," Marshall said. The realization hit hard. "They're doing everything they can, but they're still losing."

"You're ArmoTech!" the woman said. "Haven't your people got *something* we can use to fight the Rage?"

"We've got plenty," Marshall said. "At Porton Station, orbiting LV-244 in the Alpha quadrant, I have an engineered plague that will kill any living thing. *Any* living thing. It'll wipe out mammals and insects, reptiles and fish, and all known bacteria. We've found nothing that can withstand it. The plague survives temperatures of over a thousand degrees, and if exposed to deep space it'll exist for a hundred years. But how can we ever use it?"

"We need to stop the spread," Maxwell said. "We need to shut down the dropholes."

A stunned silence filled the cabin. He remembered General Bassett's reaction when Marshall had suggested the very same thing. *"Shut down all six hundred Gamma quadrant dropholes and you doom everyone out there to die a cold, lonely death."*

"Don't be a fool," someone said.

Another voice whispered, "That'll be the end of us."

"It's not feasible," Marshall said. "If we do that, we'd be giving up the areas of the Sphere where the Rage have already infiltrated."

"To save the rest," Maxwell said.

"Impossible," Barclay said. "Throw away five hundred years of advancement and exploration?"

"We'd get it back."

"At what cost? No. That's not an option. This war has come as a surprise to us, but we are far from defeated. We all have work to do. First, find out just who or what the Rage are, what they want, and how they can be stopped. Second, acquire a sample of their Xenomorph soldiers, experiment on it, analyze it, find its weak spot. If they're under control of these monstrous androids, as seems to be the case, then that control can be usurped, or even hijacked.

"Imagine if *we* could control them!"

For a moment, the Thirteen imagined. Marshall knew where each of their thoughts lay—beyond victory, and how they might then benefit from possessing the means to control the mighty Xenomorphs. It was a long-held Company desire.

Barclay continued, "Lastly, we need any means necessary to defend the Sphere's most important populated and settled areas. Sol System goes without saying, but Weaver's World, Addison Prime, and the other major settled planets must be protected at all costs. I'll initiate contact with Elder Kalakta myself, and ask for the Yautja's help."

Barclay paused as if to invite dissent. There was none.

"As a Company, we've been building and maintaining the Colonial Marines for centuries. We've always feared something like this. Internal strife is bad enough, but a threat from outside, initiated by a force we can hardly know, and with which we cannot reckon... No, this isn't just something to fear. We can't leap to knee-jerk reactions. We pool our intelligence, think outside the box, and come up with a way to *win* this."

Mutters of agreement. Even Marshall, so close to the

realities of their situation, felt inspired by Barclay's words.

"We speak every day from now on, at this time," Barclay said. "Get to work."

The holo screens fizzled out, plunging Marshall's cabin into a temporary murkiness, lit only by his tactical screen. He let out a breath he didn't know he'd been holding.

One of the blank screens turned opaque again, and moments later James Barclay was there, staring at him as if he was in the same room. Marshall had never seen the man looking so serious.

"Gerard," Barclay said, "we need to talk about those dropholes."

"Shutting down the entire network," Marshall said, nodding slowly.

"It's a doomsday scenario," Barclay said. "This is between you and me. Always. But talk me through how it would be done."

6

BEATRIX MALONEY

Outer Rim
December 2692 AD

"Do you want to go across to see it, Mistress?" Dana asked.

"No," Beatrix Maloney said. "No, I can see it from here." She had not been off the *Macbeth* in more than a dozen years, and she had no desire to leave it now. She was old and frail. Although the life-giving gel they had found on their long journey was keeping her alive— she could feel it coursing through her veins, filling her, surrounding her in her containment pod—she could not deny her vulnerability.

The next time she left the *Macbeth* would be to step out onto Earth once again, victorious at the end of her mission. That was a promise she had already made herself. Until the Rage triumphed, this ship was her home.

That didn't mean that she could not look.

"It's amazing," Dana said.

"Incredible," Kareth agreed from Maloney's other side. She floated between them on her support platform, torso and shrunken limbs contained within the gel pod, head still exposed.

"I think it's almost done," Maloney said. "Summon Challar to me. I want him to see."

"Yes, Mistress." As her helpers Dana and Kareth left to bring Challar, Maloney floated closer to the viewing portal and watched the Faze at work.

They had been in geostationary orbit around the drophole for almost forty days, and for all that time the Faze had been working on the vast object's superstructure and controls. The being was as mysterious now as it had been when they'd found it and its cousin, deep in that alien habitat of *Midsummer*. The other Faze was dead now, destroyed with the *Othello*. The loss of both had planted a cold seed in Maloney's heart.

But her Faze still flourished, and it had been working nonstop ever since leaving the *Macbeth*.

As ever, the being had known what she desired of it. No one—Rage, shipborn, or android—had ever successfully communicated with the creature. There were some who remained unconvinced that it even *was* a creature. It might have been manufactured by an ancient, unknowable intelligence, and left behind on *Midsummer* to continue its work. Perhaps it *was* a machine, almost as old as the galaxy itself, so advanced in its own constant reimaginings that it resembled nothing they had known before.

Perhaps it was a god.

Maloney watched it now from afar. Though she was old and jaded, and her mind had been alive and conscious far longer than was natural, still she enjoyed experiencing a glimmering spark of wonder.

The drophole ring was huge, almost two miles in diameter. Over the past forty days the Faze had traveled the entire circle five times, extruding new material from its amazing body, reshaping, reforming, breaking down the structure here, constructing something new there. The drophole mechanism retained its previous shape, but there could be no doubt that it was now something different.

At six points around its circumference were the nodes, where the real technical guts of the drophole were housed.

The Faze had remade these from scratch. They now resembled bulbous growths, randomly shaped and filled with technology that no one on the *Macbeth* could hope to understand.

Maloney did not need to understand.

As ever, the Faze seemed to instinctively know what was desired of it, and it worked nonstop until that task was complete.

Even from several miles away, she could see it slowly circling the drophole's outer ring, moving between one control node and the next. A haze of gas accompanied it as it laid what Maloney hoped was the final layer of material upon the ring's outer shell. Several long limbs that had formed across the being's back worked hard at the material it expelled, twisting and knotting, turning and smoothing it into shape, like a massive spider manipulating its silk.

Somehow the Faze could work in deep space with no breathing apparatus or protective clothing. Maybe it really was a construct, and the true Faze was a being inside, that they could never see. Or perhaps it was something unknowable by a human mind, even one as advanced as Maloney's.

Long ago she had ceased concerning herself with the hows and whys. The Faze served them, made everything they possessed better, stronger, faster, and it had not once failed in a task Maloney desired of it.

Even now, General Alexander hunted down the eloped

android Liliya, using the Watcher that the Faze had supplied. She expected news from him soon, hopefully before this drophole was complete, and the *Macbeth*'s contingent readied for their final journey.

It would be the longest, most ambitious drop ever performed. Usually such technology was limited, and could only take a ship between eight and ten light years. And even then, only to a neighboring hole. After the Faze had finished its work, however, Maloney planned on dropping five hundred light years, traveling directly to the center of the Human Sphere.

There, she would attack its beating heart.

The Sol System, and Earth.

"Fucking incredible," Challar's augmented voice said. Maloney sighed. Considering the fact that he was one of a handful of the longest-lived humans in history, she constantly hoped to hear something more eloquent coming from his artificial mouth. But no. Challar always had been his own man.

"We'll be ready soon," Maloney said.

"Really? You're sure?"

"What's wrong, Challar?" she asked, chiding him. "Scared?" He floated beside her in his crystal globe, entirely submerged in the life-giving gel. His legs and one arm were missing, the other arm shriveled. The gel was mostly clear, although some flakes of skin and other detritus from his body floated here and there. Sometimes his eyes were enlarged by light diffraction through the fluid, and other times they appeared shrunken. He hadn't breathed air in almost four decades.

Yet little about his personality had changed.

"I'm too old to be scared," he said.

"Good," she said. "Soon General Mashima will arrive at Weaver's World and launch his attack, if he hasn't already begun. As soon as that happens, and we detect reaction across the Sphere, we'll perform our drop."

"Then we might only be days away," Challar said, eyes widening grotesquely with a childlike wonder. Bubbles rose within his globe and drifted here and there, as if seeking one another. "We've been traveling so long, and now we're so close."

"I feel it too," Maloney said, "but it's not yet time for celebration. I have a job for you to perform, Challar, as soon as we arrive on the outskirts of Sol System. By my reckoning, we'll be dropping through close to Charon Station. When we arrive and the *Macbeth* breaks down into its separate ships, I want you to take charge of two of them and destroy the station. Crush the heart of the Colonial Marines, cut off their head, and they'll be lost."

Challar smiled and nodded. "I'll take three thousand troops."

"Have five thousand," she replied. "*Macbeth*'s main holds contain ten times that many."

"And you?"

"I'll be commanding four of the ships and heading for Earth. The other six will scatter around the system under the command of the other original Rage."

"No shipborn in charge?" he asked. "I thought we'd been training them for this day. They'll be disappointed."

"The shipborn will lead the ground assaults, along with the generals. Every member of the Rage will take part. Every one of us will fight. By the end of the year, the entire Sol System will be in our hands."

"Yes," Challar breathed, his voice seeming to carry the weight of emotion, even though it was electronically formed. He stared out across space at the Faze completing its work upon the drophole, making it better, more powerful, and safe for them to perform such an unprecedented drop. "We've been waiting for so long. Now we're unstoppable."

I hope, Maloney thought, but the niggling fear remained—that Liliya would continue to evade Alexander. That the tech she had stolen and carried in her blood would fall into Weyland-Yutani hands. If that happened, there was no telling just how quickly they could study it, and devise a defensive plan.

"Mistress!" Kareth said, rushing along the hallway toward them. His appearance startled her. "We've received a sub-space transmission from General Mashima. The *Aaron-Percival* has arrived in orbit around Weaver's World, and his attack has begun."

A chill went through Maloney's body, even immersed as she was in the gel. She had initiated a slaughter.

"Good," she said, smiling. "Good. Send a signal to all ships. We'll be dropping in two days. It took Wordsworth and his Founders centuries to travel the distance we're going to cover in the blink of an eye. His retreat from humanity was performed in secret.

"Our return will be triumphant."

7

VICTIMS

Various locations, Weaver's World
December 2692 AD

Jemima Jones wanted to be an explorer. She came from a long line of adventurers—or so she told her friends—and her parents rarely did anything to discourage this idea.

She could trace her bloodline back to the year 2000, and a young woman named Tracey Jones who had spent almost three months crossing the Antarctic continent on Earth, unsupported and unaided. Jemima even had a picture of this woman from almost seven hundred years earlier—huddled in a bright blue coat, hood pulled around her ears, exposed skin speckled with ice and frost, and smiling the biggest smile Jemima had ever seen.

"You have her smile," her mother had told her the first time she'd seen the picture. Yet her parents displayed little interest about this distant ancestor. Jemima had printed the picture, and she kept it on her at all times.

There were other pictures, too. Nathan Jones, an astronaut who had been a first-generation Mars colonist in 2044. Angharad Jones, a botanist who had spent the last ten years of her life on Europa before a tragic asteroid strike had destroyed the research base there in 2203. Leyton Jones, a pilot who had allegedly become a pirate, killed in a brush with Colonial Marines in 2393. And there were others. Some might have been true ancestors, others might merely have shared her name.

Jemima took inspiration from them all.

She had become another famous Jones explorer. Perhaps she shared most of her interests with that first woman in her bloodline, Tracey Jones, because the place she and her parents had settled was on the freezing northern shores of Ellia. The largest landmass on Weaver's World, Ellia was almost six thousand miles wide and four thousand from north to south, and their research base—her parents and their friends had named it Land's End—was on the very northernmost peninsula. Beyond lay two thousand miles of unexplored open ocean, stretching between them and the ice-covered north pole of the world.

It had been snowing for fifteen days without a break, and this was the first day of clear, beautiful blue skies.

"Nibbs!" she called. Across the field of snow she saw a flurry of movement, then the dog came bounding. Fifteen decades before, when the first colonists came to Weaver's World, they hadn't been allowed to introduce any alien species to the ecosystem. That strict edict was still observed, although with over nine million people now living on the planet and exploring its surface, they were hardly keeping the world pure and untouched.

The wonderful flora and fauna were still being categorized. Much use had been made of the commonest cattle-type animals, sacrificed for food and clothing, and then the dogs had been discovered. Wolf-like, curious, intelligent and friendly, they had made perfect pets.

Nibbs bounded toward her, kicking up snow in his

wake, tail whipping from side to side in delight. Jemima laughed and threw a snowball. He jumped, caught it, and it exploded in his mouth. He shook his head as he landed, then ran toward her once more.

"Jem! We'll be heading back soon," her father called out.

"Okay, Dad."

"We're going down to the beach to collect the last few sample pods. You stay here with the convoy."

Jemima waved to her mother and father. They waved back. The whole team wore blue insulated clothing, and it reminded her of the picture of Tracey Jones.

They'd been camped on this coastline for eighteen days. Fifty adults and thirteen children had come, separate groups tasked with cataloguing flora and fauna, taking geological samples, assessing weather patterns, and mapping the area in detail. The mapping hadn't been easy because of the snowstorm that had started only days after they'd arrived, but they'd enjoyed a comfortable time camped out on this most glorious of locations.

Behind them, hills rose steadily inland, and to the far south they could see the snowcapped mountains they had driven through on the way here. To the north lay the sea, endless and filled with mystery.

On their fifth day here Jemima had been the first to see a group of giant animals breaching several miles out, huge tentacles snatching birds from the air, smooth curved backs cutting through the waves, water exploding upward as blowholes were cleared and deep breaths taken. Her father guessed each beast at over fifty yards long. They hadn't been seen again.

"You wait!" she said to Nibbs. The panting dog dropped to its front in the snow, almost buried to the top of its head. Jemima giggled. Sometimes she saw a startling intelligence in the animal's eyes, other times an alienness that still troubled her. Her mother had once said, *"I wonder who's playing with who?"*

"Are you a clever boy?" she asked.

Nibbs panted, stomped his feet, staring at her hand as she pulled a treat from her pocket.

A few other children were enjoying their last moments playing in the snow, while the adults finished packing up the camp. The twenty heavy-wheeled transports they'd come in had doubled as their living quarters. Some of the kids complained about living three, four, or even five to a vehicle, but Jemima loved it. Wherever she was with her family, it felt like home.

Ellia was a giant place, and she was young. Her ambition was to spend her life exploring every mile of its more than twenty thousand miles of coastline. Nine million people might live here, but the bulk of them existed in the five cities straddling the equator, four hundred miles to the south of where she was now. Weaver's World was still young, and there was so much left to discover.

As Jemima played with Nibbs, she became aware of a stillness that had settled around the camp and vehicles. She glanced up. Everyone was looking past her, to the north, toward the slope that led down to the beach and out over the sea.

"What?" Jemima asked. Her heart thumped.

"Something," a woman said.

Jemima turned around. Far out over the ocean, a craft of some kind was approaching. It flew so low that its shockwave was visible on the waters below, smashing the tops off waves in clouds of white spray.

The adults huddled together, some of them talking, a few others jumping into the transport cabins and reaching for communicators.

Nibbs nudged her hand with his wet nose, whining.

"Mother," Jemima said. "Father." For some reason she suddenly felt scared. She started running, kicking through the snow with her heavy boots. It was hard going. She tried to follow paths that had been trodden over their time here, but they had been compacted and frozen into treacherous ice. She fell a couple of times, and both times Nibbs was there to fuss around her.

He was still whining.

Even her dog knew this was no longer a game.

Jemima focused on the aircraft as it rolled in toward land. She had never seen anything moving like that before, nor anything with that strange, globular appearance, and just for a moment she thought perhaps it was alive. She'd been the first to spot those leviathans from the deep, far out to sea, and perhaps now she would be able to name this new airborne creature.

But it's huge! she thought. *Bigger than a transporter.* Probably larger than their house, back on the outskirts of New Cardiff.

As she ran faster, the shapes began to fall.

She heard them splashing into the sea and striking the snow-covered beach as the thing passed above her, moving slower now. Nibbs began growling at the shape as it hovered above the camp a couple of hundred yards behind them.

A dozen more shapes dropped from the vessel and struck the ground, and then it rocketed away inland, heading for the mountains and throwing up a trail of powdered snow behind it.

As Jemima ran down the slope and the beach came into view, she heard the first screams from the camp behind her.

"Mother!" she shouted. "Father!"

Nibbs moved ahead of her, snarling and growling as he ran. He headed across the rocky dunes and toward the strange thing she'd seen in the snow close to the water's edge. The thing that looked so wrong, and which for a moment her mind refused to acknowledge.

The spread of blood and body parts, marring the pure white snow.

"Mother…" she breathed, barely a whisper.

Nibbs barked as a dark shape darted across the snow, then howled as he was speared by a limb and hoisted aloft. A twist, a wrench, and his blood painted the snowscape.

Jemima opened her mouth to scream. As a nightmare burst through the snow toward her, she knew that her brave explorer's blood would be next.

Devon liked hanging around the spaceport. It was a waystation, and anyone arriving or leaving New Cardiff probably wouldn't know him. They'd see signs of his phrail addiction, if they knew where to look—the dilated pupils, swollen fingers, thinning hair—but most of them didn't know, and many were too exhausted from their journeys, or too excited about leaving, to notice.

He could wander the roads and parks outside the spaceport without interruption, sometimes sleeping in the shadows of trees, other times sitting beside the paths and playing his guitar. He wasn't a great player, but he'd invested in a small insert that filtered his strums and converted them into something resembling music. Most people knew. Few cared.

On a good day he could leave with over a hundred credits, and that was enough to buy a meal, a drink, and a couple of vials of phrail. Though not necessarily in that order.

Another reason Devon liked the spaceport was that he had never stopped dreaming. His life was a mess, and had been for ten years. Soon after arriving on Weaver's World and finding employment in New Cardiff, he'd fallen in with a small group of people whose vision had seemed clear and unique. They believed in a deity called Sang, a god supposedly stepping from world to world and granting life to those planets that could support it.

They worshipped Sang by traveling out from New Cardiff into the wilds, on unsupported trips in unsafe vehicles. Devon's sense of adventure took him with them. His vulnerability and naiveté led him to experiment with the other ways they worshipped their god.

The group sex was fine, day-long orgies out in the wilds beneath Weaver's World's comfortable summer sun.

The phrail was not. He was soon hooked, and he fell deeper than most. Then one day his friends vanished, like the god they had manufactured. Devon had never moved on.

Today was a day like any other. He'd watched a ship landing, one of the smaller in-system freighters that took people and supplies out to the planet's three moons. There were research and mining colonies out there, and Devon found it difficult to understand why people would live in such harsh conditions when they were so close to such a planet. Weaver's World was like Earth, but without all the industrialization, wars, pollution, disease, and overpopulation.

He'd watched another ship take off, a private vessel owned by someone worth more than he could imagine, but what he was really waiting for today was the arrival of the weekly passenger ship. These vast transports would fall into orbit and then ferry their passengers down via dropships. Depending on the numbers involved, this could mean a daily drop for up to twelve days, with perhaps five hundred passengers per drop.

That was a lot of guitar playing to welcome them to Weaver's World, and a lot of credits with which to buy phrail.

He sat beside the main path leading out from the landing bays and arrival quad. To his right was the spaceport itself, a wide, open area enclosed within a high circular building that housed processing, border control, restaurants, storage, hangars, and everything else involved in a busy arrival and departure site.

To his left, New Cardiff lay sprawled across the valley floor. The city was over two hundred years old. Its original buildings were still there, encased now in diamond-shield and maintained as a museum in honor of those who had first settled this world. Around this central portion, and following the course of the wide river, stood buildings and skyscrapers that were home to almost a million people.

The area around the spaceport was bustling with street vendors, pedestrians, and others like him awaiting the new arrivals. There were always those keen to exploit or prey upon newcomers to Weaver's World.

Devon looked up, away from the city and into the deep blue sky. No clouds today. One of the moons was a pale ghost, and another was peering between the mountains to the north, like a face watching from afar. He was resigned to never traveling in space again, and sometimes, when his addiction and personality weren't so enmeshed, and he found his old self coming to the fore, he felt a deep, soul-sapping sadness.

At least I can still sing, he thought. He strummed the guitar and hummed a song. *I'm not that worthless*.

Right. Singing for his next fix.

A roar in the distance grabbed his attention. He looked up, surprised, because the first dropship wasn't due for at least another hour.

Yet there it was, swinging in toward the city from above the mountains. A distant speck at first, a dark spot on the sky moving closer, the pounding of its engines echoing against the peaks and drifting ahead of it across the valley plain. It quickly drew closer, and a few more people paused to stare.

It didn't resemble any dropship Devon had seen before.

"Is that a Marine ship?" someone asked nearby. There was a permanent Colonial Marine presence on Weaver's World, with bases in each city and several larger outlying facilities. Their numbers had increased recently, especially following the tragic attack on Swartwood Station 3, where almost two thousand people had been killed. That had hit the whole planet hard. It seemed as if everyone knew someone who had been affected by those deaths.

"Not Marine," Devon said.

"Then what?" the person replied. "'Cos that's like no dropship I've ever—"

Objects started falling from the ship. They landed far away, across the river and behind buildings, but the vessel still drew closer. Upon nearing the spaceport it shifted direction, banking, rolling, aiming directly for the facility.

"Bombing!" someone else shouted.

But there were no explosions.

Devon stood, guitar in one hand, the other delving into his pocket to clasp the three phrail vials resting there. He tried not to use during the day, especially when he was busking, but grabbing hold of them made him feel safe.

The craft flew across the river, about half a mile from the spaceport. More objects dropped, and even before they hit the ground Devon saw them unfurling, long limbs sharp in the stark sunlight.

"Oh, no," someone said. "Oh no, it's them, it's the Rage. It's the Xenomorphs!"

Devon didn't understand. He didn't keep up to date with developments in the Sphere, because all his interests were on this planet. Nothing beyond concerned him anymore.

People started to run and scatter. They tripped, fell, shouted, and then screaming began as the things dropping from the aircraft began to kill.

Devon ducked down and looked up as the craft roared directly above him, passing over the spaceport's boundary buildings and disgorging many more of those dark shapes as it went. He heard a heavy thud behind him, felt it through the ground.

He turned around, guitar raised in both hands.

Two weird, sharp-edged creatures were ripping through a group of people. Blood flew, spattering the bright green grass. Screams rose and were cut off. Vicious tails whipped, a head rolled, limbs fell, guts spewed and were trodden into the ground by harsh, sharp feet.

A set of teeth snapped out and punched right through someone's chest.

Devon dropped his guitar and fell onto his rump, phrail vials clasped in his left hand.

A Xenomorph ran at him. It was coated in gore from the people it had already killed, blood and skin hanging from its claws.

Devon didn't even open the vials. He dropped all three into his mouth and bit, crunching the glass, swallowing the shards and the sickly sweet fluid. Blood filled his mouth. He took in a huge breath, and moments before the nightmare beast reached him, the drug carried him away.

* * *

Corporal Dentz had once seen some headcam footage of a Xenomorph attack. It had been lifted from a Company quantum fold by an info-pirate, and if anyone knew he'd seen it he would have been dishonorably discharged, at the very least. But of course he'd watched. Sickly fascinated. Terrified.

Now he was about to face the real thing.

Everyone in the rolling troop carrier was wide-eyed and silent with shock. He had fifteen Colonial Marines under his command, and he was doing his best to rein in his terror at what was happening. However well trained they all were, this was the last thing they'd been expecting. Posted to Weaver's World after the disastrous and tragic attack on Swartwood Station 3, they had only arrived several days ago, after a long space journey involving two drops.

Despite what was happening in Gamma quadrant, Dentz had considered this a cushy posting. Weaver's World wasn't a military target. It was also a posting with benefits, because where there was a large civilian population, there were plenty of sons and daughters wanting to meet marines.

He hadn't even had a chance to go off-base.

"All units, listen up," their lieutenant said through his comm. "It's looking messy. Reports coming in from across the inhabited zone. Xenomorph attacks everywhere, and they're coordinated and brutal. Largely civilian targets. It's a massacre, not an assault, so we've got to do what we can."

"Where are we heading, L-T?" Dentz asked.

"Penperlleni Plains," she replied. "The villages out there are getting hit hard."

"Shouldn't we be defending the cities?"

"We're responding to reports and defending what

we can." Their lieutenant went quiet for a moment, and Dentz was sure he heard a deep sigh, despite the noise the vehicle made rolling across the terrain. "There's a big enemy ship dropped into orbit. There's been fighting up there, too, and it sounds like the 7th Spaceborne has lost a destroyer already. This is a sustained, well-planned attack. Enemy dropships have been reported in over twenty locations. We're doing what we can." He paused and glanced at his screen. "Okay, ten minutes."

Their lieutenant signed off, and Dentz looked around the troop carrier's interior.

"Check suits and weapons," he said. "Carry all the ammo you can. Double up on grenades." He hefted his own weapon, knowing he should have felt comforted by the blistering firepower he was carrying. He did not.

Ten minutes passed quickly, and Dentz's visor screen revealed that they were heading across the Penperlleni Plains. Eight troop carriers came with them, over a hundred Marines, all packing serious weaponry. Each carrier would launch a drone upon deployment, and the lieutenant would follow and oversee the operation. They were a formidable unit.

"Holy fuck," the lieutenant said.

"L-T?"

"Deploy. Deploy! Units one to four, swing north. Five and six, direct assault. Seven and eight, swing south. Go, people, go!"

The carriers screeched to a halt and doors opened. The air was cool after the heat of the vehicle. Dentz and his unit stormed out.

He led the assault.

Ahead of them, on the banks of a small river, the village burned. Smoke rose from several locations, and at its center a large building was blazing, pouring smoke into the sky. A schematic showed him that it was a school.

"Contact?" the lieutenant asked.

"Negative," came the reply from all eight units.

"Whatever happened here's already over," Dentz said.

"Don't be so sure, Corporal. Head into the village and…" Her voice trailed off as she saw what every other soldier saw.

Dentz slowed. Shock weighed him down. He'd been in combat before, had seen people die, and he'd killed three people by his own hand.

But he'd never seen anything like this.

The village was red. People lay dead in the streets, some of them huddled in groups against the walls of buildings, others on their own where they'd attempted to flee. Their bodies bore terrible wounds. Blood flowed in the gutters. Adults and children alike, the dead were still warm, their insides steaming into the fine summer air.

"Move in," Dentz said. He led his unit, entering the village past a building with holes blasted in its walls and windows smashed. Someone had attempted to fight back. He saw a man lying dead on the road, his head a bloodied ruin. In one hand he still clasped a blaster. His other hand and arm were melted, and patches of acid sizzled on the road surface.

"Don't step on that," Dentz said. "Movement?"

"Negative."

"Move forward. Teams of three."

They penetrated deeper into the village, and with each step the horrors mounted. Close to the school they found a mass of dead children. Teachers had attempted to protect them. Nothing had stopped the Xenomorphs.

They didn't go too close to the dead kids.

Dentz felt his fury rising. This was senseless, random,

and whoever the Rage were he wished their leaders were here with him now, tied up and facing the justice these marines would be happy to give them.

"Contact, north end of village!" the lieutenant said through Dentz's comm. He accessed his visor screen and saw the schematic, with gunfire marked by red points to the north.

Audio brought the sounds of heavy laser fire from com-rifles, and the sounds of squealing and screaming as Xenomorphs died.

"Hold position here," Dentz said. "They might be trying to—"

"Ten o'clock!" one of his unit shouted, and then all hell broke loose.

The creatures came pouring out of the buildings. They ran across the corpses of those they had already killed, closing on the marines and being cut down by heavy fire. Six fell, nine, and as they hit the ground they burst apart in some sort of self-destruct, spewing burning acidic remains across the ground.

Dentz and his unit put down a defensive fire, forming a rough circle and keeping the creatures away from them. But there were too many.

"We need help!" Dentz shouted, but his plea was met with desperate shouts from the other units. Shouts, and screams.

"Drone support!" the lieutenant shouted.

Drones whistled in, firing on the Xenomorphs from above.

Dentz checked his visor schematic for life signs. All he saw were the Colonial Marines, and the Xenomorphs. More and more were making themselves known now, emerging from the buildings where they'd been hiding. Launching attacks in a well-coordinated effort.

Two of his unit fell, and when the Xenomorph that had dropped them was struck by laser, it erupted and splashed its insides across the other soldiers. Molecular acid worked at their combat suits. Dentz felt the heat, all too aware that their resistance would last only so long.

Past the attacking creatures he could just make out the square at the center of the village, a place where its inhabitants would gather to socialize and enjoy themselves. It was piled with dozens of dead, maybe hundreds. Almost as if the Xenomorphs had dragged them there to kill them in the open. A display. A gruesome point to be made.

Someone screamed, and a woman beside him fell with her head torn apart. Another marine blasted the creature that had killed her. They were down to three marines now, the others wounded or dead, and the attacking beasts pushed in from all sides. They did not pause. They would show no mercy.

Sweating, heart hammering, Corporal Dentz knew that this was the end.

He dropped his com-rifle and grasped a grenade in each hand.

From: Major Sergei Budanov, Weaver's World Garrison

To: General Paul Bassett

The death toll is catastrophic. The attack was sudden and huge, and early estimates put Xenomorph numbers on the surface at over five thousand. The ships dropping them have concentrated on heavily populated areas, ignoring most military targets.

A Fiennes ship identified as the *Aaron-Percival* is in orbit, along with at least six accompanying vessels and an unknown number of dropships. All assaults on the *Aaron-Percival* have resulted in heavy Colonial Marine losses, including two destroyers and a dozen manned drones from the 7th Spaceborne. We are concentrating our forces on defending the cities, but they are already under sustained attack, and the dropships are landing Xenomorphs scattered over hundreds of areas. However fast our response, we are usually too late.

I hereby request full reinforcements. I've never known such willful destruction or slaughter on this scale. We are living through a tragedy the likes of which humanity has not seen in many centuries, if ever before.

I fear for Weaver's World. I fear for us all.

8

AKOKO HALLEY

Gamma Quadrant
December 2692 AD

Halley wasn't used to inaction. Especially considering recent events, remaining cooped up inside the Yautja asteroid seemed… disingenuous. They should have been out there fighting, taking part in the defense of the Human Sphere. Halley was an intelligent woman, and she knew what they were doing was the right thing, but sometimes it felt like sitting down and ignoring reality.

Despite appearances, she knew that her crew felt the same. Bestwick was reclined on one of the soft beds extruded from the floor, reading a book contained on her datapad. Sprenkel and Huyck were servicing their weapons. The Yautja had allowed them to retain their com-rifles. Halley suspected a certain element of trust lay behind that, but also confidence on the part of the alien warriors. If she and her DevilDogs did decide to cause trouble, the Yautja would be able to isolate and neutralize them instantly. This was their base, after all.

The room they were staying in was just off the large

lab, where even now Isa Palant and that spooky-looking Yautja were still trying to glean information from the captured android. Since the Yautja's troubled turn a few hours before—uttering the word "Drukathi" and stating how that changed everything—Halley and the others had performed as many searches as they could on the name. But the limited computing power in their suits yielded nothing. If they were outside the asteroid, perhaps they'd have been able to hack some of the Company's quantum folds. However, the Yautja base was heavily shielded.

They were trapped.

"Drukathi," Halley muttered. The name sounded heavy and alien in her mouth. There was nothing familiar about it. The Yautja had appeared worried, even seeming to fear what it represented.

The Major was eager to speak to Palant alone, but the scientist and the Yautja hadn't taken a break in hours.

Halley paced the room. It was circular, cave-like, walls lined with a smooth, almost fluid material from which beds and seating areas had extruded as soon as they had entered. The chamber seemed to perceive their needs, with a water dispenser and food replicator also appearing. The doors remained open. They weren't prisoners in here, yet none of the Colonial Marines were comfortable, and all were well aware that they were guarded guests of the Yautja.

"Huyck, c'mere," Halley said. She gestured to him, and he strolled across to her, carrying his partly stripped com-rifle in one hand. He and Sprenkel were each dealing with one weapon at a time, always ensuring they had others to hand.

"Major?"

"I want to take a walk," she said. "Look around. You and the others stay here, relax, keep calm. Exude chill. I'm not sure whether or not they'll let me out, but if they do,

I want to sniff around. Something's happening here, and I don't want to wait for Palant to finish playing with her new toy to find out what."

"I could come with you."

"No, you're in charge while I'm gone."

"You sure?"

She didn't like having her orders questioned, but these were unusual circumstances. In truth, no, she wasn't sure at all.

"It'll be fine," she said. "I don't trust them one bit, but they could have taken us out a thousand times already. I think this is all as it seems, for now. I just want to know more. If they don't want me wandering around their rock, they won't let me."

"Okay, Major." He glanced down at her sidearm.

"I'm taking it. They've let us keep our weapons up to now."

"I can't help thinking that's because we're completely outgunned," Huyck said.

Halley looked around the room at the strange walls. Anything might have been hiding behind or within them.

"Yeah, I think you're right," she said. "Perhaps it should make us feel safe."

"I just feel twitchy."

"We're not built for sitting back and being passive," she said. She even offered him a smile.

"Be safe," he said. "You're the only one who can handle Sprenkel."

"An hour, that's all." She slapped his shoulder and left the room.

Passing into the lab, she was hit by the smell. It was a warm, singed stench, like an electrical short, and beneath it was something altogether more biological. She took several deep breaths, trying to identify the constituent aromas, but failing.

Palant and the legless Yautja were working within the central blue containment field, the android splayed on a raised platform between them. While Palant seemed to be questioning the android itself, datapad in one hand while she spoke to it, the Yautja was slightly removed, consulting various displays on a sphere that had risen from the floor.

It was odd watching human and Yautja working together. Halley had developed a huge respect for Palant, for the way she had handled herself and pulled through violent and dangerous events, and also for what she had achieved. Because of her there was peace between Yautja and humanity, when it could have escalated into all-out war. That in turn led to the possibility of the two radically different species working together.

Like now. If what Halley saw could be replicated elsewhere, perhaps they could stand against the Rage.

Palant looked up and caught her eye. Halley cocked her head, eyebrow raised. *Anything?* she mouthed.

Palant shook her head.

Yaquita had yet to enlighten them about who or what the name "Drukathi" applied to, or even if it *was* a name, for that matter. Halley suspected the Yautja was waiting for permission from a higher source. That, or perhaps it didn't consider humans important enough to share the information.

A worried and scared Yautja. That was enough to concern and frighten Halley.

She nodded at Palant, then started walking toward the lab's entrance doors. She expected at any moment to be called back, or for the doors to open and reveal a couple of heavily armed Yautja standing guard. But neither happened. As she neared the doors they misted away to nothing, and she passed through into the hall beyond.

Ahead of her was the passageway they'd followed down from their moored ship. The *Pixie* felt like a very desirable destination right then, but Halley wasn't out here to find somewhere comfortable and familiar.

She looked left and right. Left, the passage curved around the lab and led somewhere out of sight. Right, it headed down a nearby series of deep steps, illuminated far below by a subtle glow emanating from the walls. She chose the steps. Deeper into the asteroid somehow felt like the way to go.

Checking her sidearm, running a rapid diagnostic on her combat suit and finding all systems functioning, she started down.

Walking these corridors, it was the first time she'd been on her own in longer than she could recall. There were moments on the *Pixie*, but it was a small ship, and even in her sleeping bay she was never more than a couple of yards from another crew member sleeping or walking or floating past. Back at Charon Station she had been surrounded by thousands of other spacefarers— Colonial Marines, scientists, support crews, and the upper echelons of the Company and military.

Now, it truly felt like she was walking alone, unfollowed and unobserved. The deeper she descended into the asteroid base, the more she felt her mind settling. She and her crew had been dragged along by events, tumbled here, rolled there, and she'd hardly had time to gather herself. Even waiting for Palant to recuperate, Halley had felt pressure building all around her.

Now at last she had time to think.

She could never trust the Yautja. True, they'd helped them win the battle at LV-1657, and then actually handed over the android on the ruined Fiennes ship. Bringing them here with the android might have been a masterstroke, though. No doubt the base was shielded from any form of detection, and it seemed perfectly equipped for Palant to be able to extract all the information she could from the Rage general.

But Yautja were Yautja, implacable, unreliable. Always one of the Colonial Marines' most feared enemies, because there was no hope of negotiation with them.

Until now.

Halley remained unsettled by Palant's communication with the beasts, but she had to admit it was working to their benefit, so far.

There was more than that to concern her, however. Technically she and her crew had gone AWOL, killing McIlveen, the Company man, and then hiding away with the one thing that might help humanity fight the Rage. She *had* to believe it was all for the best, but her mind remained on edge—and she *wanted* that edge, because it meant she stayed sharp. She could see no good end for her and her crew, but this went way beyond personal considerations. They were doing what they genuinely thought best for the entire human race.

Still walking, she passed several arches in the walls that might have indicated doorways. She'd seen the walls fading and hardening again to allow them access to the lab, and she approached one of these arches to see if the same thing would happen.

It didn't.

Maybe some doors only worked for Yautja. If that was the case, it was a perfect security device. They had been allowed access into a place the Yautja must have been keeping secret for decades, if not much longer. There was doubtless so much more they weren't being permitted to see.

What might happen when the time came to leave?

The smells, the sounds, the sights, everything felt alien. She'd become used to the smell of Yautja—had experienced it in battle, and when Palant and Elder Kalakta had met to make peace. Here it was heavier, the warm spicy aroma seemingly a part of the atmosphere, imbued in the walls. There was a steady background grumble, almost sub-audible. It was probably life support systems and augmented gravity, but she couldn't help imagining it coming from a Yautja throat, or perhaps a group of them.

She pictured a dozen of them, more, squatting motionless in a room and sending the hum vibrating through the asteroid.

Descending more large steps, Halley came to a junction of several passageways. She instructed her suit to compose a map of their route and went in a random direction.

The place felt deserted. It was evidently a large base, but didn't seem to be heavily occupied. Then again, Yautja weren't thought to be a particularly social species.

Twenty minutes after setting out, she heard human voices.

She paused, crouched, and drew her weapon. Consulting her suit, she made sure she hadn't simply walked in a wide circle and returned to the area of the labs. But she didn't recognize these voices. Whoever it was, they were talking with an urgency she did not like.

As she moved along the passage and closer to the source, she started to identify clicks and buzzes that indicated these were transmissions. The revelation relaxed her a little, but not the tone of the voices.

A few yards ahead of her stood an open archway in the wall. The voices came from within. She edged closer, sidearm held down by her side. When she reached the opening and peered inside, she holstered her weapon.

The room was empty. A bank of communication equipment lined one wall, objects she hardly recognized— hollow crystal globes, tubes throbbing with pulses of light, banks of a papery material stacked like layers of a bees' nest. She couldn't see precisely where the voices issued from. They faded in and out, and she only caught snippets.

Those were enough.

She stood in the middle of that strange room and listened.

…at least ten thousand, maybe more, and they're landing…

…wiped out, just murdered, none of them taken prisoner…

…over two thousand dead, and that's just in one village. The cities…

…Weaver's World, but we won't even reach orbit for another eight days…

…massacre. A massacre! I've never seen anything like it. It's…

…horrible. Help us. Someone help us!

There was more. The gruesome picture grew more layered and detailed, and in her mind's eye she saw terrible things.

"Weaver's World," Halley muttered. She had family there, cousins she hadn't seen for decades. She was pretty sure Bestwick had a brother there, too. She'd been panicked when they heard about the sabotage at Swartwood Station 3, but he'd been down on the planet at the time. He probably still was.

There were nine million settlers on Weaver's World.

Heart hammering, she looked around the communications room. It was an intelligence gathering center. She should have been concerned at that, because this was espionage on a grand scale. She also should have wondered just how the Yautja were receiving these communications from so far away.

All that mattered right then was what she heard.

Halley turned and ran from the room, sprinting back the way she had come.

Her crew were where she had left them. Sprenkel and Huyck had finished servicing and rearming their com-rifles, and Bestwick was eating. They presented a scene of faux relaxation, although Halley knew they were just as coiled as her.

"Weaver's World is under attack," she said.

"What?" Bestwick said. "How do you know?"

She told them about the room she'd found, the transmissions that were being intercepted.

"We have to go," Bestwick said.

"Your brother's there," Halley said. "I know that makes it personal, but we need to plan."

"Plan how? Plan what?"

"It's a fucking long way," Sprenkel said. He'd already accessed his suit computer, contacted the ship's computer, Billy, and processed a travel plan. "Three drops, with travel time in between. And there's no saying all three dropholes are still in human hands."

"How much travel time?"

"Over forty days at *Pixie*'s top speed."

"Maybe the Yautja have faster ships," Huyck said.

Halley shook her head. She turned and paced to the door. When she'd returned and rushed back through the lab, Palant and the Yautja had been in the same position, android spread across the surface before them, leads and wires protruding. They had come here for this, to learn whatever they could from this Rage general.

"We can't just leave," she said.

"But there are millions of people on Weaver's World."

"Yes, and thousands of Marines probably heading there right now. One more ship and four more Marines won't make much difference."

"It's our duty!" Sprenkel said.

"Your duty is to obey my orders!" Halley snapped, and immediately she was sorry. They knew that. None of them held it against her.

"The major's right," Huyck said, nodding past her. "That's what matters. If anything the Yautja Woman finds out can help us, that's more important now."

Halley nodded, then headed across the lab. The others came with her. She felt a kinship with them that was deeper than family, stronger than simple friendship. They had killed and faced death together, and that gave them a bond no one else could understand.

Facing their android enemy as a team made them feel stronger than ever before.

They listened, and watched, and hoped that progress was being made. But Halley quickly found her hopes fading.

"What are your strengths?" Palant asked the android.

"Without limit."

"Yet your ship was destroyed."

"I allowed that."

"Really? So what was that, a strategic decision?"

"Of course." The mechanical's voice was strange, strained, yet not without character. Halley could hear the humor underscoring every word.

"It seems a strange way to win a war."

"It got me here, didn't it?"

Palant glanced around at Yaquita. The Yautja on her wheeled platform was listening to the android's translated words, and processing information on the large globe by her side. She didn't seem startled or troubled.

They're not stupid, Halley thought. *They'd have never*

brought us and the android here if they thought it was a threat.

"Your self-destruct is disabled," Halley said.

"Is it really?"

"The base is shielded. No transmissions in or out."

"I seriously doubt that." The android's single eye turned wetly in its head and fixed upon Halley. Surprised, still she did not look away. She wouldn't give it the satisfaction.

"A word," Halley said.

Palant raised a hand to show that she'd heard, then continued questioning the android.

"You're vulnerable," she said. "You're ruined."

"My shell is ruined."

"And your mind?"

The android gurgled something unintelligible. The Yautja spoke back. The android hissed, and a cloud of vapor rose from its mouth and lacerated face.

Palant consulted the datapad beside her, and smiled.

"That's not a very nice thing to say."

"It's fucking with you," Sprenkel said, and Palant looked back over her shoulder at them.

"Of course it is." She stood, stretched, and paused beside Yaquita for a while. She leaned in close and looked at several screens on the globe. Palant pointed at one reading. Yaquita growled something in her strange language, and Palant glanced at her datapad. Again she smiled.

"I really need a word," Halley said. "Preferably away from that thing."

Palant nodded. She tossed a glance at Yaquita, the pale blue containment field faded, and she stepped through.

"I need to eat anyway," she said. "What's the food like here?"

No one replied.

"I take that to mean surprisingly good."

"We're not used to complimenting Yautja on their

culinary expertise," Halley said. "Come on… our room."

Once Palant was standing at the food replicator waiting for her choice, Halley told her what she knew.

Palant's face turned pale. She leaned against the counter.

"I was afraid of this," she said. "All-out war."

"It sounds like a massacre," Halley said.

"It's a distraction," Palant said. "It has to be. What other reason to slaughter an entire planet?"

"So what I need to know is, how much have you found out from that bastard?"

"And can I fire a laser through its head yet?" Bestwick said.

"We're discovering more with every moment," Palant said. "Or rather, Yaquita is. The Yautja technology is… way ahead of ours. While I speak to Oscar and it teases me back, trying to tie me in knots, Yaquita is plumbing the depths of its damaged mind."

"And it doesn't know?" Halley asked.

"I'm sure it suspects, but it's more hurt than it admits, and whatever defenses it might once have had against such interrogation have fallen. It's hanging on by a thread, and it's only the power we're feeding it that's keeping it alive."

"So what have you found out?" Sprenkel asked.

"Lots of minor stuff," Palant said. "Some history. Names, hierarchy. The aspect that seems of most interest to Yaquita is the Drukathi, who or whatever that is. But I think we've found something else. I think I know how to make it self-destruct."

Halley blinked, then gasped as realization dawned.

"And all the others?" she asked. "All the other Rage generals?"

"Perhaps. There might be a way. But…"

"There's always a but," Bestwick said.

"*But* we need to get on board their main control ship," Halley said. "Is that it?"

"Yeah. I think so." Palant nodded. "It's not just a case of transmitting a sub-space signal, and then all the generals go bang. There's a deep link between them and their Xenomorph troops, and we haven't even got close to understanding it with Oscar yet. There's also a definite link between the android generals and who or whatever controls them. A link that's beyond any technology I know about, or can understand."

"A psychic link?" Halley said.

Palant nodded.

"So we need to find the central control hub."

"We certainly need to start looking," Palant said.

"And we don't know anything about it."

"Well…"

Halley raised an eyebrow.

"It's called the *Macbeth*," Palant said. "As for where it is, I still don't know."

"You have to find out."

"I'm working on it, Major. Meanwhile, you need to work with the Yautja, and come up with a plan. Elder Kalakta wants to communicate with me soon, perhaps we'll know more then. Once we know where the *Macbeth* is, that'll be our one and only target."

"But Weaver's World?" Bestwick said.

"We can't let that distract us," Palant said. "We need to win the war, not join the battle."

"What about the Drukathi?"

Palant shook her head. "Yaquita won't say anything. I think she's waiting for Elder Kalakta. Maybe he'll tell me."

"She said it changes everything," Halley said.

"We'll see." Palant took a drink of her coffee and sighed. "Yeah. That's not bad."

9

BEATRIX MALONEY

Outer Rim
December 2692 AD

"Mistress Maloney," Karath said, standing nervously just inside her cabin door. "Something's happening."

"To the drophole?"

"No. To the Faze."

"*What?*"

"It's... it's coming apart."

"Dying?"

"I don't think so," Kareth said. He was frowning, afraid, and Maloney felt something that might have been maternal concern. She had never had children, and had never regretted the fact. The Rage was her family now, and even when she was young enough to consider conceiving, when she had been with the Founders—a loyal disciple of Wordsworth—she had never thought of herself as a mother. The idea of something growing inside her had seemed alien, and repulsive.

Kareth and Dana were her children. Helpers and servants, they had also grown to fulfil other tasks never assigned to them. Neither of them had ever called her mother, but she saw the way they sometimes looked at her, with fear and love.

"Don't worry," she said, drifting across her cabin and nudging against Kareth at the door. "It's never done anything to harm us."

"I've never liked it," he whispered. He looked down at the floor, as if having muttered a dark secret.

"I don't think we were ever supposed to," Maloney said. "Now guide me to a viewing portal, will you? My platform isn't fully charged, and I like it when you or Dana push me."

"Dana's on her way," he said, happily now. "She's been to the welfare suites with Challar, preparing *Macbeth* for the drop."

"The cryo-pods are still in working order?"

"I believe so. We don't need as many as we believed. There are fewer shipborn than ever."

Maloney knew the numbers. There were a dozen original Founders left, now the elders of the Rage. All of them were approaching three centuries old. As for those who had never seen or known Earth or the Human Sphere, there were only a hundred shipborn left alive. Genetic doctoring meant that interbreeding did not present any problems, although no new child had been born for a dozen years.

Maloney had put a hold on procreation once she knew that their journey back to the Sphere was well underway, their arrival due in a handful of years. She wanted no children to distract the crew from their tasks.

That was yet another reason why the loss of the *Othello* had come as such a shock.

But as well as the hundred humans and dozen elders, the Rage also had the generals and, under the androids' direct command, tens of thousands of Xenomorph soldiers. The *Macbeth* was a powerful ship. The Faze had performed adaptations that made it and its constituent vessels almost perfect weapons of war.

They might be few, but they would be unstoppable.

Once the *Macbeth* dropped through into Sol System, the ship would break down into a dozen individual craft, each of them heavily armed and bearing an army the likes of which the Colonial Marines had never faced before. Challar and the other Rage elders would command a ship each, with the Xenomorphs under the android generals' control. Maloney would command the largest, main vessel, still called *Macbeth*.

Everyone had their orders. Everything was ready.

The Faze doing something unexpected troubled Maloney, but she did her best not to display her concern.

Kareth pushed her through the ship's passageways, past bulkheads adapted by the Faze, through chambers filled with new equipment that strange being had constructed. Eventually they arrived at a portal that presented the best view of the huge drophole.

They were only two miles away, and the Faze was clearly visible. It drifted toward them slowly, the limbs it had been using to work on the drophole now absorbed back into its strange body. As it grew closer, Maloney could see what Kareth had meant.

No longer a single, cohesive being, the Faze was now more of a cloud. It drifted toward them in a close formation, but as it neared *Maceth* its portions shifted apart.

"Magnify," Maloney said. The viewing portal hummed and the image before them grew larger.

"Twelve," Kareth said.

"Yes," Maloney said. "Of course." It was preparing to board *Macbeth* again, and attach a part of itself to each of the large vessel's individual components. Once through the drophole, each Rage ship would still contain an element of the Faze.

"It's controlling us," Kareth said.

"What? No," Maloney said. "It's helping us."

"I'm sorry, Mistress," Kareth muttered.

"No, say your piece." Maloney felt a chill passing through her body. Impossible, she knew, because the gel kept her perfectly maintained at the optimum levels for her enhanced life. Yet she shivered, because Kareth was voicing an idea that had haunted her for years.

"It's just... it does everything to help us, and to make our ships better," Kareth said. "The *Macbeth* travels much faster than it was ever designed for. Our systems are almost too advanced for us to control, the weaponry is powerful, warp drives have been refined to such a degree that the wastage is a portion of one percent.

"We've always accepted that, just as we've always been at peace with the Faze seeming to know just what we want of it. But what if that isn't the case at all? What if it's just making us *think* that, and in fact we end up desiring what it wants of *us*?"

"A return to the Sphere has always been my intention," Maloney said, her voice stern. She saw the effect this had on Kareth, and she felt almost sorry for the man. But she would not have her authority and control questioned. Not even here, in private, by one of the two humans she loved.

"Of course, Mistress," Kareth said. "But the Faze dictates our ways and means."

"It helps."

"But why?"

Maloney did not answer. She didn't know.

"I don't believe it acts on its own," Kareth said. "I've had… dreams. Ideas. I think it's a tool of something far greater."

"I've considered that," Maloney said. "The Rage elders have debated it, many times over the decades. Of course we have! But even if that proves to be the case, we see no harm. Our aims are intact—the Faze simply gives us the means."

"But the idea of some other intelligence controlling it…" Kareth said, drifting off as he watched the image of the Faze spreading, its smaller part approaching the *Macbeth* and disappearing from view. Each part penetrated the ship through a different exterior door. Once on board, they would move under their own propulsion, settle somewhere in each section of the ship.

Waiting for the drop, and whatever came next.

Maloney remembered the fossilized remains of those dog-like aliens they had discovered deep in *Midsummer*. She often wondered about them.

"We are in control," Maloney said. "*I* am in control! Never forget that, Kareth."

"I won't, Mistress." He bowed, eyes averted.

Maloney stared at the drophole that would soon transport them into the heart of a war she had begun. She swallowed her doubts, and wondered what might happen if the time came when she sought to destroy the Faze.

"Everything is ready," Dana said. She'd run from the welfare suites, her excitement obvious. Born after the Rage coup, she and Kareth had been waiting for these events their entire lives. For them, this was destiny coming home to roost.

"Good!" Maloney said. "So tell me."

Dana grinned, delighted to be asked.

"All of the cryo-pods are prepared," she said. "The adapted pods for yourself and the other Rage elders are also ready. All Xenomorph hatching is complete, and the soldiers have been distributed to the relevant holds. Full links have been confirmed through the hub to their respective generals, and the generals are seeing that their troops are ready for action.

"The Faze has…" Her smile dropped, voice sounding more troubled.

"We saw," Maloney said.

"They've each settled into the separate ships' warp containment fields."

"Their own method of surviving the long drop, perhaps," Kareth said.

"The Faze is still with us," Maloney said. "That's all that matters. The queen?"

"She's still laying," Kareth said.

Maloney nodded. The Xenomorph queen would remain in the *Macbeth*'s central core, which would form the part of the ship Maloney herself would command. The beast had been with them for a long time, and perhaps she might yet enter into the war with them. Restrained for so long, fed a diet of humans. Maloney often imagined the magnificent creature, unleashed and raging through a human ship, or through the densely populated, polluted cities of Earth.

"And the generals?"

"The generals have opted to remain conscious during the drop, in case we emerge into trouble." Dana seemed proud of the androids' decision.

"Good," Maloney said, nodding. That made sense. It was known that androids could withstand a drophole journey, while humans had to be placed in cryo-suspension for the short timespan a drop would take. Yet even for an android the effects could be debilitating, and this was a drop the like of which no one had ever made.

Nevertheless, it was still the correct choice. There was no way of knowing what they were jumping into, three thousand trillion miles away. Anything could be waiting for them when they emerged.

With the generals waiting, fingers on triggers, their safety would be assured.

"This is science we don't know," Kareth said. "What if we drop through, and a million years have gone by? What if—"

"Enough," Maloney said. "We're close to victory." She should have berated him, but she did not. His fear came from wonder, and she felt it herself.

"Yes, Mistress," he said.

"Schedule the drop for twelve hours from now. Inform everyone that I want a conference in three hours. Elders, shipborn, generals—everyone is to congregate in the central chamber. I'll address the remainder of the Rage face to face, before we travel into battle, and victory."

1 0

MAJOR SERGEI BUDANOV

Weaver's World
December 2692 AD

There was a story about how Weaver's World got its name. Major Budanov had heard it on his first posting here, and it had done little to settle his nerves at the time.

His previous postings had been to desolate asteroids, space stations, or habitats built and expanded over centuries, artificial places or bases where every part had a purpose, and his surroundings were angular and formed. Weaver's World was a Goldilocks planet, rich in flora and fauna, much of it unknown to science. Most people would have been excited.

Budanov heard about the spiders, and any excitement he might have felt had faded away.

Thing was, they weren't even dangerous. There was some scientific name they'd been given, but they were commonly known as jewel spiders because of their remarkable colorings and ability to chameleon from one pattern and shade to another depending on their surroundings. They frequently swarmed, nests of billions of creatures covering hillsides and valleys in swathes of glimmering, iridescent webbing. They caught insects and small birds, and frequent birthings of young filled the air with countless floating skeins of gossamer strands, each of them carrying an arachnid the size of a pinhead.

They were beautiful, amazing, harmless. They had given the planet its name. Budanov had hated them even before he'd landed, and nothing that had happened to him had shaken that feeling.

Until now. Now, he'd happily be thrown naked into a jewel spider's nest rather than do what he had to do.

The creatures they fought were a million times larger, and there was nothing beautiful about them.

"Major, we've got reports coming in—"

"No more death tolls," Budanov said. "Tell me something useful, or don't tell me anything at all."

The corporal beside him fell silent.

There is no good news, Budanov thought. *This is like the end*.

They rode in one of the skimmers often used for transport on Weaver's World. This one was adapted for Colonial Marine use, its fuselage reinforced, heavy laser cannons and a plasma gun fixed to its wings. They were escorted by two fighters, fast craft that the garrison had been developing and improving over the many decades they had been stationed here.

The sky was bright blue and cloudless. In the distance he could just make out the shining spires and graceful skyscrapers of Boston Three. Several years ago he'd visited Boston Two on Addison Prime, and that had proven to be a seedy, run-down city, once part of that planet's settlers' base, now little more than a hive of criminality and illegal shipping. It had been haunted by indies and pirates, and even as a Colonial Marine major, he'd felt danger stalking him.

Boston Three was very different. Perhaps the most cosmopolitan city on Weaver's World, it was home to the best theaters and arts centers, the food was exquisite and celebrated across the Sphere, and its science institute was the greatest outside of Sol System. Of particular interest to Budanov were the coffee plantations stretching out beyond its eastern extremes. The Boston Three bean was widely regarded as the best coffee bean grown anywhere in the known galaxy.

Now, Boston Three was burning.

"Two miles!" the corporal snapped.

"Lock on and fire," Budanov said. Their skimmer shuddered as the plasma gun unleashed a blazing hail of fire toward the small object in the distance. The Rage dropship was one of seven that had been detected heading for Boston Three, and Budanov had issued orders that the dropships should be targeted as a priority. Once they landed and disgorged their infernal occupants, the Xenomorphs became shadows, flitting through the settlements and cities like dark ghosts, slaughtering as they went. Street-to-street, hand-to-hand fighting was proving costly to the Marine contingent, and already combat losses were high.

Death tolls among civilians were unbearable.

Hitting the dropships before they landed was the best way of combating the Rage right now. He knew that the battle in orbit continued, and that the 7th Spaceborne were suffering crippling losses. He would never, ever admit aloud that they were fighting a losing battle, but the truth hung heavy around his heart.

"Direct hit!" the corporal said.

"Deflected," the gunner said. "It's got shields, just like the others."

"Hit it again," Budanov said. "Fighters, peel away and strike it from both sides. Combined assault should knock it down, even if it does have shields."

"They're locking on!" the corporal said, and their skimmer spun and spiraled as he performed avoidance maneuvers. The skies outside flared briefly as the dropship's return fire sizzled past.

Budanov felt his stomach lurch and drop, then the ground rushed up at them. The corporal piloted the craft a few yards above the ground, skimming the landscape and then twitching their nose upward so that they were screaming in toward the dropship's underside.

"Let's see if they've got a soft belly," the corporal said as the gunner locked on and opened fire.

Twin spears of laser blasted out from the skimmer, followed by a searing white blast from the plasma gun. At the same time the fighters fired solid-state missiles, the constructs exploding on impact. The dropship disappeared for a moment in a blast of blinding light, the skimmer's cockpit screen darkening to protect its passengers' eyes.

The corporal swung them around into another crazy spin, then leveled again.

The dropship had fallen to within a dozen yards of the ground, and accelerated. It left a trail of smoke behind it, but there appeared to be no damage whatsoever to the fuselage.

"How the fuck do we bring these things down?" the gunner shouted.

"Open channel," Budanov said, and he heard the subtle click as the skimmer's computer opened comms. "This is Major Budanov. Have any air units managed to bring down a dropship?"

"Negative…"

"No, sir…"

"Shielded…"

"We used a nuke." It was a voice he recognized. Lieutenant Seeton. "Knocked it out of the sky, bounced down a mountainside. We went back in and blew it to hell."

"Use nukes if you can," Budanov said. "But only if it's safe! Enough of our people are dying."

They were within a mile of Boston Three now, and already he could see how much the city was suffering. Fires had erupted in countless places, columns of smoke reaching for the sky in the still air. They spread above the city like a cloak. Flashes of laser fire flickered here and there like static, although they were too far away to make out individual incidents of combat. There were at least five hundred Marines on the ground, combating the Xenomorphs that had already landed.

"Corporal, take us low and quiet," Budanov said. "Hold fire until the dropship's disgorging its cargo."

"Sir."

The fighters whisked by above them, unable to hover. They roared over the city and then began circling, laser cannons arcing down as they picked out individual targets. But they didn't fire very often. Their big weapons were too destructive for such surgical strikes.

The dropship, still smoking, hovered in closer to the city, and its big bay doors dropped open.

"Ready," Budanov said.

"I'll blow them to—"

The dropship flashed.

"Lock on!" the corporal shouted. Then the skimmer was struck by a heavy blast, cockpit window exploding inward. Budanov's combat suit hardened and protected him from some of the blast, but he felt a rush of heat across his shoulders and neck.

Someone screamed.

Through the flames, and the hail of molten glass and

metal, and the smoke, Budanov saw the pilot slumped low at the controls, half of his head blown off. He wiped at his visor, smearing red.

The skimmer was spinning.

Budanov unclasped his straps and threw himself forward, landing across the corporal's splayed legs and grasping onto the controls. They thrashed against his hands. Air screamed through the broken window and fuselage, and Budanov leaned heavily on the controls, dragging them down and to the left to try and take the skimmer out of its deadly spin.

"Brace!" the gunner shouted. Budanov hadn't even noticed she was still alive. "Brace for—"

The craft slammed into the ground. A copse of trees broke some of their fall, trunks exploding all around them, leaves and splintered branches pouring through the broken window until at last they came to a halt.

Fires roared. The engine hammered, still cycling, and Budanov smelled the rancid scent of melting metals and plastics, flowing together.

"Out!" he shouted. "Now!" He and the gunner helped each other, struggling up the sloping floor to the smashed cockpit window and hauling themselves outside. The chance of surviving a crash like that was minimal, but Budanov didn't give himself time to feel lucky.

They had to get away before the skimmer exploded.

Dropping to the ground, the Major wiped his combat suit's visor again, worried that his vision was hazing and perhaps he was losing consciousness. But then the gunner was beside him, and her reaction chilled him to the core.

"I fucking hate these things."

The woodland they had crashed into was a spiders' nest. Their webbing was everywhere—hanging from trees, splayed from branch to branch—and the extravagantly colored arachnids were skittering all around, disturbed by the violence that had crashed down into their midst.

Budanov felt panic grabbing him, but he closed his eyes and took in a few deep breaths. He felt a hand close around his.

"We're fine," the gunner said. It was an intimate gesture, far removed from their position and relative status. He smiled at her, grateful.

"This way," Budanov said, and they headed in the direction of the fighting. They could hear the sizzle of laser blasts and, less frequently, the unmistakable screech of Xenomorphs on the hunt. The woodland they'd landed in was on the outskirts of Boston Three, part of a wild park that formed the city's eastern border. They didn't have very far to go.

To Budanov, it looked as if it would take forever.

The webbing tore as they pushed through, ripping like thin cloth. Spiders scrambled away from them, but they still had to push aside countless strands and sheets of web laden with old, dried meals. Budanov constantly wiped his visor free of webbing, and he found himself speckled with a fine silver dust that drifted on subtle breezes. He didn't know what it was. He didn't *want* to know.

Twenty minutes of effort and they emerged from the nesting area. The gunner was swathed in webs, only a few parts of her uniform visible, and she grinned as she looked him up and down.

"Fetching," she said.

"Are you flirting with me because you're a spider lover, Private?"

"Not at all, Major. I wouldn't—" She looked past him, eyes wide. "Oh, fuck."

Budanov spun around, drawing his sidearm and expecting to see the spiderish dash of a Xenomorph.

But this was something else.

The Rage dropship was aflame, drifting down and to the left until it disappeared behind buildings. Moments later, there was a huge explosion.

"What the hell?" Budanov said.

A ship streaked through the cloud of smoke and flame, banking over the city in a tight circle and firing another salvo at the downed craft.

"Not Marine," the gunner said.

"No," Budanov said. "That's Yautja."

Three more ships appeared low to the horizon, and moments later another dropship—so far across the city that Budanov hadn't noticed it—bloomed into flames and dropped from the sky. Instinctively the Major felt a surge of elation.

The Yautja ships began to land. The one that had taken out the first dropship banked right and descended close to them, settling in the park area.

"They've come for a hunt," the gunner said. "I just hope we aren't considered prey." She drew her sidearm, but Budanov held her arm.

"Holster it." He did the same with his weapon.

"Sir?"

"They've been fighting with us, on our side," he said. "That's what I've heard, at least. Though I don't really know *what* to trust anymore."

The ship was almost a mile away, its engine rapidly winding down to a gentle hum. A doorway appeared in the fuselage and then a tall creature stepped out, jumping to the ground, pausing, looking around to take stock.

Its gaze fell upon them.

Budanov felt it, like a weight. A targeting laser spiked red fingers at them, playing across his chest and the gunner's torso.

And now it blasts out my guts to prove me wrong, he thought.

The Yautja turned and moved rapidly toward the city.

"Come on," Budanov said. "We've got work to do."

As they ran after the striding Yautja, it crossed a roadway and passed between the first buildings. Two shadows came at it from the building on the left, spiked, skittering things larger than a man.

The Yautja paused and blasted them to pieces. They burst apart, their dregs splashing and sizzling across the ground. The hunter screamed, a cry of bloodlust and triumph that echoed between the buildings.

For just a moment, the sounds of chaos and violence seemed to pause, as the place took heed of this new arrival.

By the time they reached the dead Xenomorphs, Budanov had seen two more Yautja ships appearing overhead. As they passed into the first shadows cast by Boston Three's buildings, he allowed himself to feel hope.

That hope fled as they entered the city.

Major Budanov had seen plenty of death, and had dealt it himself on occasion, but he had never seen anything like this. He'd viewed holos of the slaughter, read reports, and flying across the vast continent of Ellia toward Boston Three, they had skirted the equator and witnessed the scenes of destruction around the space elevator and its infrastructure and ports.

The elevator had been blown by a contingent of the 7th Spaceborne when they discovered it was being used by the Rage to ferry down their Xenomorph troops. That great structure, eighteen years in the making and seeming to exist in defiance of the laws of physics, had fallen like a colossus and smashed across the land. Its upper sections were shattered and sent spinning into low orbits, where huge portions burned up in the atmosphere, adding flaming yellow exclamation marks across the heavens.

Flying above such scenes of destruction, Budanov hadn't been close enough to witness the true extent of the massacres. He'd seen the evidence of bodies, however, piled here and there like tangles of clothing.

Entering Boston Three gave him the full, first-hand experience.

There were hundreds of dead scattered through the streets. Some were marines, their combat suits ripped and shredded, their flesh the same. Others were people who had simply been fleeing the carnage. Men, women, children, torn asunder and cast aside. Flesh was torn from bones. Bones were snapped. Heads were crushed by the dreadful Xenomorph teeth. Clothes had been cut and holed, revealing insides that were red. Children lay huddled beneath the useless protection of their parents' bodies, drowned in blood.

"Oh, my God," the gunner said.

"Not here," Budanov said. "Not now." He retained some belief in a form of god, though he didn't ally himself with any organized religion. This stretched his faith so far that he felt it readying to snap.

In the distance were sounds of battle, but here the battle had already happened.

"A dead one," the gunner said, pointing across the street toward the base of a building. The structure was crazed and burnt with the familiar trace of laser fire, and spread across the heavy crystal doors they saw a different type of burn. The acid splash of a Xenomorph kill.

"Only one," Budanov said. "I don't see any more. Do you?"

"No, sir," the gunner replied. "No more dead Xenos.

Only our dead. And there are…"

"Thousands."

The streets of Boston Three were set like spokes on a wheel, all leading from the large central area which housed markets and theaters, food stalls, and a hub of commerce, art, and entertainment. Two miles distant, usually it was clearly visible down one of the spokes, but it was invisible now because of the clouds of smoke. As far as they could see, the road they followed was paved with the dead.

"Movement!" the gunner said.

"Got it. Let's move." Much as Budanov hoped it meant survivors, they had to assume it meant the enemy. At least until they could confirm, one way or another. He gripped his sidearm tightly.

They dashed along toward a large domed structure, doing their best not to tread on the dead or slip in spilled blood and gore. It was difficult. Several times he felt his boots landing on something softer than the road's surface, but he never looked down.

The movement was a single trace, and now that they moved it shifted direction, and began moving directly toward them.

Halfway to the dome, Budanov paused next to a dead marine and scooped up a com-rifle. The soldier's head was a squashed mess, and he silently gave thanks. Pairing the weapon to his suit and assessing its status, he found that it was seventy percent armed. That was good. It made him feel safer. Today was a day for heavier firepower.

"Twenty yards," the gunner said. "It'll be in sight soon."

Nothing moved. They reached the domed building and hunkered down behind two of the heavy stone planters that encircled its forecourt. Three dead people shared their hiding place. It had done them no good.

"It's close," Budanov said.

"We should be able to see it!" the gunner said. "Ten yards, dead ahead, and…" She trailed off, just as she saw what Budanov also saw.

A smear in the air. A smudge, like haze generated by the heat, moving of its own accord.

"Lower your weapon," Budanov said.

"Sir?"

"Do it!" Budanov lowered the com-rifle and his gunner did the same. He stood slowly from behind the planter, just as the strange disturbance in the air changed. It settled before them, sparking and quivering as the Yautja appeared as if from thin air. It was barely ten yards away.

Tall, broad chested, it wore its battle helmet and carried a long spear in its right hand. Its left arm was damaged, dripping green blood, and smoke rose from its injured hand. It was shivering a little, but its head remained still. The targeting laser coming from its shoulder settled on the planter between Budanov and the gunner, ready to flit up at a moment's notice.

Budanov held out his left hand, palm facing the Yautja.

"We're… on your side," he said. He had no idea if the thing heard or understood.

It clicked, croaked, and then it spoke in a spooky impersonation of his voice. "We're… on your side." It then waved behind it with the spear and said something else, a series of noises that made no sense.

"Major," the gunner said. "Big movement, closing quickly."

"I see it," Budanov said.

"It led them right to us!"

"Yeah, so we could help." He glanced at the big alien's injured arm, and thought he understood. "Get ready. Pick your targets, and don't assume one shot will bring them down."

The Yautja strode right over the planter and stood just to their right, the building to their backs. Budanov could smell the creature, and could feel the heat radiating from its body. It was terrifying and amazing, but he didn't have time to dwell on it.

The Xenomorphs burst from a building across the street, and a narrow pathway that ran beside it. Limbs clicking, they came across the paved road, hissing softly, aiming for them in a concerted, organized attack. There must have been twenty of them, spread out to offer difficult targets, passing over the bodies of dead civilians.

A blast from the Yautja's shoulder cannon took down the first one. It burst apart.

Budanov's combat suit gave him a firing option and he took it, firing a burst of nano ordnance that impacted the advancing creatures and exploded, shearing off limbs, blasting chunks out of their heads. A couple of them fell and seemed to explode across the ground, but others came on, ignoring their injuries and spraying deadly acid from their wounds. He shifted to plasma bursts and took out the two leading Xenos in a blazing white-hot fire. His suit darkened its visor against the glare.

His gunner started shooting, laser sprays that cut down the beasts one by one. As each alien fell, its destruction sent up a haze of gases, and another would leap through the cloud, using the death of its companion as cover.

The Yautja stepped left and right. Its sighting laser cast a bloody, probing finger through the mists of battle, blaster singling out and taking down the attackers.

Budanov's com-rifle chimed to signal the end of his plasma charge, and he switched to laser.

The noise was deafening, the violence shocking.

The paved area became a scene of chaos, Xenomorph corpses sizzling, melting the dead civilians that lay in their path. The smells were sickening, even filtered through the suit masks.

Then, as quickly as it had begun, the assault was over.

"Holy fuck," the gunner said. She was breathing fast and hard, and Budanov clasped her shoulder and squeezed.

He glanced at the Yautja. Its breathing was labored, and he noticed for the first time that the damage to its left arm also extended to its side, acid burns that still smoked as its skin and flesh was eaten away. There was nothing he could do.

"Thanks," he said. "Er…"

A screech, the whip of something whisking through the air, and the Yautja leapt forward, shoving past Budanov and the gunner and spearing a leaping Xenomorph through the head. The beast cried out, and the Yautja jumped onto the planter and heaved the dying creature away. It let go of its spear and fell back, landing heavily between the Marines just as the Xenomorph melted down into a foul soup.

Budanov reached for the Yautja, instinctively seeking to help. He felt its huge hand close around his own, and he knew it could crush his bones and pulp his fingers, even through the protective suit.

He pulled, and it allowed him to help it stand.

"Maybe we should stay together," Budanov said.

"We're… on your side," the Yautja said again, in his voice. Then it jumped over the planter, retrieved its spear from the melted-down Xenomorph, and sprinted away along the road. They watched as it skirted left and disappeared between buildings, cloaking as it went, becoming a phantom.

"Holy fuck," the gunner said again.

"Come on," Budanov said. "We've got to find a decent transmitter. People need telling about this."

"Yeah, right—but what *is* this?"

"Weirder by the minute."

They went from door to door, always with half an eye on their trackers. A couple of times they saw traces of movement, drawing close and then moving away again, and Budanov had to assume they were Yautja approaching to see whether or not they were Xenomorphs.

Though they could still hear the sounds of battle in the distance, the immediate vicinity was eerily quiet. When they saw the troop carrier parked askew along a side street, Budanov called a pause.

"Doors are open," he said. "No sign of life."

"No sign of movement," the gunner corrected. "Could be anything waiting inside that thing."

The troop carrier was a purely functional vehicle, a box with a motor, wheels designed for difficult terrain, and a hover facility for softer passage across paved areas. The hover was off now, wheels deployed. Even from this distance Budanov could see the mess ingrained in the wheel's treads. The detritus of the dead.

"Oh shit," the gunner said. "They've been driving over people."

"And over those bastard things," Budanov said. "Focus in on the front left wheel."

It was melted. There were also burn marks across the vehicle's side, and splashed around the door. Surrounding buildings showed scarring from laser fire, and the circular pits of exploding nano-shot. The road's surface was cratered from a dozen explosions.

"Split up, ten yards between us," Major Budanov said. "Slow advance. Eyes on the movement detector."

They moved closer. It was only as they neared the troop carrier that they saw the dead.

There were three marines lying in one of the craters. They'd been taken apart, but they had died bravely. Several acid patches—areas of disturbed ground melted and set again—showed where Xenomorphs had been taken out. Close to the vehicle were more bodies, and blood dripped steadily from inside. It pooled beneath the door, forming a dark mirror that reflected the cloudless blue sky.

Budanov signaled for the gunner to hold back. "You're carrying an old shotgun," he whispered.

"Erm… yessir." Private weapons were against regulations. "My great-grandfather's."

"Put a round through the door." Budanov knew that a laser blast might do more damage to the equipment inside the vehicle, and a plasma shot would fry it for sure. A few pellets from an old projectile weapon wouldn't harm anything that wasn't already fucked, and it might just stir up whatever might be waiting inside.

The gunner drew the weapon from her backpack, aimed, and fired. The shot was loud, quickly echoing away along the street. Nothing reacted. Budanov kept a careful eye on his suit's readouts, and there was no sign that anything still lived, anywhere in the vicinity.

The gunner ran toward the carrier, com-rifle at the ready once more. She paused at the doorway and looked inside.

"Clear," she said, voice small and weak.

Budanov went closer. He knew what he was going to see inside, but it was still a sickening shock. There might have been four of them, or perhaps as many as six or seven, but the marines had been taken apart, pulped, smashed to pieces by the Xenomorphs that had killed them. They hadn't even had a chance to use their weapons.

"Here," the gunner said. "In the cab. Comm unit's still pretty intact."

Budanov paired his suit to the transporter, and then accessed the Colonial Marine mainframe. His voice command opened an all-channel broadcast. Nodding to the gunner, he pointed to his eyes and then gestured all around them.

Keep watch. She already was.

"This is Major Sergei Budanov to all forces," he said into the comm. "The Yautja have joined the assault, and they're fighting with us. Do not engage them. Repeat, do *not* engage. Assist them where possible, join forces if they show the inclination. Their vessels can take out the Rage dropships, and on the ground they're combatting the Xenomorph troops.

"Fight hard. Continue fighting to protect and defend the civilians of Weaver's World." He paused, lost for words. The slaughter was already so horrific.

But now they knew what was happening. They could regroup, and they had the Yautja on their side.

"To the last Marine?" the gunner asked.

"To the last Marine," Budanov said, his words transmitted to ground and spaceborne troops all across and around Weaver's World.

In the distance, close to the center of Boston Three, the sound of combat grew more frenzied.

11

ISA PALANT

Gamma Quadrant
December 2692 AD

Elder Kalakta was more than three feet taller than Isa Palant, and perhaps a thousand years old. He exuded age. It came off him in waves, as if each breath she took was painted by scenes from his past, images and experiences, hunts and kills.

He was decorated with trophies she recognized, and some she did not. The ones she knew were worse. How could she speak with him when he sported a human spine, curled around one thigh? How could they collaborate when a mummified hand, tattooed with a Colonial Marine sigil and curled like a dead spider, hung on a cord around his neck?

She had to get past these doubts. She had done so before, and managed to bring about a delicate peace between human and Yautja. Again it was time for her to do the job that had been entrusted to her.

Kalakta wasn't actually there. He might have been a thousand miles away, or ten trillion, but the Yautja's communication suite made it seem as if they were in the same room. When Yaquita had taken her there, it had seemed like an ordinary cave, hewn from the asteroid in a roughly spherical shape. Only the door was artificial, and once they had passed through, that had hardened again behind her, leaving a smooth surface set among tool-scarred rock.

Then a brief hiss, and the entire chamber changed.

Abruptly she stood in a jungle, teeming with the sounds of unseen creatures, a warm breeze playing against her skin, and even the scents were vivid. It seemed as if, had she started to walk, she would encounter the thick undergrowth, rather than butt up against an unyielding wall.

It was more than a holo suite. It was amazing.

But fascination would have to wait.

Elder Kalakta stood before her, and it was the first time she'd seen him without guards. The illusion was so perfect that she thought she could reach out and touch him.

"Yaquita of the Wounded Clan has told me a shocking truth," Kalakta said. The datapad Palant carried translated his words almost instantaneously now, such was the program's progress.

"She mentioned Drukathi," Palant said, "but wouldn't tell me any more."

"Under my orders." Kalakta fell silent, leaning both hands on the head of a long stick, its point planted between his feet. It might have been a weapon—Palant wasn't sure. He regarded her with his piercing alien eyes, and she could discern nothing from his gaze. She hoped she held his respect, but she couldn't be sure. Perhaps he still considered her pathetic and weak.

"I can tell you some," he said finally. "Enough to illuminate. Enough to serve your purpose—and our purpose—in fighting the Rage. But the Drukathi have a history deeper, and older than anything you comprehend. Their history with the Yautja is… long. To us, your human lives are a fleeting thing. You are whispers in the dark, hardly heard. I can hear your heart now… bang, bang, bang, rushing toward your end. As if eager. To the Drukathi, Yautja lives would seem the same."

"Would?"

"Drukathi are long gone from here. Perhaps a million years ago there might have been a few left behind, but even then I believe they had moved on."

"To where? Another part of the galaxy?"

"Their time in this galaxy was over."

"Another galaxy completely?" she asked. "But that's…"

"Impossible," Kalakta said. He laughed softly. "What would your dropholes have looked like to your ancestors, just a thousand years ago?"

"The Yautja have been there?"

"Yautja history is not your concern." Palant was starting to pick up tones in the complex and very alien Yautja tongue. She thought Kalakta sounded cool, or perhaps angry.

"I apologize," she said, and the datapad translated. He seemed to accept.

"Even long-since departed, the Drukathi exert their influence," Kalakta said. His fingers tightened around the heavy head of the staff. "Their will."

Palant thought she understood.

"The things Yaquita has mined, and found traces of in the android's data memories," she said. "The habitat they found and called *Midsummer*, the beings they brought from deep down."

"Yes," Kalakta said, "and the remains they discovered.

Even the Yautja have never found anything like that."

Palant frowned, trying to understand. She decided to take a chance...

"Are you afraid of the Drukathi?"

"Afraid of something that is no longer here?"

Palant tilted her head.

"Perhaps," Kalakta admitted, his words swallowed in something that might have been a sigh. Palant knew that the admission of fear would be difficult for him, because fear implied weakness. She sensed that he was opening up to her, more than he'd ever intended, and she felt honored. Yet his fear made her afraid, as well.

"Can they really influence events?" she asked. "If they're so far away, if they've truly gone, what would be their interests, or their reasons?"

"That, I cannot know," he replied. "I suspect the things they left behind, some of which the Rage has found and used, were designed to prevent other civilizations from becoming too..." He trailed off.

"Warlike?"

Kalakta looked upward, as if considering the heavens.

"Advanced," he said.

"Have they interfered with Yautja in the past?" she asked.

He glared at her, offering nothing.

"It's still the Rage," Palant said. "They're the ones we have to defeat."

"If the Drukathi are aiding them, however passively, then they will be unbeatable."

"No," Palant said. She began to pace, forgetting that she wasn't really in that jungle, with that huge alien. The scene shimmered slightly and a force repulsed her, air thickening and edging her back toward where she'd been standing.

"It may not be the Rage the Drukathi remnants

consider too advanced," he said. "Their influence may have a broader purpose."

"You think they engineered this war? To hold us back?" The concept seemed so impossibly huge.

"I think aided, rather than engineered."

Palant shook her head, trying to absorb everything Kalakta had said. Trying to believe it.

"It doesn't matter," she said at last. "This changes nothing. We still have to fight, and knowing that the Rage's technology comes from somewhere else, well, it's irrelevant." She looked at Kalakta, eyebrows raised. "Isn't it?"

"Perhaps," he said. "The Yautja have known of the Drukathi for… longer than I can say. In all that time, we never found cause to go against them."

"But the Rage have killed your people," she persisted. "Destroyed your habitats. It's *them* you're going against."

"I simply seek to warn you," Kalakta said.

"Thank you for that, but I can't accept that the Rage are unbeatable. I *won't* accept that." She paused, and added, "I've begun to form a plan, and Yaquita will help me."

"You are a brave human."

"You are an honorable Yautja."

Kalakta's face twisted. It might have been a smile.

"I've always liked that name." His image faded, the jungle suddenly twisted and roared as if a hurricane had stormed in. Moments later she was alone in that room again, the darkness pressing in heavily.

The door faded open. Yaquita was there on her wheeled platform.

"You should come," she said.

"Something's happened?"

"Something's changed." Yaquita of the Wounded Clan turned and wheeled herself away, and Palant followed.

* * *

"He's dying," Palant said.

Oscar the android was shaking, jerking, and bleeding out across the examination table. Halley and her crew were gathered outside the containment field to watch, but Palant didn't like the look of satisfaction on their faces.

Do they still not understand?

"I thought we had control?" Palant asked.

"We did," Yaquita said. "We do."

"He's doing this himself, then. He's shutting his systems down, bypassing whatever blocks we've put on him."

"I'm doing everything I can." The Yautja ran her hands across the globe by her side, swiping screens, long taloned fingers tapping on the crystal surface.

"That won't be enough." Palant went to the android and leaned in close. His eye followed her, rolling in its fractured socket, pupil dilating as she drew close.

"Fail..." he croaked. "Fail..."

"Shut up." Palant started delving into the networks of wires and light cables snaking around and into him. She thrust her hands into his chest cavity, rooting deep, no longer careful to preserve any structures. They'd learned all they could from this thing, and now her priority was to save his data memories, in case they could access more.

First, however, she had to make sure he couldn't blow them all to hell.

"It's isolated," Yaquita said.

"You told me that about his support systems, and he's shutting them down. Let me work." She strained, pushed, pulled, tearing out handfuls of cool matter that dripped milky blood as she cast them aside. She heard one of the marines muttering in disgust, but she had no time to acknowledge them.

"This containment field…" she began.

"No," Yaquita said. "Of course not. If he detonates, it'll take out most of our base."

She finally uncovered the android's heart. It was still warm—not a true heart, yet she regarded this organ as the center of him. While his brain ran all functions, and stored data and programs, this was what *drove* him. Several light probes were attached, trailing like tendrils as she tugged the organ from his body.

Oscar might have gasped.

She held it tight and felt its potential, destruction as hot as a star's core, intent as cold as deep space. As well as the android's self-destruct nuke, she believed this was also the object that had provided him control over his dead Xenomorph army.

This might be their method to win the war.

"It's growing warm," she said.

"Impossible," Yaquita said. "It's disconnected, no longer part of him, and all his systems are under my control."

"Obviously that's not the fucking case!" The datapad translated her angry outburst into clicks and rattles, and she wondered whether "fucking" had a corresponding word or sound in Yautja.

Oscar was shaking even more now, bits of him slipping off of the table, slick trails of white blood and thick matter spilling over the edge. She felt it landing on her feet, cool and intimate. His eye was wide, and dead, and she felt a curious pang at his sudden lack of expression. She had always known they were interrogating a machine, but his personality had made dealing with it somehow… different.

"Hotter!" she said. She turned the wet heart in her hands, making certain there really were no connections left leading to his body. Pulling out the light probes, searching for a way in. If she simply ripped it apart, would that work? She tried.

It was tough, pliable but untearable. Blood seeped out as she squeezed.

"Palant!" Bestwick shouted. "Containment! Palant, shut down the—"

A hum, and the blue glow of the containment field faded away.

"Back!"

Yaquita picked her up, a hand under each arm, and her wheeled platform drew them quickly backward, dodging the other alien samples situated around the large room.

"Plasma!" Palant heard, and she knew to close her eyes.

The heat washed over her, the blast punched her in the face and chest, and then Yaquita was spinning and protecting her with her own body. Palant opened her eyes and saw their shadow thrown long across the room by the flaring plasma explosion.

Palant still grasped the heart in her hands.

Will I see it? she wondered, holding her breath. *Will I have time to see it burst apart, and feel the new sun growing in my hands?* But of course, she would not. When the nuke blew, her eyes, her brain would be blasted to atoms at the speed of light.

Then…

"It's cooling," she said. "It's stopped." The heart was lifeless, wet, and dead in her hands.

Yaquita turned around slowly, and placed her down again. Together, human and Yautja saw what had been done.

Oscar and the table were gone, melted into a boiling mess. The Marines were backed up against other displays, guns still aimed at what remained of him.

Halley's com-rifle smoked softly.

"Sometimes the old ways are the best," she said.

Palant closed her eyes and released a heavy sigh of relief.

"Tell us you can do something with that," Bestwick said.

"Perhaps," Palant said. "If we can find their ship the *Macbeth*, get there, board it, defeat the Rage on board…"

"No problem," Sprenkel said. "Just point us."

Palant looked helplessly at the dripping thing, all that remained of the android.

Yaquita spoke.

The datapad translated.

"I know where the *Macbeth* is."

1 2

LILIYA

Gamma Quadrant
December 2692 AD

It reminded Liliya of her time being tortured at Hashori's hand. Only this time she was being given something to help with the pain, and there was a purpose to the mutilation.

"You sure that's comfortable?" Yvette Tann asked.

"I didn't say it was comfortable," Liliya said.

"You can put up with it, though."

"Yes." Liliya nodded. She had no right trying to be light-hearted with these people. They had recently fled their home, and they knew the probable fate of those left behind. Many days later, they were still awaiting word from Hell.

Captain Ware and her crew of indies had fallen silent following the destruction of Alexander's ship. It was a respectful silence, during which they performed efficient and familiar routines around their ship the *Satan's Savior*, and allowed their group of unusual passengers time and space.

Yvette and Jiango Tann had wanted to make themselves busy. Liliya understood this immediate need, and their urgency quickly translated to her. It wasn't simply a desire to occupy themselves—it was an understanding about the future, and what it might bring. They'd all witnessed how powerful Alexander and his small fleet had been, and even though the Yautja had defeated them in the end, the thought of many other such attacks was sobering.

So they had commenced their experiments upon Liliya—experiments that had continued for fifteen days.

In the beginning the procedures were non-intrusive. Yvette performed some basic medical routines, and took readings that would set certain baselines for later tests. Jiango, meanwhile, spent the time unpacking the scientific equipment he'd managed to bring with him, and pairing it with some of the ship's systems. He seemed pleased to find that much of his equipment was compatible with the *Satan's Savior*'s computers, and went about setting up a small lab in a spare cabin.

That was where the real testing had begun.

Among them, they'd agreed upon a destination—Addison Prime, the huge inhabited planet that was also a major Colonial Marine base. Weyland-Yutani maintained a large presence there. Their plan was to discover as much information as possible about the strange tech Liliya carried in her blood, and do so by the time they arrived.

Then they would face the decision of how much to hand over to the Company.

Millard, the ship's navigator, had estimated that Addison Prime was twenty-nine days and four drops away. Thus they were halfway there, and approaching the first drophole on their journey.

"Shouldn't you be getting ready for the drop?" Liliya asked. The Tanns were both fussing around her. They looked tired, faces drawn, and they had long ago run out of small talk to exchange with this android they hardly knew.

She could also sense the sadness that was haunting them, and hated herself for that, just a little. She'd brought so much sadness.

"Couple of hours yet," Jiango said without looking at her. He was busy with a chroma sampler, breaking down a sample of her blood for a spectrograph analysis. "Just want to finish this."

"You sure that's okay?" Yvette asked one more time.

"Yes. Sure."

There was an opening cut in Liliya's chest. It was four inches long, and Yvette had used a clamp to hold it open. Through it they could access her heart, drawing blood samples from whichever location they deemed appropriate for a particular test—valves, veins, arteries, or the small reservoirs of milky white blood that hung around her heart. These reservoirs filled and emptied according to her levels of exertion and the atmosphere around her.

They were the best locations for harvesting the tech she'd injected into her blood, so Jiango focused his efforts on them.

They'd gathered plenty of samples, but much of the testing they were performing destroyed what fluids they drew. When those were exhausted, they needed more.

"We'll finish this and seal you up," Jiango said. "You'll be needing to go into suspension, too."

"No, I'm fine," Liliya said. "I don't need to. I don't really want to. I'd rather stay… awake."

"Is that wise?"

"I did it with Hashori," she said. As if bidden, the huge Yautja shadowed the doorway. She had removed her battle helmet following Alexander's defeat and not worn it since, yet it still hung at her belt, as if she constantly expected more violence. Liliya supposed it was a logical expectation. Violence seemed to follow her.

"Well, I really don't think Captain Ware will want to go under, and leave you and Hashori awake," Yvette said.

The Yautja started to speak. Liliya tilted her head, listening, and then began to translate.

"News from Hell," she said. "There are pockets of survivors. They're transmitting requests for help. The space station's main areas are overrun, and the Xenomorph soldiers continue to press with their attack." Even when the words became hard, and she saw the effect they were having on the Tanns, she did not deviate. To lie would have been unfair, and would merely mean holding the terrible truth for another time. "Three areas have been barricaded, all of them in one of the station's docking arms. The enemy is breaking down the barricades."

Hashori said a little more, but this time Liliya held back. She felt the Tanns watching her, but she could not meet their gaze.

"Liliya," Jiango said. His voice was empty.

"There are less than thirty survivors," Liliya said, completing the translation. "They're running out of ammunition and supplies, Xenomorphs are breaking through bulkheads and sacrificing themselves in order to further their efforts. The survivors estimate they have two days left."

Jiango and Yvette leaned in close to each other, and once again Liliya was jealous of the warmth they shared. Even though it made nothing better, it was still comfort.

"I'm sorry," she said.

"Not your fault," Jiango responded. He turned again to his test. Hashori remained in the doorway. Then Ware's voice came over the intercom.

"Hey, guys, better get up to the bridge," she said. "We're approaching the drophole, and there might be a problem."

"What problem?" Jiango asked.

"To the bridge," Ware said again, and she disconnected.

Jiango sighed, and Yvette reached for the wound in Liliya's chest.

"I can walk like this," Liliya said. "We should go."

On the bridge, Ware and her crew were all in their seats, and holo screens displayed various views and readings.

"Tell me this hole's not taken by the Rage," Liliya said.

"On the contrary," Captain Ware said. "I've never seen a drophole so heavily defended. This is Gamma 67, its control base on a space station seven hundred miles away. I count five Colonial Marine destroyers, and about twenty smaller ships. We'll have to submit ourselves to their inspection."

"I'm guessing they'll want to board and search," Hoot said.

"Right." Ware looked at the tall Yautja, and the android with a hole in her chest. "Right."

"Maybe this is when we submit ourselves to the Company," Robo said.

"No!" Jiango said. "No. We don't know enough yet. Liliya will be taken away, she'll disappear and—"

"And it's them that need her," Ware said. "The Rage are coming, launching an assault against the whole Sphere, not just us and your friends back on Hell."

"It *is* what I came for," Liliya agreed.

"You don't know the Company like I know them," Jiango said. "And you work for me. I hired you to help us avoid them, until the time was right."

"Okay, you've got issues with them," Ware said. "But

they were the ones who sent us to find you, in the first place."

"It's not just issues," Yvette said. "It's a matter of trust."

Hashori started talking. Her strange voice silenced everyone, and the humans looked to Liliya to translate.

"There is a message coming for me," she said. "I need to access a receiver." Without another word Hashori stepped forward and grabbed Robo, starting to lift her from the flight seat. Instantly Robo's arm mechanism whirred as she pulled a gun and pressed it against the Yautja's stomach.

They both froze, the huge Yautja and the human warrior straining against her grasp.

"Robo, let it do what it needs," Ware said.

Liliya spoke in Yautja. "They will let you. You don't need force."

Hashori eased back, and Robo slowly holstered her weapon, then backed away from her seat. The Yautja looked around at them all, then started accessing communications channels. She worked quickly and confidently, even though the controls should have been unknown to her. This fascinated Liliya and she wondered how many human ships, missing in the infinite depths of space, had fallen prey to Hashori's people.

Moments later, a series of strange noises burst through the ship's speakers. Hashori tilted her head and opened a panel on her arm unit, standing motionless while the sounds continued. After a minute they ceased, leaving only the cool white noise of deep space.

The bridge remained silent, heavy with expectation. Robo edged closer to her station again, shoving past Hashori to drop into her seat again. The Yautja took one step back to enable her to do so, then turned to stare at Liliya.

As usual, the Yautja's mood was unreadable.

"You need to tell us what that was about," Captain

Ware said, and as Liliya prepared to translate, Hashori cut in and started talking. Her strange, guttural language spoke into silence, and Liliya translated as best she could.

"My people have taken a Rage general," she said. "It's damaged and uncooperative, but with the aid of a human and a group of captured Colonial Marines, it's being interrogated, and information is being extracted."

Hashori glanced at Liliya as she said this, and Liliya was sure she saw something in the big creature's eyes. She couldn't tell whether it was a flicker of humor, or something else. Then the Yautja continued speaking.

"Yaquita of the Wounded Clan has extracted some deep information from the android's shielded mind. We know where the Rage mothership is. We believe it won't be there for long."

"Shit! We need to go there!" Hoot said. "*Everyone* needs to go there! Where is it?"

Hashori continued talking as if no one had spoken.

"The human working with Yaquita of the Wounded Clan has forged a peace with Elder Kalakta. She is currently examining data from the Rage android, in an attempt to understand its strange technologies."

Hashori stopped speaking and looked around the bridge, as if expecting others to start talking.

"Fuck me," Robo said.

"Very eloquent," Jiango said.

"So this tech," Ware said. "It's the same thing you're trying to work out? From her blood, yeah?"

"Partly, yes," Yvette said, "but if they have a general, they'll be trying to find out how it's connected with its troops. We need—"

Hashori started talking again. Liliya translated.

"The human and Yaquita work together at a Yautja base. The work I've been watching you humans perform here is linked to their work. We should go there."

"Screw that," Hoot said. "If we know where the Rage bastards are hiding, that's where—"

"The *Macbeth* will be heavily defended and virtually indestructible," Liliya said. "We go against them, and we'll die."

"You know this how?" Ware asked.

"I'm from there," Liliya said. "Believe me, our best chance of defeating them is to fully understand this technology, and use it against them."

"You're from there, but you don't know the tech?"

"No, I don't," she replied. "That's why I stole it."

"We never hired you as a warship," Jiango said. "Our cargo is far too precious to go to war." He nodded toward Liliya.

"It's nice to feel wanted," she said.

"Oh, you're not wanted," Yvette said. "I feel sorry for you, and I understand that you've suffered, but I wish none of us had ever met you."

Silence fell again. Liliya wasn't surprised by the woman's honesty.

"Where is the Yautja base?" Liliya asked Hashori.

"I can transmit its location to this ship's computer," Hashori said. "We should go there. It's a safe place. We can combine what Yaquita has discovered with the knowledge these people have gleaned from you. It might help us defeat our common enemy."

Liliya translated, and this time no one objected.

"How close?" Tann asked.

Hashori moved to Hoot's station, and glanced over the navigational holo currently on screen. She tapped at her arm pad, and a new holo appeared, turning slowly as a red destination dot orientated itself in the display.

"Seven days and one drop," Hoot said, reading the

new information. "But…" He turned to face them. "I'm pretty sure records show that the drophole has been taken by the Rage."

Ware nodded slowly. The Tanns glanced at Liliya, Jiango smiling.

I'm no more than a specimen to them, she thought. Sometimes, she had to remind herself that she was not human. They seemed to have no such difficulty.

"Well, then," Ware said, "we'd better prepare to take it back. Looks like we *are* a warship, after all."

Alexander kept the Yautja vessel cloaked.

Liliya and the ship she'd used to escape had a good head start. But Alexander had the Watcher. It remained beside him in the strange Yautja vessel, sometimes floating close to the control panel, other times attaching itself to the ceiling or floor. It pushed a continuous signal to the navigational computers, and the general was content for the ship to follow its directions.

He was settling into this new version of his body. The Xenomorph grafts worked well, and his damaged mind found some gentle irony in their presence. He had been joined with his army on a deeply psychological level, and now he was part Xenomorph himself.

He could not wait to confront Liliya, face to face.

Her ship, far ahead of his, seemed to pause for a time. Then it changed direction. His stolen ship did the same.

They were heading for a drophole that had already been taken by the Rage. Alexander smiled. He would not allow the forces there to steal his destiny. Capturing or killing Liliya had become a very personal mission for him.

But they could help him slow her down.

1 3

BEATRIX MALONEY

Drophole Rage One, Outer Rim
December 2692 AD

Her audience was dispersing.

Beatrix Maloney had given the speech of her life, and many were moved to tears. At the end of her speech she had renamed the Faze-adapted drophole Rage One, to a raucous round of applause.

The central chamber of the *Macbeth* was a mass of movement as personnel left to make final preparations for their drop into Sol System.

Almost a hundred shipborn dispersed to the component parts of the *Macbeth*, ready for the sections to separate once they'd made the drop. Eight or nine people would crew each ship.

Pilots, navigators, communications experts, maintenance and upkeep crew, medics and loadmasters, all were assigned specific tasks for which they had been training for many years. They'd been born soldiers, and now these men and women were the human element in a very finely honed military machine.

Inhuman elements were locked away in the dozen separate holds. The Rage kept these places dark and dank, the air heavy with moisture, the Xenomorphs' own extrusions landscaping the chambers and providing the perfect habitats in which they could bide their time. Soon, these soldiers would be unleashed.

"Mistress, that was inspirational," Challar said, drifting over to Maloney's side. Contained inside his crystal globe, the Elder's skin looked more flushed than usual, his eyes wider and gleaming through the gel.

"It is an important time," Maloney said. "I wished to inspire."

"And you have, for every moment of your rule."

Maloney glanced around the chamber. Other Elders were hovering close by, and she could see that some of them were nervous. Challar's words hadn't been a simple vote of praise.

"What is it, Challar?" she asked.

He waited as the last of the generals left, and the shipborn streamed out, hugging as they went their separate ways. This wasn't a time for long goodbyes, though. Before they saw each other next, they would enter into the heart of this war, and she had promised them victory. They would meet each other again on the other side, and the Human Sphere would be a very different place.

The Rage would be in command. Weyland-Yutani would cease to exist, and any remaining Colonial Marines would fall under Rage control. Those who refused would perish.

When the chamber was cleared of all but Elders, Maloney turned toward Challar and waited for him to say his piece.

"We're taking a huge risk, Mistress," Challar said

finally. "Some of us feel... it's a risk too far."

"What risk?" Maloney asked, though she knew. She was simply playing with him.

Challar's gel enclosure bubbled as his globe shifted from side to side.

"The drop," he said. "We'll be traveling hundreds of light years in an instant. It's something that has never been done before, and—"

"Never been done by *humans*," Maloney said, cutting him off. She smiled. They all still thought of themselves as human, despite what they had become. She and these others were the only remaining members of the Rage who remembered what it was like to really be a human, within the Human Sphere, centuries before. Maloney had long ago ceased thinking of herself as such. She had no name for what she had become, other than Rage.

"The Faze is an unknown quantity," Challar said.

"You are afraid?" Maloney asked.

"Of dying?" Challar scoffed. "Of course not. Look at me, Beatrix. You think dying would be any worse than this?"

She shrugged her one good arm. At least she was able to do that.

"We're afraid of what the Faze is leading us into," he said. "We don't have the capability of placing the Xenomorph army into cryo-sleep. What if the drop kills a large portion of them. Perhaps even a majority?

"What if some of the generals are damaged? They're remaining awake, so they can take control of the ships the moment we drop through. What if the cryo-pods deteriorate while we're... traveling? The Faze has adapted the drophole itself, but the cryo-pods are mostly as they were when we left the Sphere. What if—?"

"What if we *don't* drop through?" Maloney asked. "In that case, we work our way into the Sphere hole by hole.

We come up against Marine resistance, and the Yautja are out for our blood, as well. What if the war we've begun lasts for another hundred years? What of us then, Challar?"

She looked around at the other Rage members, all of them in some form of gel enclosure. That almost magical gel that kept them all alive. It was an alien artifact that they had only just begun to understand, yet they used it because it worked.

"I understand," Challar said. "Truly I do, but... this is a huge risk."

"It is a risk we're taking," she said, raising her voice so that they could all hear. "We've been traveling for so very long, and the destination is in sight. In three hours we drop into the heart of the Human Sphere, and soon after that we will have achieved everything we've dreamed of." She looked back to Challar. "Do you really want fear to hold us back from that? Do you think we should be afraid?"

"I'm not—" Challar began, but Maloney hovered forward and knocked him aside. He spun, bounced from a wall, and a gasp went up from the other Elders. But Maloney was angry now, and the more she spoke, the more that anger grew.

"Questioning me after so long, Challar. It hurts. It stings. I've led you this far, and it's just one more step to what we've dreamed of for over a hundred years."

Challar was gathered, calming his gel levels and righting his suspension unit. She could tell that he had more to say, but she wasn't about to give him the opportunity.

"To your ships!" she said, turning to address them all. "Be brave. Be furious. Our time is at hand, and you all know what to do. Let there be no more talk of fear, or failure. We are the Rage!"

The Elders parted, and as each of them left they

came close to Maloney and offered some form of acknowledgement—a smile, a nudge, a nod. Challar was last. Eyes downcast, he paused before her.

"No need to say anything," Maloney said. "All of our lives change today."

Challar met her eyes, then backed out of the chamber, leaving her alone.

Maloney silently called for Kareth and Dana. There was much for her to do before the drop, and they would be moving down to the suspension suite very soon. But there was one creature she still had to visit.

"She's still beautiful," Maloney said.

The Xenomorph queen, chained and suspended in her hold as she had been for decades, sat among the mess of her recent meals. Human body parts and skeletal remains lay strewn around. Her head hung down, steam hazing around her. Moisture condensed across her carapace, shiny black. She laid another egg, her huge egg sac pulsing as shadows moved and passed along its insides.

She was not mindless, but she was committed to her task. Maloney could relate very closely.

"Mistress, we really should proceed to the suspension suite," Kareth said. "There are only two hours to go, and Dana and I need to get you into your pod."

"Yes. Of course. We should go." Maloney took one last, lingering look at the beast that had given them their army, then she let her helpers guide her back toward the suite.

It took a while. The *Macbeth* was huge.

Once there, she saw the other shipborn who would crew her portion of the *Macbeth*, once the drop was complete. The rest had already settled into their suspension pods. The lids were closed and slightly misted over, their faces peaceful in repose.

Maloney's own pod was set aside from the others, and heavily adapted to incorporate her augmented form.

"One short sleep," she said as Kareth and Dana went about connecting tubes, hoses, and wires to her gel unit.

"One short sleep," Dana echoed. Her eyes sparkled with excitement and delight. Maloney only wished that she could still be so young.

Wordsworth sits across from her, old and decrepit, whiskey glass in one hand, an old book in the other. Maloney has never asked him what he was reading. It seems private, and somehow intimate, and she's never felt that close to him.

Much less so now.

The leader of the Founders is dying.

But not quickly enough.

"We have to bring it on board!" Maloney says. They've been in orbit around *Midsummer* for almost twelve years, and continue their study of the creatures they call the Faze. That, and many other studies. *Midsummer* is a precious place, and Maloney wants to rush forward, and use more of the gifts they've found.

Wordsworth, as usual, is slow and contemplative. He takes a small sip of whiskey, and eyes Maloney over the edge of the glass.

"Beatrix," he says. "You've wanted me gone for years."

"No!" she gasps. *Yes*, she thinks. *Useless, dried out old bastard, holding us back, holding us here*.

Wordsworth raises an eyebrow and drinks again. He can see the truth.

"I'm almost dead," he says. "The gel we found, that sustains me, but… it's unnatural. Alien. Humans weren't *meant* to live this long."

"You look good."

"For my age?" He laughs, and she feels a tingle of reaction. His laugh is part of what makes him great, filled with charisma and confidence. When Wordsworth laughs, he can make friends with anyone.

"Your mind is older than your body," Maloney says. She, too, is old, but she feels strong. She feels ready to continue. That is why she has come to see him.

"Not really," he says. "Perhaps wiser, though. It always has been, and that's why the Founders followed me. Follow me still."

"Most do." She puts down her drink.

"Why did you come to see me, Beatrix?" he asks. "You've made no secret about your growing hatred for me."

She stands, joints creaking.

"If you've come to ask my permission to bring the Faze on board," he continues, "we've already discussed that."

She shakes her head.

"The gel, then. A use for it other than mere medicine?"

Maloney says nothing. The time for talk, for requests, for appealing to Wordsworth's better nature, is over. He may have brought them all from the Sphere, but this old Founder is still stuck in the past.

As she takes a step toward him, she draws the syringe from her pocket.

"Murder, then," Wordsworth says. "It's murder." He laughs again.

She only slows for a second, before proving him right.

"Mistress."

The word came in from a vast distance, whispered a million years before and left to echo forever through the galaxy. The voice was imbued with ancient knowledge and experience long-since faded away to memory, drifting now through cold, empty space.

"*Mistress.*"

Beatrix Maloney tried to open her eyes. Her eyelids were too heavy—and apart from that, she was still content to exist in this inner world, where she was young and filled with vigor. Not like now. Not old, failing, and kept alive by the slick, intimate touch of an alien gel.

"Please, Mistress, you must wake."

The voice was filled with pain and fear. Wordsworth had shown neither as she slid the needle into his arm. Sometimes, when she was in pain and afraid, she wondered whether the wrong one of them had died.

She opened her eyes to a harsh glare, and a whisper from nearby turned down the lighting.

A heavy vibration shook her body, causing painful ripples to spread throughout her enclosed gel globe.

"Did we…" she said, words failing.

"We're through," Dana said, "but not undamaged." Something in her voice brought Maloney around quicker, and she blinked against the light.

"The ship's shaking."

"We're trying to get it under control."

"Why didn't you wake me sooner?"

"We tried, Mistress. Shipborn came around first, but for some reason it's been more difficult for the Elders to wake." She paused, then added, "And not all of them will."

Maloney breathed deeply as Dana and another shipborn tended her. They disconnected her from the adapted cryo-pod and pulled her out, bustling as they went through the unfamiliar procedures. Her gel felt sluggish, slow, and spells of dizziness washed through her. She took another deep breath, and then asked the question.

"How many, Dana?"

"Mistress, three Elders have yet to awaken."

"What about the rest of the crew?"

"Seven cryo-pods failed. Five occupants died, two have survived but… they're raving."

"The generals? The ship?"

"The generals are all fine, and preparing the *Macbeth* for separation. The ship itself is rolling, but the pilots are slowing the spin in increments. They predict we'll be leveled again within an hour. And the Xenomorphs seem to have come through the drop relatively undamaged. They seem more… agitated than usual, but the generals suggest that this will benefit the battles to come. They're stronger than us, and more ready to fight than ever before."

Still Dana was not meeting Maloney's eye.

"Dana," Maloney said, voice soft.

"Kareth," Dana said, and she paused to look at Maloney, tears brimming. "He's one of the ones who…"

"Take me to him."

"Mistress?"

Maloney knew this was wrong. The most important moment in the history of the Rage, their ship damaged, people dead, her duty and priority would be to reach the bridge, and take control. And yet…

"Take me to Kareth."

Dana finished tending to Maloney, grabbed a couple more medical items from the cart she had brought, and started to push her mistress out through the suspension suite. Here the pods had been adapted by the Faze, for use by the Elders, and most of them were open, their occupants being tended by their helpers.

She saw Challar and nodded, acknowledged several others, then saw a closed pod. Several people were gathered around the unit, and inside sat Dariel, completely enclosed within his gel suit. She could already see that he was dead. The gel was cloudy and still, a deep blue instead of its usual pale, translucent color, and there were areas of debris that should have been automatically expunged.

They left the suite and approached the shipborn suspension area. Pods lined each wall, all of them open. As Dana pushed her toward a door in the far wall, she could already hear the screaming.

"That's him?" she asked.

"He makes no sense," Dana said. "We've tried everything."

"He was awake," Maloney said. His screaming hurt her to hear, she could only imagine the pain it caused him.

In the small side room, Kareth and another shipborn lay on restraining beds. They thrashed and squirmed, blood puddling the floor from wounds sustained from them straining against their bonds.

Kareth's wide-open eyes were deep, dark pits of despair. He didn't appear to be blinking, as if afraid to close the lids and see what lay behind them. Awake through such an extreme drop, he must have lived lifetimes in the blink of an eye, all of them motionless, restrained, still and silent. She could hardly comprehend what his mind had been through.

He turned his head slightly as they entered, but didn't seem to recognize either of them. She knew that her two helpers were a couple. This must have been painful for Dana.

"We will win for him," Maloney said. "Win the war."

"Yes, Mistress."

"Say goodbye to your friend," she instructed. "Then take me to the bridge."

"Mistress," Dana whispered. She knew what Maloney meant.

It was the kindest way.

"Report," Maloney said loudly as Dana pushed her onto the bridge. It was already bustling, and a dozen holo screens each showed the status of one of *Macbeth*'s soon-to-be-separate vessels.

Her crew, her Rage, issued their reports.

"The drop was successful. We've emerged through drophole Alpha 7, a billion miles beyond the orbit of Pluto. Automated weapons systems engaged the enemy's defensive positions and neutralized them."

"*Macbeth* is still in a spin," another man said, "but we're preparing for separation within the next seventeen minutes. All crews are aboard their ships, and Elders are being transported now."

"Xenomorph status is all green. The queen is still laying."

"Additional Colonial Marine units are approaching, with contact expected in a little over one hour. Most of *Macbeth*'s segments will have jumped away by then."

Maloney looked around the bridge at the separate holo screens, feeling her heart settle into a familiar rhythm, her body relaxing, her mind alight with the possibilities of what might come.

"This is our greatest hour," she said. "Regarding those who did not survive the drop, we fight for their future, as well as our own. Good luck to *every* ship. You know your duties. Use your rage."

Dana stood beside her, and Maloney wished she could reach out to hold her hand.

"We're going to win," Dana said.

"Of course," Maloney said. "There was never any doubt."

1 4

GERARD MARSHALL

Charon Station
December 2692 AD

Gerard Marshall was walking in the wild countryside of his South African childhood home, his faithful dog by his side. Nomad barked in delight, but each bark emerged as an electrical sound.

Realization slammed home harder than it ever had before. He was on Charon Station, billions of miles from home, and space only wanted to kill him. He rolled over, and even as he answered the call he recognized something different.

His main holo screen kept a constant, silent data feed flowing from throughout the station. The volume was kept muted while he was asleep, but relevant and important events were recorded for when he woke.

On the screen, Charon was in turmoil.

"Gerard, they're here." It was Bassett, calling from his control pod.

"What? Who?" Marshall wiped his eyes.

"The Rage."

"But that's…"

"Impossible." Bassett looked impatient in the small holo frame. "Yet it's true. They dropped through Alpha 7 a while ago, took out the defensive positions, and now their ship is spinning away from the hole, apparently out of control. Three destroyers are en route, and I'm hoping we'll hit them before they can recover."

"There's no way they could have reached the center of the Sphere so quickly," Marshall protested.

"I agree, but it can't be denied. There's no record of the ship that's come through, either. It's massive, heavily armed, and it wiped out all four defending ships and seventeen drones even while still reeling from the drop. It *has* to be them. We have to take all necessary precautions."

Marshall sat up quickly, rubbing his eyes. "I have to tell the Thirteen."

"That's why I woke you."

Marshall's blood ran cold as he imagined what was to come.

"Can you defend against them?"

"Of course," Bassett said flatly. He glanced around as if to ensure no one could hear him, then continued, his voice lower. "We'll do everything we can, but I can't pretend to be completely confident. Not after everything that's happened, and is *still* happening. The situation on Weaver's World remains dire, death tolls are huge, and we're throwing a massive number of resources in that direction."

"A distraction," Marshall said. "It was a distraction. A massacre, staged just to draw our attention."

"Perhaps." The General shook his head. "But we didn't send everything. Sol System has a defensive force greater than humanity has ever seen before, anywhere. Charon Station is the best-defended Marine establishment anywhere in the Sphere, including on Earth. Coming straight to us might have been the Rage's worst mistake. This is where we win."

Marshall nodded, but before he could respond, Bassett cut the connection, leaving Marshall alone in his cabin.

He dressed quickly, instructed his welfare bot to make coffee, then sent a signal to James Barclay, requesting an audience with the Thirteen. Drinking his drink, he sat back and viewed events and information streams playing out on the main holo screen.

The station was in full defensive mode. Its seven main constituent parts—huge vessels interconnected by a series of diamond elevators, transport tubes, and heavier structural elements—were all abuzz with activity, and Marshall felt slightly aggrieved at being left sleeping while all of this was happening. But he was a visitor, not an active member of its crew.

Several Marine destroyers floated in geostationary orbit around the station, supply ships flitting back and forth. General Bassett's control pod was one of the smaller elements of Charon, yet also the most heavily defended. The Sleek-class destroyer docked against the pod was permanently crewed and ready for launch in thirty seconds.

That pod was also heavily protected by networks of nano-filament, a haze of intercepting wires stretching far out from the solid hub itself. This soft cloud was usually illuminated, but as Marshall watched those subtle glows were extinguished, and he knew that the mechanism itself would be expanding, stretching to surround the entire station, dark and imperceptible, the routes through it known only to the relevant ship's computers. At full extent, the nano-filament would stretch several miles out from the structure, ready to intercept and destroy any enemy craft, missile, or laser blast.

It should have made Marshall feel safe. It didn't.

They're really here, he thought, watching the frantic preparations taking place throughout the facility. Beyond Earth, Charon was the main control hub of the Colonial Marines, and it would inevitably have become a target of the Rage. But judging from enemy positions, analysts had predicted the attack for next March or April at the very earliest, more than fourteen weeks away. Somehow, this Rage ship had dropped from the fringes of the Sphere. If they had transport technology like that, who knew what more advanced weaponry they might be carrying?

Marshall felt a twinge of excitement at that. Capture the ships, kill the Rage, and their tech would belong to the Company. Weyland-Yutani would be more powerful than ever before. Ready for any incursion or invasion that might launch from the endless depths of unknown, unexplored space.

With the excitement came a fear he had never known before. Bassett himself had admitted that the Colonial Marines weren't faring well against *this* enemy, human and yet unknown. With the Yautja joining in the fight, some negligible victories had been recorded. Generally, however, humanity was being battered down beneath the Rage's onslaught.

"This is where we win," Marshall said, echoing the General's words and trying to imbue them with the weight of confidence.

His comms unit chimed, and moments later the holo of James Barclay, leader of the Thirteen, appeared across the room.

"Gerard, I've heard the news," Barclay said. "The Thirteen will be online soon, but first, I wanted this private chat. Just you and me. We need to discuss the doomsday scenario, should these bastards actually win."

* * *

"Who goes there?"

The marine in her combat suit barred the door to Bassett's main control pod. It was at the end of a 450-yard-long diamond bridge, and walking across, Marshall had been more aware than ever of the explosive rings that could vent and destroy the walkway in milliseconds. Yet another of many security features designed to make this place impregnable.

"Really?" he asked.

"Sorry, Mr. Marshall, but we're on a war footing." The marine brought her com-rifle down and aimed it at Marshall's stomach. "Second warning—who goes there?"

"Gerard Marshall. As you well know. Seventh chair of the Weyland-Yutani Thirteen. Your boss. Your *boss's* boss. You want my ID code?"

"Yes, sir."

"Same as it ever was. Same as it was three days ago when I saw you here. Seven-one-gamma-three-November."

The marine stood aside. "Just doing my job, sir."

"Yes. Right. Fine." *As am I*, he thought, and a shiver of pure terror ran down his spine at what he might have to do. He paused while the door opened, and glanced sidelong at the marine. "Where's your family?"

"Sir?" She sounded confused.

"You do have family, don't you? I'm assuming you're not an android."

"Oh, yes," the marine replied. "My parents are on Earth, they live in Spain. I have a brother in the 7th Spaceborne. My sister was in the 13th… she was recently killed in action on Priest's World."

"I'm sorry," he said. "The 7th are defending Weaver's World, aren't they?"

"Yes, sir."

"I hope he's well," Marshall said. "I hope…"

"Thank you, sir." There was hardly any emotion in her voice, and she stared straight ahead, along the diamond bridge between the control pod and the neighboring unit of Charon Station.

Marshall said no more as he passed through the doorway and it closed behind him. He imagined never being able to open that door again. Never being able to open *any* door, being trapped, finding himself in a room far from home with people he didn't know, unable to travel or communicate.

He closed his eyes, then walked through the inner doors that gave access to Bassett's main command sphere.

It was chaotic, but there was order among the chaos. Loud, frenetic, people hustled left and right, holo screens displayed various scenes, and data drifted from console to console. Service drones flitted along their regulated flight paths, and people drifted from terminal to terminal on air chairs. It was a constant whirl of movement that for a moment made Marshall dizzy.

The globe was fifty yards across, and General Bassett was at the center of it. A platform had extruded from the wall and he paced slowly along its length, observing activity around him, taking reports from staff. He looked even taller than Marshall remembered, standing stiffer and more upright, and perhaps that was because he was doing his best to withstand the weight that threatened to crush him down.

Two marines guarded each end of the platform, and Marshall expected to go through the same foolish "Who goes there?" procedure. But Bassett saw him as he approached, waved him on, and the marines stepped aside.

Marshall walked along the unprotected platform

and looked down at the control center floor twenty-five yards below. He felt momentarily dizzy. Ridiculous, he told himself, being afraid of heights when he was in deep space.

He so wished for solid ground beneath his feet.

"Gerard," the General said. "I thought you'd come. You'll forgive me if…" A marine drifted up to the platform and handed over a datapad. Bassett scanned it briefly, nodded, handed it back, and the marine drifted away again on her chair, dropping quickly to a terminal below. The pad lasered a signal across to the terminal, and its screen lit up with data.

"Of course," Marshall said. "I know you're busy. I just came to observe." That wasn't quite true.

"For the Thirteen?"

"Yes." That also wasn't quite true.

Marshall stood slightly back from the General and looked around, trying to make out the state of things.

One large holo screen showed an array of data, ranging from 3D coordinates to ship numbers and compositions, contact times and points, to suspected target destinations. The information flickered and changed constantly, and when called on by different personnel, portions of it flitted across the control globe to other terminals and screens. It was confusing, but there was also an order to it that instilled confidence.

Some, at least.

"How long until they reach us?" Marshall asked.

"We're not yet sure they're coming for Charon Station."

"Of course they are."

The General half-turned, then nodded at something whispered in his earpiece, and muttered an order.

"Alpha 7 is a billion miles beyond Pluto's orbit," he said. "That makes them a little over three billion miles away from us right now. Local sources indicate that it's just one ship, but its spin is lessening."

"The spin doesn't seem to have affected its defensive capabilities."

Bassett didn't answer that. However many Spaceborne Marines had died out there, that number was merely added to the terrible toll already borne.

"Just one ship?" Marshall said. "That's strange."

"My guess is that it'll split into component parts, and do so very soon," the General said. "Its configuration suggests such a capability. We're trying to get fresh units there as quickly as possible, to stop it before that happens."

Marshall nodded. Looked around. Saw barely contained panic in some faces, fear in others. People here knew better than anyone how the Rage War had unfolded, very little of it in the Marines' favor. Most would have friends or loved ones, or at least people they knew, on Weaver's World. The massacres being perpetrated there were too painful to contemplate, and they had to be put aside for the moment.

All that mattered was defending the Sol System. Charon Station, the main control center for the Colonial Marines. The inhabited planets and moons—Io, Europa, Mars, the moon, Phobos, Ganymede, and many others—with more than a billion inhabitants spread across a hundred orbital bodies. And Earth, the hub of humanity, bustling with more life now than it ever had before.

Perhaps they had left it too late.

That was Marshall's fear, and he'd been surprised to see such terror in James Barclay's eyes, too. When it was just the two of them, alone in his cabin though billions of miles apart.

"They're here already," Barclay had said, *"and even the doomsday scenario might not save us all."* When the full

Thirteen had convened, he had been as confident, as in control as ever, yet Marshall hadn't been able to shake the fear he'd seen.

"I need to ask you a favor," Marshall said. "I need a ship and a crew."

"Really?" Bassett turned and glared at him. "Now?"

"Something fast."

The General seemed to consider for a moment, frowning, looking into some middle distance that no one else could see. He'd lost his son to this war. Seen his Colonial Marines badly defeated in places, obliterated in others. Abruptly he grabbed Marshall's arm and shoved him back toward the beginning of the platform.

"Keep streaming," he said aloud, and a couple of heads turned their way, then back again.

If Marshall hadn't walked, he'd have been dragged. The General was stronger than he looked, and probably far more dangerous than Marshall had ever given him credit for.

"It's not—" he started to say, but Bassett grasped his arm tighter.

"Wait!"

They left the platform and the side wall opened up, revealing the entry to Bassett's private rooms. Marshall had been in there a dozen times, but never like this. Never feeling as if he was in danger.

"Paul—"

"Doors!" the General snapped. They closed, and the two men stood in the silent, cool chamber. It felt empty and unused. The General probably hadn't slept in days.

"It's not what you think," Marshall said.

"You're running," Bassett said. "Fucking coward. So where are you going, you and the rest of the fucking Company? Got a ship tucked away somewhere, I'll bet.

Ready to put yourself to sleep and blast out of the Sphere. Twenty years of warp drive and you'll wake up to see what's left."

"No," Marshall said. He was shocked that Bassett would think such a thing, but he supposed it was understandable. Marshall was a Company man, first and foremost, and the General had always known it. Whatever gentle dance they performed around each other, they could have never been friends.

Bassett reached up to make sure his microphone was switched off.

"This might be the end," he said. His voice was low and tight, and everything about him changed in that instant. He went from tall and powerful to stooped and vulnerable in the blink of an eye. His face fell, his eyes glimmered. In the silence of the chamber, Marshall could hear the constant whispering in the General's earpiece. He wondered what was being said.

"They've come too far," Marshall admitted. "They'll never take Sol, though. The system's too heavily protected."

"But what if they land them on Earth?" Bassett asked. "Those things. Those monsters. They'll be unstoppable. It's like no army we've ever confronted, or been trained to fight. It's like… fighting ants with nukes."

"Listen to me!" Marshall snapped, deeply troubled by the General's sudden, unexpected display of weakness.

Bassett looked directly at him.

"I'm not running away," Marshall said. "I need to get somewhere, quickly and safely."

"Where?"

Marshall remained silent. He had been instructed to tell no one of his purpose. *"Especially not that fucking soldier,"* Barclay had said. But Barclay was a long way off. He and the rest of the Thirteen weren't yet in danger, although it was closing in. They didn't have their fingers on the pulse—that's why Gerard had been sent.

They didn't know Bassett like he hoped he did.

"There's a place where I can shut down the drophole network," he said. "I have the ability, and the codes."

Bassett's eyes went wide. His mouth opened, but it took a while for him to speak.

"You're really going to do it?"

"I hope not," Marshall responded. "Doomsday scenario, Paul. But I have to be there, and be ready."

Bassett smiled. Then he laughed, soft and brief.

"Have you ever heard the phrase, shutting the stable door after the horse has bolted?"

"Yeah."

"This is… different. Like dodging a bullet after you've already blown your brains out. What good will it do, shutting down the dropholes, if the Rage take the whole of the Sol System?"

"Fucking hell," Marshall said. He stepped back and leaned against a bulkhead, shaking his head, struggling to compute that possibility.

"It might happen," Bassett said. "I can't guarantee that it won't. They're relentless. Brutal. Their tech is far superior to ours."

"Yeah, and if it does happen, Earth is gone." Marshall steadied himself. "The Colonial Marines are left leaderless and adrift. Sol System is infested with Xenomorph soldiers—every planet, every moon, every space station and habitat and ship. The Human Sphere has its head cut off, and without its head… it can't think for itself. Not as it is, not as a whole. But if the Sphere fragments and becomes a vast congregation of human settlements, all of them at incomprehensible distances from one another, those distances will be our saving grace."

Bassett shook his head. He still didn't understand.

"If we shut down the dropholes, we halt their ability to expand," Marshall said. "We abandon everywhere they've already taken."

"Yet to get everywhere *else* will take years of travel," Bassett countered. "It's the end of humanity as we know it."

"No, Paul," Marshall said. "The end of the *Sphere* as we know it. The beginning of something else. It won't even end the war, but we'll stretch it out over decades, instead of losing it in months. In that time we'll learn more about them, and be able to present better defenses. Even counterattacks."

"And Weyland-Yutani will allow this?"

"Not as such," Marshall said. This was where his request might stand or fall. Bassett was general because he knew the chain of command, and though he was a military man—first and foremost—he also knew who he served.

"Not you alone," the General said.

"No. James Barclay and I consider this the only viable option. There are others in the Thirteen, too, but it's not a Company decision. It's those of us who have the ability to see it through."

"Where is this place?" Bassett asked. "What will you need? What are the safeguards?"

"For that information, you and I need something I'm not sure we have." He reached out a hand.

"What's that?" the General asked.

Marshall grabbed Bassett's right hand in his and squeezed hard. "Trust," he said.

1 5

LILIYA

Drophole Gamma 117
December 2692 AD

Satan's Savior came out of warp half a million miles
from the drophole, the crew ready for a fight, the Tanns
strapped into their seats, Liliya still pierced with wires
and tubes from the experiments they'd been performing
on her.

Hashori was the first to speak, in her language of clicks
and groans.

"She needs to access communications," Liliya said.
The big Yautja looked even larger, squeezed into a human
seat, wearing her helmet and grasping her battle spear as
if ready for a one-on-one confrontation.

"Drophole ahead," Millard announced, bringing up
various views on the bridge's holo screens.

"Defenses?" Captain Ware asked.

"Scanning," Hoot said. He worked his control station
with fluid grace, never still. "Three ships."

"I must have communications!" Hashori said via the
android.

"Not now, big girl," Ware said. "Can't you see we're—"

Before she could finish, Hashori was already unstrapped and drifting across to Robo's communications station, expertly managing the zero-G.

"Hoot?" Ware prompted. Then she glanced back at Liliya.

"I don't know what's wrong," Liliya said.

"Don't recognize the ships's traces," Hoot said. "Assume they're Rage. Gamma 117's central control was on a close-orbit station. It looks like it's powerless, and stuck in an irregular elliptical orbit."

"It's been blasted," Millard said.

"Ships have seen us," Hoot said. "They're swinging around."

"All yours," Ware said.

Hoot opened up with everything the *Satan's Savior* had. The plan had been to drop out of warp and attack the moment they confirmed that the drophole was guarded by Rage ships, using surprise to their advantage. It appeared to Liliya, however, that these ships did not seem very surprised.

Satan's Savior shuddered as a range of weapons opened fire. Laser blasts streaked across the space between them and the huge drophole. A plasma spurt followed, and six drones carved their own random paths across space. Explosions appeared on the holo screens, smaller detonations marking the Rage ships' countermeasures.

"Now!" Hashori said, looming over Robo.

"Okay," Ware said, and the crew member surrendered her comms unit to the big Yautja once again.

Liliya glanced to her right, at the Tanns. The husband and wife sat side by side, but did not look afraid. She supposed their expressions might have been resignation.

"A hit!" Hoot exclaimed. "It's damaged and venting,

but still functioning. The other two ships are coming right at us."

"No way it could survive impacts like that," Ware said.

"They're shielded," Liliya said. "Most of your munitions will ricochet away from them."

"Ricochet this," Hoot said, and another shattering burst of fire erupted toward the enemy vessels.

Without sitting Hashori connected to the communications point, the forearm panel of her battle suit open and flickering. She tilted her head to one side.

"Damaged ship's toast," Hoot said.

"They're opening fire," Ware said.

"Initiating avoidance measures." Millard sent the ship into a pre-programmed series of ducks and dives, and the view from the ports spun and streaked as distant stars danced. They shook as a detonation erupted nearby, and several warnings chimed.

Liliya's eyes were on Hashori. She was almost ignoring the battle, and for a Yautja that was extremely unusual. Though not a direct part of it, she should have been soaking up the action, thriving on the violence, and itching to join in herself. But there was something about her stance that made Liliya think they were in more trouble than they thought.

"Hashori?" she asked. The Yautja didn't even acknowledge that she'd heard.

Another huge thump shoved the ship, sending it spinning. A red light burst across the bridge and was immediately extinguished. Somewhere out of sight, something hissed—atmosphere venting, gas escaping.

"Too fast!" Hoot said. "Our targeting computers can't lock on and—"

"Everyone brace!" Ware said. "Millard, jump us past the hole, two light seconds, on my mark."

"Hashori!" Liliya said again. A jump beyond light speed in these circumstances would deliver a heavy blow to anyone, let alone a Yautja no longer strapped into her seat. She glanced across at Liliya at the last moment, and her eyes had gone wide.

Something's wrong, Liliya thought…

…and the *Satan's Savior* jumped.

A rush, a thud, and her almost sense of humanity was left behind, struggling to catch up. Then Liliya opened her eyes again. Beside her the Tanns were gasping, Jiango wiping his mouth from where he'd vomited.

Hashori was crouched down beside the comms unit, holding on tight.

"Hoot!" Ware said.

Hoot opened fire again, the full array of their weaponry targeting the rear of one of the ships. Their jump had confused the enemy, and the ship was engulfed in a storm of laser blasts and plasma bursts.

It exploded in a rapidly expanding cloud of gas.

"Alexander is not dead," Hashori said.

Liliya felt her android heart stutter, as if overloaded with energy.

"We saw his ship destroyed," she said.

"He survived," the Yautja insisted. "Took over one of my brethren's vessels, and now he pursues us. Two Yautja also pursue him. He'll be here—"

"Now!" Ware said. "Holy shit, Millard, didn't you see that coming?"

Another ship appeared in the vicinity, a blue blur on the locational holo screen. It was closing rapidly.

"That's a Yautja warship," Hoot said.

"Take us out of here," Jiango Tann said. "We can't face both of them!"

"How far away are your pursuing ships?" Liliya asked.

"Too far behind to help. We are on our own," Hashori told the crew. She stared at the blue smear that was closing on them.

Will he never, ever give up? Liliya had no idea how General Alexander could have survived the conflagration, but she had to trust Hashori's claim.

"Okay," Ware said, and for a second the captain seemed to hesitate.

I could give myself up, Liliya thought. The Tanns had taken as much information as they could from her blood, and perhaps with everything they knew, they could find some way to use the tech against the Rage. Maybe a way could be found to fight back.

There were no more reasons for her to flee.

"Don't even think it," Yvette Tann said beside her. Liliya stared at her. She hadn't presented any of her thoughts outwardly. The older woman just smiled back. "It's a human thing," she said.

Liliya sighed deeply.

"I can help you fight the Yautja ship," Hashori said. "I know the wavelength of its—"

A massive blast hit the *Satan's Savior*. Hashori was blown from her feet, tossed around the bridge's interior like a piece of loose equipment, her battle spear spinning and then piercing a bulkhead.

Someone screamed.

Liliya looked to her right and saw the Tanns pressed back in their seats, eyes closed and hands clasped.

Let no one else die because of me.

Her entire existence was tainted with countless deaths in her name.

But fate did not listen. Another explosion rattled through the ship, a compartment bulkhead blew out, and flames seared across the bridge, fueled by the high-pressure jet from a severed oxygen pipe. Millard screamed. His seat harness kept him in place as the flames played across his body, limbs waving, torso writhing as the seat melted and his combat suit burst beneath the heat.

The stink of burning flesh filled the cabin.

"No!" Hoot shouted. "Noooo!"

Maintenance drones came to life around the bridge, converging on the damage and extinguishing the fire. One of them caught the end of the severed pipe and sealed it, while three others went about performing a temporary repair to the tear in the bulkhead.

None of them approached Millard's smoking corpse. It spat, molten fat still superheated. It dripped, but he was dead, so none of the drones recognized any need to waste time on his ruined body.

"Incoming!" Ware shouted. "Six objects, heading from one of the enemy ships. Hoot, take them out."

"Weapons array is down."

"All weapons?"

"Yeah."

Hashori, bumped and bleeding, grabbed onto her spear where it had pierced the wall, and dragged herself upright.

"I can perform the dead one's duties," she said.

Ware hesitated for just an instant. "Do it," she said.

"We need to get away from here," Liliya said. "No more deaths. We'll run, repair—"

"Impact in six," Hoot said quietly, and an image appeared on a holo screen that made Liliya's android blood run cold.

The things fired toward them across the space between ships weren't drones, torpedos, or munitions of any kind. They were much, much worse.

"Hull status!" Ware snapped.

"Secure, no breaches," Robo said. "We've suffered

some interior damage, computer's trying to patch through emergency repairs. We've lost weapons and…"

"And?"

"Drive control is offline."

The bridge fell silent. Air whispered as environmental controls struggled to cope with the smoke and stench from Millard's body. Liliya's eyes kept flicking back to him, blackened and wet in his seat. Hashori stood beside him, spear in one hand, the other moving above his control desk.

"We're crippled," Ware said. "Until systems realign, we can't go anywhere."

"Look," Robo said, pointing with her mechanical arm. "Lining up for the final shot." On a holo screen, the two ships were drifting in closer, following parallel courses. The Rage vessel was almost circular, its surface uneven, and it seemed to spin slowly. The Yautja ship was sleek and powerful.

"No," Liliya said. "He'll want me alive."

"Well, he won't get you alive!" Ware said. She glared back, then her eyes softened. "We won't let him. Everyone, arm up. Hoot, turn on the artificial gravity."

With a whirr, they all found weight again. Someone groaned.

The crew stood, and started checking their combat suits and weaponry.

"What about us?" Jiango asked.

"Can you fight?" Ware asked.

"Of course," Yvette said. "Anyone can fight, if they have to."

Robo lobbed weapons over to them.

"And me," Liliya said.

"Not you," Ware said. "You don't fight. You're the bait."

From elsewhere in the ship came the sound of something hammering on the hull.

They came in through the emergency airlock.

"Breach, level two," Hoot said. "Emergency airlock's been forced, safety drones have already resealed, atmosphere being leveled."

"So they can breathe in space?" Ware asked.

No one answered. None of them knew.

From somewhere far away, Jiango Tann heard the sound of sharp limbs skittering against metal.

He carried the gun as if it were hot. He'd fired guns before, as had his wife, but not for a long time, and never at anything alive. Back on Hell, there had been a firing range, housed in the VR pod and blasting imaginary ammunition at make-believe enemies. He'd been there once for a friend's seventieth birthday celebrations. He'd given it a try, and hadn't found the experience particularly enjoyable.

This weapon didn't feel much different, but its potential was vastly so. There was nothing virtual here. This was reality.

"Stay here," Robo said. "The bridge will be sealed, so you'll be safe while we get rid of them."

Hashori pushed forward, past the Tanns and Liliya, her spear pointing ahead.

"Our ship, our problem!" Robo said. Her voice shook, heavy with the emotion of seeing her friend cooked alive. "You stay here and protect—"

The Yautja towered over Robo, staring her down.

"It's not in a Yautja's makeup to miss out on a fight," Liliya said. "Really. Best let her come with you. Trying to stop her will just waste time."

"You'll need everyone," Jiango said. His heart

hammered, breath light and fast, but he had already considered the outcome. The idea of being trapped on the bridge with the android, everyone else dead, while those things smashed their way through the bridge's sealed door… that was worse than a quick death.

With his wife by his side, he pressed up behind the Yautja.

"Fucking hell," Robo said. The Yautja seemed to sense that she'd relented.

Behind Jiango and Yvette, the bridge door began to close. He turned around and caught Liliya's eye. She nodded and smiled, and her deep history once again impressed itself upon him. She had traveled so far, seen and done so much. The wound that he and his wife had put in her chest still gaped, wet and vulnerable. She looked so alone.

The doors closed and Robo waved her hand across the panel, locking them shut.

"Hoot and I take point," Ware said. "You two follow up, and Robo will—"

Hashori shoved past the captain in the narrow corridor and paused, head tilted. Her helmet cast an inhuman shadow, and her long, heavy spear should have been cumbersome in the confined space. But she carried it deftly. The targeting laser on her helmet flashed on, and lanced along the short passageway, swinging slowly left and right. On her shoulder, her blaster followed the path of the laser.

She was testing her systems.

"I think the Yautja's on point," Jiango said, offering Ware a smile.

The captain stared back, expressionless.

"We're sorry about Millard," Yvette said.

"Risk we take," Ware said, and she nodded. "Come on."

Hashori headed along the short corridor. The *Satan's Savior* wasn't a large ship, but there were plenty of places where a Xenomorph might hide—nooks and crannies, storage rooms, service ducting.

Jiango expected that they wouldn't be hiding, however. They'd be moving toward the bridge even now, checking room by room for Liliya, their target. He couldn't help imagining the fate of his friends on Hell.

At the end of the corridor a staircase led down, with a closed door on either side. Hashori glanced back, and Ware signaled down. The Yautja ducked and took her first step onto the staircase.

There was a flurry of movement, a loud scratching and banging, and Hashori's targeting laser flickered and flashed. Her blaster fired and, further down the short staircase, out of sight, something screeched.

Ware and Hoot dashed to either side of the Yautja and aimed their guns down. Then they froze.

Jiango heard a dull explosion, saw the fluid splash across Hashori's legs and their combat suits, and then the sizzling began. The suits handled the molecular acid, but Hashori hissed loudly as her legs were burned. She tugged a canister from her belt and sprayed something up and down her shins.

"Contact!" Hoot shouted. He ducked ahead of Hashori and down the staircase, his rifle coughing as lasers blasted out and down. Something screamed.

Jiango and Yvette dashed forward, following the others down the few stairs. In the area below was a scene of chaos. The floor bubbled and spat where one Xenomorph had been killed, and another was crouched against the far wall, a limb blown off. It leapt at them, a blur of sharp edges and shadow, and Hashori darted forward to meet it. Her spear pierced its torso and she heaved and twisted, using the creature's momentum to swing it around and slam it against a wall.

"Cover!" Robo shouted. She'd come down the few steps behind them, and now she shoved Jiango and Yvette to the left as she started firing.

Two more Xenomorphs slammed through an open doorway. They were inconceivably fast. Robo's gunfire scarred the wall behind them and then they were on Hashori, grasping and lashing out, driving her down.

Jiango crouched so that his angle of fire wouldn't hit the Yautja, aimed, pulled the trigger. The gun pulsed in his hand and a laser blast seemed to ricochet off one of the creatures' terrible curved heads.

Hashori roared. She threw one opponent away from her, and a long silver blade extruded from her armored arm. With it she slashed out at the other creature. Part of it flipped aside, spraying acid as it went.

"Get down!" Ware shouted, pointing at Yvette and Jiango.

Jiango turned and gathered his wife in his arms, pushing her down, feeling the spatter of something across his right shoulder. Something wet. Then hot. Growling as the pain bit in, he drew a knife from his belt and slashed at the clothing, letting the burned material flap down.

The indies concentrated their fire on one of the creatures, blasting it to pieces across the open area. The gunfire was causing terrible damage to their ship, but they couldn't take time to worry about it. This was a fight to the death. None of them could afford to look beyond it.

Hashori dropped her spear and used both hands to grasp the crippled beast. She shoved it against a wall and drew her bladed hand back, ducking her head quickly to the side as its inner teeth snapped out with a sound that Jiango heard even above the gunfire and shouting.

He'd never seen anything like it. He'd heard about these beasts, but never believed he'd lay eyes on one.

And now, he never wanted to again.

The Xenomorph's tail lashed around, sharp tip kissing across Hoot's combat suit and opening it up, impacting hard across Hashori's back. She took no notice. Driving the blade forward and up, she twisted her arm and opened a wide wound through the center of the beast's head.

A gush of fluid spattered out and down across her arm, and she drew back, dropping her prey.

She retrieved the canister again, spraying the sticky acid with the contents as it started to smoke and sizzle on her skin.

Hoot grabbed his torn suit, then drove forward with Ware and Robo. The three of them kicked through the open doorway, disappearing inside the recreation room. As soon as they did, Jiango heard shooting beginning again.

Hashori stood amid a scene of devastation, scarred and wounded, triumphant.

"Look out!" Yvette shouted. Even as she spoke she was moving, drawing Jiango with her and going for the speared creature. Cast aside by Hashori, it was struggling to work itself free of the Yautja's weapon, its blood already working on the spear's solidity.

Jiango feinted left, Yvette right, and then he clasped the spear and leaned all his weight against it.

The Xenomorph screeched and thrashed as he drove it across the molten floor and against a wall. He could hardly breathe, choking on the acrid fumes. His eyes were watering, and he saw the sharp shadows of the monster's limbs lashing out for him.

Yvette stood with him, adding her weight against the spear. A strange thought struck Jiango then, almost placid and removed from this violence and terror—

This is how we'll die, side by side.

It was almost calming.

A shadow fell on them, and then Hashori took hold of her spear and jerked it to the right. Jiango and Yvette let go and stumbled back, just as the weapon ripped its way from the Xenomorph's body, leaving a gaping, dripping wound. The creature slumped down, shivering as if it was cold.

"Come on!" Jiango said, grasping Hashori's arm. She felt cool, damp beneath his hand, and her head jerked around as she looked at him. "We need to move," he said.

They stepped away just as the creature disintegrated, a soft explosion that spilled its acidic innards across the floor.

The floor began to melt.

Gunfire came from further into the ship, and Hashori quickly followed. Jiango and Yvette shared a glance, and he saw the same understanding in her eyes that he'd just experienced himself.

They followed the Yautja into battle.

There were two more Xenomorphs on the ship. The indies dispatched one, and Hashori took out the other with two perfectly targeted blasts from her shoulder cannon. But once they were dead, the creatures caused even worse problems.

Their acidic bodily fluids were eating away at the ship. Environmental systems struggled to deal with the fumes, and from all around they heard the sparks and sizzles of control routes and ducting being melted and severed. Ware viewed the data on her combat suit's visor.

"How bad?" Jiango asked.

"Imagine bad, then double it."

"We're not going anywhere," Hoot said. He looked around at the chaos, suit hanging open and blood beading down its slick surface. Robo stood beside him, her weapon still at the ready.

"So now what?" Jiango asked. "He'll send more, won't he? He'll keep sending them until we're dead, and then—"

"Not if we ram his ship," Robo suggested.

"We're not ramming anyone," Ware said. She continued to scan her data, then glanced at Hashori. The Yautja was tending her wounds, and did not seem to notice the captain's loaded expression.

"What?" Jiango asked.

"Proximity alert!" Hoot said. "It's the Yautja ship."

"Seems like we're going to meet Liliya's general," Robo said. She shared a look with her two companions, and something passed between them. An inaudible order through their combat suits, perhaps. Jiango was about to ask when the *Satan's Savior* shook, and a huge, grinding roar reverberated through the ship.

"Bridge," Ware said. "All of us." As the others obeyed orders, she stood before Hashori and pointed the way. The big Yautja stood defiant, deformed spear in one hand, limbs shivering from the acid burns.

"Ware!" Jiango called. "Come on. She won't listen." The captain peeled off her visor and tried to hold it up so that Hashori could view something on the combat suit's screen.

The Yautja stiffened, then relented, turning to follow the Tanns back up the short staircase.

They tried to move around the spreads of melted decking and bulkhead, but Jiango could hardly avoid seeing into the guts of the ship, places that should never have been seen.

He thought about the ruin of Millard's burnt body, still strapped into his flight seat, and was amazed that they hadn't lost anyone else.

Back on the bridge, doors sealed, Ware dropped into her seat and brought up the displays. Alexander's stolen Yautja ship was moored directly alongside the *Satan's Savior*. Ancient starlight silvered the hull. The remaining Rage ship stood half a mile to starboard, and a steady stream of dark objects were drifting from it toward the crippled indie ship.

Jiango counted twenty, at least.

"I won't live while you all die," Liliya said. "We all go together."

"No need," Ware said.

Hashori said something, and Jiango saw a curious expression cross Liliya's face. It might have been a smile.

On the holo screen, the Rage ship exploded into a glaring sun-hot cloud of gas, and as it expanded it enveloped the Xenomorphs that were drifting toward them, burning them from existence. Only the furthest few survived, but the blast shoved them so hard against Alexander's Yautja ship that they seemed to burst across its surface, becoming little more than smears.

"Hashori's friends are here," Ware said.

Two Yautja ships appeared on the screen, then closed in, quickly taking stations fore and aft.

Hashori spoke again, and this time Liliya translated.

"They've already taken control of the stolen ship's computer. General Alexander is trapped."

"They need to destroy him!" Ware said. "If what we've heard is true, the Rage generals have a self-destruct capability."

Liliya quizzed Hashori, and translated her answer.

"Alexander is still. Silent." The android frowned, as if looking for the correct word. "Suspended."

Jiango closed his eyes and sighed, reaching for his

wife's hand. She found his quickly, squeezed.

Not quite yet, he thought. *When the time comes we'll die together.*

But… not quite yet.

Six hours later they were ready to use the drophole. Hoot hacked its control interface on the damaged space station and programmed their coordinates. Hashori and the Yautja pilots of the other two ships held a conference on board the vessel Alexander had stolen.

The Rage general himself had been secured. The ship's main cabin had the facility to become a suspension unit in times of emergency, or for long periods of space travel, but the Yautja also had their version of suspension pods. It was into one of these that his deformed, grotesque body was placed.

He had grafted parts of a Xenomorph onto his own damaged body. Jiango had never seen or even dreamt of such a monster.

They were all glad to see the lid closed.

The *Satan's Savior* was finished. Ware and her crew were keen to effect repairs, but they quickly came to the conclusion that it was beyond their ability to fix, certainly out in deep space.

Hashori's pride came to the fore. Through Liliya, she invited the crew, along with the Tanns, to accompany her onto the Yautja ship Alexander had stolen. It was large for a Yautja vessel, with more than enough room for them all.

"You fought bravely," she said. "You are all warriors."

The other two Yautja vessels remained with them as escort.

"We have a horrible treasure on board," Jiango whispered to Yvette as they prepared for the drop. They would all be put into suspension in the main cabin, and the craft seemed to provide just the right sized and shaped seats for them all, rising from the deck in some sort of fluid mechanics.

"Two of them," Yvette corrected. "But which one do you mean?"

16

AKOKO HALLEY

Gamma Quadrant
December 2692 AD

Something was up—something big. Major Akoko
Halley, formerly of the 39th Spaceborne DevilDogs but
now gone rogue, felt the tension in the air as if it was a
physical thing.

Isa Palant was excited. Halley could see it in every
way the scientist moved, spoke, or stared silently at the
artifacts that still surrounded them. She had been pacing
the room for an hour, pausing here and there to peer
closer at this thing and that.

Before, when she and the Yautja had been examining
Oscar—and, as it turned out, digging into his memory
banks without him knowing—Palant had paid little
attention to the rest of the room. Her focus had been
entirely on the android. Now Oscar was little more than a
pile of mush, and the scientist was freed to explore.

Halley had already done so, several times. In doing
so she'd confirmed for herself that these creatures
had traveled further and advanced more than even

Weyland-Yutani had ever thought likely.

What next? she wondered.

Yaquita wheeled toward them all, and began preparing to leave. She gave no indication as to what their destination might be, however, or how they might get there. When Halley approached Palant, the scientist's reply was so vague as to be irritating.

"Yaquita's preparing," she said. "She'll tell us all soon."

"They're going to wipe us out," Bestwick predicted.

"If that's all they wanted, they wouldn't be discussing it," Palant replied, and Halley silently agreed. They'd put themselves at the mercy of the Yautja, and that was where they remained.

Yaquita paused in front of them, and Palant switched on her datapad translator.

"If the location that I gleaned from the android is accurate," the Yautja said, "the Rage ship *Macbeth* is close to one of your Outer Rim dropholes."

Too far, Halley thought. *Even with the fastest ship, that'll be—*

"We can reach this location in a little under three days."

Halley heard the collective gasp from her crew.

"Impossible," Huyck said. The datapad translated into the Yautja language, and Yaquita regarded him for a long while before responding.

"For humans, perhaps." She turned and started wheeling from the room. "You should prepare yourselves to leave."

"Wait!" Halley said. The Yautja did not pause.

"I know some of what's going to happen," Palant said. "Best let them prepare."

"Prepare for what?" Bestwick asked. She seemed agitated, twitchy, and Halley could hardly blame her. They'd been here for ten days, holed up in the guts of an asteroid, hidden away in a secret Yautja base deep in Gamma quadrant. At any other, normal time these would have been enemies. Halley hardly regarded them as friends, but they *were* the enemies of her enemies.

It was a loaded, precarious situation, and keeping them in the dark would only put her crew further on edge.

"Isa, tell us what's happening," Halley said firmly. What they'd done—keeping the android out of the hands of the Company—had essentially made them guilty of desertion. They'd done it for the good of the human species as a whole—of that she was convinced. Having done so, however, she wasn't inclined to follow blindly while others decided the agenda.

"This asteroid is more than it seems," Palant said. She looked around, then nodded across to the door that led into their communal living quarters. "Can we get a drink?"

The five of them sat on their bunks, each drinking a fluid almost passable as real coffee, even though it came from the alien replicator in the corner.

"So, this asteroid…" Halley said.

"There's something deeper inside," Palant said. "I think it's some sort of drophole."

"Not one of ours," Bestwick said.

"No, of course not. One of theirs."

"Yautja?" Sprenkel asked. "The bastards have a drophole of their own, this deep inside the Sphere?"

Palant shrugged, and drank.

"If they have this one," Huyck said, "it stands to reason they have many more. No telling how many, either."

Palant didn't respond. Halley hoped it was because she didn't know.

"So how much more did they tell you?" she asked.

"Some," the scientist said, "and some I overheard. I'm becoming pretty good at translating some of what they say, even without the datapad."

"So?"

"They don't use this drophole much. It expends a tremendous amount of energy. I don't think they're as constrained as our holes, distance-wise, and it's dangerous."

"Dangerous to use it?" Halley asked.

"Not sure, but it's definitely dangerous to the asteroid. This place has been a base of theirs for millennia. Far as I can figure, they've only used the hole a handful of times in all those years."

"To attack us," Sprenkel said. "Flit around human space, launch hunts, track us and kill us."

"Sometimes," Palant said.

"I say we nuke them to fuck."

Halley glared at Sprenkel. "Really?"

Sprenkel looked down at her feet. "Sorry, boss."

"Yeah. Right. Don't be sorry, be sensible. Do you have any idea what they're giving up just letting us onto this base, this close to the drophole?" Then it dawned on her. "That's how we're getting out of here."

"Are we sure that's what they're thinking?" Bestwick asked. "Maybe they're just going to kill us all, steal our ship, and take Yautja Woman here with them. Everything they know, and everything she knows. Why the hell do they need us anyway?"

"Nice," Palant said.

"No offence."

"Plenty taken."

"Can it, Bestwick!" Halley snapped. "They've kept us safe up to now. We have to trust them." She hoped she was right.

No one replied. No one trusted them. The Yautja were

unknowable. They weren't prone to emotions that could be easily identified, so it was impossible to read them. That made it all the more difficult to trust them.

"It's the fastest way to get to the *Macbeth*," Palant said. "And there's more. They've agreed to rendezvous with some other Yautja before going after the Rage. Another ship that claims to be carrying a living Rage android. Not a general, but one that fled them some time ago, when they were still beyond the Sphere. It stole some of their tech when it went."

"Why bother?" Halley asked. "What do they have that you and Yaquita haven't already got from our friend Oscar?"

"Plenty," Palant said. "Yaquita and I have found out lots about Oscar, but there's so much more we don't know. We could probably prompt the self-destruct, and that's why we need to be aboard their mothership to do it, but the method of linking the generals to their troops is still unclear to us. Without that, we don't know what damage we can do, if any at all. If we could find a way to link to, and destroy *all* the Rage generals, they'd take their ships with them."

"You think that's possible?" Halley asked.

Palant mused for a while, turning the cup in her hands, staring into the steam.

"No," she said at last. "I doubt it. The science is almost arcane. Way ahead of, or so different from anything I've ever seen before. But if there's even the smallest chance, then we have to take it. This android that fled the Rage might give us that chance."

"At the very least, maybe we'll take out their mothership," Huyck said. "That's gotta be worth a punt, right?"

"Right," Halley agreed, and she stood. "Okay, people, let's get ready. We've been here long enough."

As Bestwick, Huyck, and Sprenkel went about

gathering their kit, Halley sat back down next to Palant. The scientist still confused her. After McIlveen had turned on them, and tried to hijack their ship, the *Pixie*, Halley had always considered her to be on their side. Even after Sprenkel knifed McIlveen.

She still thought that now, yet Palant was as distant and shielded as ever.

Halley had always marked her as a loner. The scientist once commented that she wished nothing more than to be back in her lab at Love Grove Base, performing her experiments day in, day out, with no need to travel and *certainly* no desire to be a part of something bigger.

Now that she was involved in the war, she seemed to be handling it with the same level of detachment and isolation. Perhaps that was a good thing. Spending hours, days, with Yaquita must have been challenging, but Palant showed no signs of having missed human interaction. Even when she wasn't working, she'd spent her downtime sitting on her cot in their shared room, accessing her datapad and snoozing.

Sometimes she seemed more Yautja than human.

"You're seeing more than you ever hoped for, I'll bet," Halley said.

"Well I am the Yautja Woman."

"We don't mean anything by that."

"I don't mind," Palant said, and she sounded sincere. "I don't care what people think of me. None of it really matters. What we're doing here matters, even though no one will ever know about it."

"I'm not looking for fame and fortune."

Palant laughed softly. "Good job."

"We're behind you," Halley said. "Whatever some of the guys might say, we're here because of you, and what you think you might be able to do."

"And if Weyland-Yutani captures you?"

"Court-martial, for sure. Life in a penal colony on some cold, dead rock in the ass-end of space. This isn't about the Company, though—you know that as well as anyone. It's about humanity."

"Humanity. Right. So let's go and save it."

They stood together, warrior and scientist, and Halley felt an unfamiliar pang of fear. They were heading into the unknown.

Yaquita accompanied them on the *Pixie*. It wasn't requested, it simply happened, and Halley didn't think it wise to object. The big Yautja wheeled herself onto the bridge and secured herself beside a seat left vacant by one of the dead crew. Palant sat close to her.

Sprenkel, Bestwick, and Huyck went about their pre-flight checks, and Halley sat in the captain's chair overseeing the procedures. It felt good to be back on board their ship again, even though the view outside was still a reminder of where they were. All systems were fully functional. The ship's computer was preparing the suspension pods for their drop, and it confirmed that it had received specifications for how to adapt a pod for Yaquita.

Through all her years in the Colonial Marines, Halley had never felt so little control over her own fate. Even when she'd been addicted to phrail, she had still been fully functioning, and an important cog in the Marines' machine. Now she was being steered and instructed. Even though she sat in the *Pixie*'s captain's chair, it was the Yautja five yards away from her who was really in charge.

"How far are we dropping?" Halley said to Palant. "Can you ask her that?"

Yaquita seemed to have anticipated the question. Even

before the question was translated, she started talking. Palant's datapad was paired with the ship's computer, and Billy's smooth voice relayed the Yautja's message.

"All coordinates and other relevant information has been downloaded to your ship's computer," she said. "This data was gleaned from the android general, so there are no guarantees as to its accuracy, nor its age, but I'm as certain as I can be that he did not know I was bleeding this information from him. It's unguarded and bare, and thus I believe it was accurate. In case of an accident, your ship and the two ships accompanying us all have the same information. This is a joint effort, Major Halley."

It was the first time the Yautja had referred to Halley by name. She nodded to the alien, then looked away again.

"Billy, confirm?" she muttered.

"All good," the ship's computer said. "I've been sent a set of data from the Yautja habitat, and it correlates precisely with the data sent to the two Yautja ships currently preparing for takeoff."

"Right. Good." Halley still felt nervous. "So, coordinates of the *Macbeth*?"

"I'll put them on screen," Billy said. A holo screen emerged before them and started filling with data—star charts, coordinates, travel times.

"That's a long way off," Bestwick said. Sprenkel whistled.

"Not according to Yaquita," Halley said.

The signal came for them to disengage from the docking arm. The ship shook gently, then they were floating in the asteroid's huge interior. Two Yautja ships drifted ahead of them, then at the far side of the cavern, something began to happen.

"What the..." Huyck muttered.

The cavern wall began to disappear. It melted away

as if it had never been there at all, revealing a wide, long tunnel beyond. As the first of the Yautja ships approached, it illuminated the way. It was like flying into the mouth of a giant beast.

Halley didn't like it one bit. But they had no choice.

The tunnel led deeper into the asteroid. The ships moved slowly, not much faster than running pace, with the two Yautja vessels leading the way.

"Suspension pods are prepared," Billy said. "We'll be close to the asteroid's core in a few moments, and I believe we'll be moving on soon after that."

"I want to see it first," Halley said.

"Me, too," Palant agreed.

Yaquita said something, but the translator didn't pick it up. Perhaps it was a Yautja swear word.

As they emerged from the tunnel into the asteroid core, the view opened up around them. Halley caught her breath. She wasn't sure what she'd been expecting—a circular piece of tech, like the human dropholes, or the dark pit of a miniature black hole. What she definitely *hadn't* been expecting was something…

Beautiful.

It looked like a star had been seeded in the heart of the asteroid. A blazing white light sat at the center of the core chamber, small but glowing fiercely, throwing off rainbows of light that coated the walls like oil. Halley's vision seemed to blur whenever she tried to look at the central light. Even though Billy's viewing screens had darkened to prevent any damage to their eyes, the star seemed to sizzle, vibrating with incomprehensible energies. Looking at it felt like looking into infinity, but the opposite of the endless depths of space.

This felt like looking at the potential of forever.

Yaquita spoke, the computer translated.

"Time to enter suspension."

She wheeled herself toward the rear of the bridge, then paused and looked back at the humans.

Halley knew that the others were thinking the same thing as her.

Just one more look.

"Let's go," she said. There was no chat as they left their seats and pulled themselves toward the door. Each of them took a final glance over the shoulder at the blazing, amazing sun contained within this asteroid's heart, and then they passed through into the *Pixie*'s interior.

In the suspension suite, Halley's crew started preparing themselves for their brief sleep.

"I hate doing this," Palant said.

"We'll be fine. Awake again before you know it."

"Yeah, but what will we be waking to?"

Halley helped Palant into her pod, and when it automatically attached sensors to her chest and head, the Major checked them for her. Unnecessary, but it was a very human gesture which gave some semblance of control. The rest of her crew did the same.

"Sleep tight," Halley said. "See you in an hour, and two hundred trillion miles."

"Yeah. Right. Thanks for that."

Halley watched as the lid closed on Palant, the scientist's eyes wide and alert. Within seconds she would be asleep. The pod hummed.

"Boss?"

"Right. My turn."

Yaquita had already lifted herself from the wheeled transport and into the adapted pod, managing to squeeze in only because of her lack of legs. No one checked her connections. She didn't even glance over at them as she lay back and the lid whispered shut.

Halley climbed into her pod and relaxed, thinking of that incredible star that the Yautja had somehow harnessed. She and the others had discovered more about the Yautja in just a few days than the rest of humanity had in centuries. She wondered whether such knowledge, gained in a time of war, might one day come with a price.

That star. So powerful, so filled with energy.

Something beautiful, she thought. Then sleep took her down, deeper than dreams, and she thought nothing at all.

1 7

GERARD MARSHALL

Charon Station
December 2692 AD

The pilot was called Andrea Rodriguez. She didn't want to be there. She wanted to be on Charon Station, ready to pilot one of the attack drones the Sleek-class destroyer *Keene* would use against the incoming Rage ships. Her husband had been on one of the Marine ships patrolling in the vicinity of Alpha 7, and now he was presumed dead, along with almost three hundred other crew members on the destroyed ships.

Stern and hard, she'd told Marshall this without any apparent display of emotion. Even when he'd offered his sympathies, she had simply continued with her pre-flight checks. She was a good pilot, she'd told the Company man. The station would need her in the forthcoming struggle. That was her job, and what she had trained for over the past two years.

Being a good pilot was why General Bassett had assigned her to him. Marshall was grateful for that, but it didn't make him feel any better. Having a good pilot in control of the frigate *Hagen* wasn't any form of protection against what was about to arrive.

Their only other crew member was Lucianne, a marine who had volunteered to accompany Marshall as a navigator and comms officer. She had been Marshall's assistant intermittently over the past few months, someone who knew Charon Station well and who was also good at liaising between military and civilian staff. She had several hundred hours of ship time, all in-system, and she'd worked with Rodriguez several times before.

Marshall had never believed that he'd be sorry at leaving Charon Station. He was wearing a borrowed combat suit that was way too big for him, and data was being broadcast onto the visor from the station's central core. None of it was required. Every living and working space across the various components of Charon Station was being kept abreast of the situation through the public address system.

"Two enemy ships incoming, contact in approximately seven minutes."

They were moving even faster as they approached the station.

Marshall, Rodriguez, and Lucianne ran along the station's main docking arm, magnetic boots holding them firm, each step a long, floating leap. All artificial gravity throughout the structure had been zeroed, saving energy and slowing the station's spin so that various defensive craft could be launched. Outlying defenses were engaging the attacking vessels, but two frigates and seven drones had already been lost. The Rage ships barely seemed to notice them.

Heavily shielded, powerfully armed, each of the two approaching ships was the size of a Colonial Marine destroyer, almost four hundred yards long. They spun as they came, rolling as if not truly in control of their own velocities. Marshall knew that was an illusion. This was a definite, controlled attack.

After the enemy vessel had dropped from Alpha 7, Bassett had prepared his forces to engage one large ship. Yet seventeen minutes after arriving and destroying the dropholes' defenders, the enemy craft had split into a dozen smaller elements, each still as large as any combat craft in the Colonial Marines' armory. Two of these had streaked rapidly toward Charon Station, their intentions all too clear.

They were still tracking the other craft, and sending warnings throughout Sol System. Four of the segments had blasted in past Pluto's orbit and toward the sun. Earth seemed to be their aim, and Marshall felt a chill every time he considered it. How many Xenomorphs could a ship that size hold? Thousands?

Tens of thousands?

Six other Rage segments had peeled off and jumped away, disappearing into hyperspace, their targets across the system as yet uncertain.

Too late, Marshall kept thinking as they ran for the *Hagen*. *I've left this too late*. But regretting his missed opportunities would benefit no one. They had to reach their destination, and from there more decisions could be made.

As he'd left Bassett's room, the General had surprised him.

"It's almost like you're not a Company man anymore," Bassett said to him.

"What does that mean?" Marshall had asked.

"You're not just doing this for selfish reasons."

He'd wanted to contradict that, to tell Bassett how Company decisions were rarely selfish, and how sometimes the long view was the right one to take. But there'd been an element of truth in Bassett's comment, and Marshall had been aware of it even before the General pointed it out.

He'd recognized the change in himself. Though he was still a Company man, his actions were no longer focused entirely on profit in the moment.

"Contact in five minutes," the Charon's AI voice said. It was calm and soft, as if recounting a favorite food recipe, rather than foreshadowing the station's potential doom. "Outlying defenses are now in combat."

"How long to the *Hagen*?" Marshall asked. He wasn't used to such exertion.

"Next dock," Rodriguez said. She was fit and fast, pulling Marshall and Lucianne along with her. She grabbed a wall handle and drifted to a halt beside an airlock. Then she gasped.

Marshall followed her gaze. The window beside the airlock looked out onto the *Hagen*, the small frigate that would take them away from this place. Beyond that lay deep space.

Stars bloomed and faded in the distance. It was impossible to tell how far away the battle was—the explosions were pinpricks, quickly appearing and disappearing back into darkness. That they were close enough to see with the naked eye meant they were far too close for comfort.

"We don't have long," Rodriguez said. "Into the ship, and I'll be taking off as quickly as possible. You'll have to make sure you're strapped in safe and sound before we go. My record's twenty-six seconds from taking the pilot's seat."

"Looks like you're about to get your wish," Lucianne said.

"And what's that?" Marshall asked.

"Getting the fuck off this station."

Rodriguez laughed, the sound complemented by the harsh hiss of the airlock doors opening. As they waited for pressures to equalize, she spoke with traffic control and confirmed their permission to leave.

On their visors, they all watched the distant space battle drawing closer.

"They'll want to take the station," Lucianne said. "They'd have been launching against us from a million miles distant if that wasn't the case."

Marshall found no comfort in this. He knew what they'd use to take the station, and he thought about everyone they were leaving behind. He'd made no real friends up here— he was a Company man, and being one of the Thirteen put a distance between him and everyone else. It was a gap he'd never been able, or even eager, to bridge. Bassett was as close to a friend as he had this far from home.

Yet he hoped more than anything that they could all escape the dreadful fate that was coming for them.

The doors opened and they were on the frigate *Hagen*, rushing through to the bridge, pulling themselves into seats, strapping in. Rodriguez muttered as she went, counting in an attempt to break her own record.

Twenty seconds after taking their seats, doors locked and secured, engines fired up, system checks carried out by the ship's computer, and docking arm withdrawn, she fired the retro flares and edged them away from the space station.

"Six second record!" Rodriguez said. "Wait 'til I tell—"

An explosion illuminated the bridge, flashing in from outside and only fading when the computer reacted and clouded the windows. Something rattled against the hull. The whole ship shook.

"Holo screen," Lucianne said. The ship reacted instantly, forming a screen and projecting a view of Charon Station taken from a drone three miles out.

The results of the explosion were evident. A haulage vessel had launched and been taken out by some of the defensive nano-filament net, projecting miles out from the station in every direction. Whoever had launched the ship had done so without flight control approval, and they'd met an unfortunate end.

The station's seven main structural elements were intact, including the General's control hub. His Sleek-class destroyer had launched and was holding station, and Marshall knew that several other destroyers orbited Charon at various distances.

"Their own stupid fault," Rodriguez said. "Sixteen seconds through the filament field, then we'll hit it."

In the distance, the space battle had ended. All indications were that the two Rage ships had triumphed, although one of them seemed to be damaged, leaving a trail of atmosphere venting into the vacuum as it hurtled toward Charon Station.

The first ship, larger than any destroyer, arrived three seconds later.

"Holy fuck, it's huge," Lucianne said. "And ugly." Her description was apt.

The destroyers attacked, pincering in from three directions and unleashing a barrage of munitions. The Rage ship rolled and shifted, dodging some, absorbing other explosions with what appeared to be little or no damage. Returning fire blasted out from the enemy, pulsing glows of laser fire heavier than any Marshall had ever seen. The destroyers launched countermeasures and darted away, complex flight movements dictated by computers so much faster than human reactions.

Boosters and retros fired in harmony, throwing the ships into staggered movements across the battlefield that dodged the bulk of incoming fire. A few blasts found home, flaring across one ship's left flank. Flames erupted outward, fueled by explosive decompression. Debris powered out through the dying flames. Some of the debris had limbs.

The second Rage ship arrived, damaged and dragging a long tail of wreckage and escaping atmosphere. It didn't appear to be in any way disabled. It launched into the fray, unleashing an assault on the damaged Marine destroyer while ignoring the fire directed at it.

The destroyer's boosters blasted it away from the battle, but too late.

It erupted in flames, coming apart as its fuel drive failed and ignited, spreading wreckage far and wide.

"We'll be out of the filament field in seven seconds," Rodriguez said. "The explosions are shifting its placement, computer's recalculating every millisecond."

"The station can't fall, can it?" Lucianne asked. "I mean, Charon Station."

"They'll put up a good fight," Rodriguez said. That was no real answer at all.

Marshall knew the truth. He'd seen it in General Bassett's eyes.

The *Hagen* shook as it moved away from the station, countless course changes shifting it safely through the filament field. It would only take one spray of filaments to wrap around the ship and explode. That would cripple them, and then they'd be a sitting target for the Rage ships.

For now, the two attacking craft were being kept busy with the station's outlying defenses. Destroyers piled fire at them, the smaller ships darting miles across space in the blink of an eye, firing, then moving again. More cannon rounds came from the station itself, gun towers unleashing a withering storm of plasma and laser fire at the attackers.

Shields pulsed a faint red as impact after impact drove home, and suddenly the damaged Rage ship seemed to be floundering. An explosion ripped apart one of its protruding elements, sending the ship into a spin toward the station. It struck the filament field and countless more explosions rippled across its surface.

"Got the bastard!" Rodriguez said. "One down, and no damage yet to the station! Bring it on, fuckers."

Marshall wasn't so quick to celebrate.

"How soon until we're away?" he asked.

"Seconds," Rodriguez snapped. He could tell she still thought of this as running away, and Marshall's eagerness only seemed to make it worse.

The Rage ship was coming apart. It rolled lazily within the filament field, a constant series of explosions decorating its hull with yellow, red, and orange, while the defending ships concentrated their fire on the doomed vessel.

"Enlarge," Marshall said. The holo screen view closed in.

"We're away," Rodriguez said.

"Hit it," Marshall said, but the pilot paused for a moment when she saw the image on the screen.

"I don't understand," Lucianne said. "Is it falling apart? Is it… melting?"

"Not falling apart," Marshall said. "It's launching its final attack."

Thousands of dark specks flowed from the blazing inferno of the dying ship. Many of them were caught in the filament field and blasted from existence, but so many more drifted on toward the nearest unit of Charon Station.

"Xenomorphs," Marshall said.

It was a surreal sight, a shocking moment, and he felt removed from himself and these events. As director of ArmoTech, he'd been searching for these creatures for so long, finding samples and then losing them again, seeking the beasts that were quite simply the most efficient living killing machines humanity had ever encountered. To have possession of these things, to be able to weaponize them, had been one of Weyland-Yutani's overriding goals for the past couple of centuries.

They had failed on numerous occasions.

Sometimes spectacularly.

Now those who had succeeded were using these deadly weapons against them. The irony wasn't lost on him.

Laser fire streaked out from the space station and pulverized the drifting clouds, but there were too many of them. For every Xenomorph taken out, five more drifted through the expanding detritus of their dead cousins.

"How can they breathe?" Lucianne asked.

The first of them reached the hull of Charon's main storage hub.

"They should freeze to death," Rodriguez said.

They skittered across the surface, seeking viewing portals and airlocks.

"Get us out of here," Marshall said.

"But—"

"Get us the fuck out of here, *now*! The second ship's arrived."

Rodriguez plotted a course and punched the boosters. Their view of Charon Station, the attacking ships, and the chaos of battle shrank quickly on the screen.

Lucianne tapped into the feed from one of the many orbiting drones. Accelerating away from the Colonial Marines' besieged base, still they were offered a first-hand view of what came next.

1 8

GENERAL PAUL BASSETT

Charon Station
December 2692 AD

In the height of battle, General Bassett took time to confirm that Gerard Marshall had made it away safely.

Three other ships had left Charon Station as the Rage aggressors closed in. One was a private haulage craft whose personnel had murdered two Marine deck crew in their hurry to escape, and whose flaming fate Bassett did not dwell upon. Another was a passenger ship carrying seventeen civilians who had chosen not to remain on the station, preferring their chances in deep space. The crew had made the same choice, and so Bassett had little power to hold them back. They appeared to have escaped whole, and were now heading in-system.

The third was the Sleek-class destroyer *Keene*, formerly moored alongside the control pod where he spent most of his life. It was now in battle with the Rage ships.

As he received data confirming that the *Hagen* had made it away, Bassett breathed a sigh of relief. He'd never liked Marshall, the Company man. Not really. But a degree of trust had grown between them, and even a grudging respect that he hoped went both ways. When Marshall had arrived, the General had seen him as a complaining, spoiled bore, a man always used to getting his way, whatever that way might be. By the time he left the station, perhaps he had become almost heroic.

I pray to God he doesn't have to do what he's gone to do, Bassett thought, but he couldn't stop to dwell on only one person. No sooner had Marshall's ship made it away than a whole new flood of data assailed him.

Standing on the platform at the center of the base's control sphere, the General was the focal point of all incoming information. His combat suit received it, transcribed it through a complex sequence of triage programs he had written and continually refined himself, sorted and categorized it, and then fed him the salient headline points. At the switch of a synapse he could retrieve any more in-depth portions of data or information. It was as if his brain had been enlarged, streamlined and refined, and he stood at the center of the battle. Every shot fired, every impact made, every blast missed, every ship movement and return fire from the Rage ships, he knew about it.

"The first Rage ship is breaking up!" someone shouted. "Just over two miles out, it's coming apart. Station gunners are taking out the smaller wreckage. Anticipate some secondary damage, but slight."

"Concentrate fire on the second ship," Bassett said. The order was unnecessary—the Marine Spaceborne units were already attacking, along with the *Keene*, and the gun towers across Charon Station were pumping plasma and laser fire toward the second ship as it stalked beyond the filament web. He allowed himself a brief flare of hope, then shut it down again.

He could not afford that.

Since the Rage assault on the Sphere had begun, hope had become so alien.

"Sir, something's happening…"

Bassett glanced around at various holo screens. Data speckled the air in front of him, changing tone and color to maximize readability. The destroyed ship was breaking up, internal explosions accelerating its demise, jagged chunks of hull flipping away only to be blasted to fragments by the Marines' continuing assault. Among the debris, there was something else. Black points spewed across space.

They looked like fleas escaping a burning dog.

"Xenomorphs," he said. "Don't let them drift close to the station!"

An even more furious fusillade began, blasting the hundreds, *thousands* of Xenomorphs pouring from the stricken vessel and drifting rapidly toward Charon's large storage unit. Many of them impacted the filament field and died. Others clung together in groups, the outer creatures subjected to the withering fire, those inside each huddle drawing closer and closer to the station.

Bassett knew that if they reached the storage section and made their way inside, their route through the station was assured.

His large control hub could be isolated by blowing all of the footways and bridges, a fact he had taken pleasure in telling the nervous Marshall on many of his visits. All other separate units of Charon Station were permanently linked—diamond bridges, elevators, heavier structures incorporating docking arms. Blast doors could be lowered. Corridors could be vented. But none of these measures would be a solid defense against a sustained Xenomorph assault.

Even with the first ship destroyed, still its threat remained extant.

"Filament field down to thirty-seven percent effectiveness."

"Draw it in," Bassett said. With many of the nano-filaments expended, drawing them in would concentrate those that remained primed. It might also destroy many more of the drifting Xenomorphs before they reached any part of the main structure.

The second ship rolled and started firing a heavy plasma cannon, vast flaming stars streaming toward the station's heart. Countermeasures commenced taking them out. Laser shots diverted then destroyed them, and those they missed were intercepted by unmanned drones. More than a hundred drones were circling the station, and a hundred more had streaked away to a dozen miles distant, orbiting and probing the Rage ship for weak spots. Most of them were wiped out by wave fields or automatic defenses, but a few made it through. They detonated against the ship's shield and faded away to nothing.

"The first Xenomorph has reached the station."

Bassett saw it. The creature landed on the storage pod and started crawling across its surface, and a probe flew by and took it out with a laser blast. But that wasn't the end of the creature's story. Its body erupted across the exterior hull, and its molecular acid started working at the many-layered skin.

Bassett accessed hull integrity. It stood at ninety-seven percent, but he put a marker on it for continuous updates.

More Xenomorphs reached the quarter mile long storage pod, and a gun tower on the adjoining welfare unit started targeting them, using short, defined shots to knock them from the hull without damaging the structure itself. Some of the impacts worked well, blasting them back into space. Others merely wounded the creatures, which then self-destructed across the surface.

Hull integrity, ninety-one percent.

The second ship started circling Charon Station, picking up speed and unleashing fire the entire time. The *Keene* pursued it, as did smaller drones and two other destroyers. Its assault was being successfully diverted, but its velocity became unmatchable, and the destroyers fell back and began matching their gunfire to every revolution. Its orbit was little more than three miles in diameter, yet it was circling the station once every four seconds.

"We're running out of drones. Filament field down to seventeen percent."

Bassett knew all that. He also knew that many more Xenomorphs had made it to the storage hub. Some were working at airlocks and portal openings, others were being picked off by defensive fire, their remains melting, working at the hull, eating inexorably inward.

Hull integrity, eighty-two percent.

"How many people remain on the storage hub?" he asked. It wasn't information that was available to him, his suit's on-board computer having relegated it to a *delete* function.

"Seventy-eight," someone replied. "Over two hundred evacuated to the central hub."

Seventy-eight, he thought. He had a great many deaths on his conscience. Seventy-eight more would only deepen the curse on his soul.

"Target access bridges and support arms for the storage hub," he said.

"Sir?"

"You heard me." He didn't need to explain himself. The Colonial Marines were trained for such eventualities. It was called "acceptable losses."

Moments later the *Keene* swung around and unleashed

a salvo of fire which took out two of the storage hub's three main support structures. The third stressed, bent and then cracked apart, and the unit started drifting inward toward the rest of the station.

Fire control took over and directed an organized stream of plasma fire against the huge unit. The explosions only scarred the surface, but succeeded in sending the storage section in an uncontrolled spin away from the base. It tangled in some of the unspent filament field and, under their detonations, it started to come apart.

Bassett closed his eyes, but only briefly. He couldn't afford to think of those still alive on that structure, smarting with betrayal, then dying.

"Sir, something else."

The rapidly orbiting second ship had ceased firing. It still circled Charon Station, but instead of energy blasts it was now firing Xenomorphs in long continuous streams, like seeds carried in an autumn breeze.

Thousands of them.

"Oh, God," Bassett muttered. It was his first external display of weakness, and he knew that many of his control-hub crew would have heard him. But he did not apologize, and could not hold it back.

Gun towers started targeting the Xenomorphs, and the rapidly moving creatures exploded in showers of acid and body parts, spattering across the extensive station's diverse structures.

The Rage ship then performed a surprise maneuver. After unleashing a final slew of Xenomorphs it slowed its rapid orbit and powered away, boosters blazing two new stars in the night as it retreated rapidly from Charon's locale.

"Pursue and destroy," Bassett said, but his order was unnecessary. The *Keene* was already chasing the ship, continuing its attack.

Sensors told Bassett that more than four thousand Xenomorphs had been unleashed, sent careering like living missiles toward the station across cold, empty space. Many were dead, but many more were already crawling across Charon's surface. Whereas their first attack had targeted the storage unit, they were now all across the vast space station's expansive structure. Scratching, probing, clawing and biting, struggling to gain access.

And something else.

While some creatures were blown into space by accurate fire from gun towers and flying drones and probes, others were self-destructing of their own accord. Some chose viewing portals, others hugged themselves around structural junctions before exploding.

Acid streaked, spattered, burned.

"Isolate the central control hub," Bassett said. Even above the cacophony of orders, alarms, and incoming messages in the control sphere, everyone heard him.

A dull thud was the only sound, and then on the outside monitors Bassett saw the bridges blasted apart. On one of them, a dozen Xenomorphs were blown back into space, dead or dying.

"Hull breach?" he asked, and the data flowed before him.

Hull breach in welfare section.

They were inside the space station.

Bassett looked around at the large control sphere from where his best people were conducting and monitoring the battle. They remained professional, attentive and alert, but he could also see the nervous glances passing between some of them, and sense the building air of tension.

"Stay sharp!" he said. "It's not over yet. Maintain fire against the Xenomorphs, and get the SpaceHawks out there."

"They're already in the airlocks," someone said.

"Good. Good." Bassett knew that the SpaceHawks

were ready for immediate action, because their status had been part of his holo screen information since the first shot was fired. The 4th Spaceborne were a specialist unit, spending most of their time training in space-walk scenarios and suit-powered zero-G combat. They were used for covert assaults on enemy craft, and were often called in if a ship was found deserted and adrift. Their main arena of operations was the Sol System. They had never expected to face anything like this.

"SpaceHawk comms," Bassett said, and he was patched through.

"Ready to go, sir," Lieutenant Podmore said. "Pressures equalizing."

"You don't need me to tell you how grave our situation is, Lieutenant."

"My girlfriend was on the storage unit."

"I'm sorry," Bassett said. He hadn't known, but he could not pause in replying, could not afford any chink in his armor.

"It had to be done," Podmore said. "But they're still inside."

"Those inside can be dealt with. It's the thousands still outside that'll cause us most grief."

"We're on it, sir. Three seconds."

Bassett watched a visual of the airlock cycling open, and then the first platoon of the SpaceHawks streamed out, thirty men and women flying like birds of prey as they expertly operated their specially adapted combat suits.

Other platoons launched from other airlocks, and a macro view of the battle lit up with their blue indicator points.

Set against the cloud of red spots illustrating Xenomorph locations, they were ridiculously outnumbered.

Their com-rifles started spewing death.

Bassett had thus far attempted to rein in his emotion.

There was no place for it in the thick of battle—that was a time for split-second decisions and objective views, and for him as their commander-in-chief, a wise and experienced eye. Emotions could delay reaction times, make a wide-ranging battle seem personal, and blur vision.

He had seen action many times in his rise up through the ranks. As a young soldier he'd fought mercenaries and, once, Colonial Marines who had gone rogue. As he'd grown older, he had embarked on two tours of duty to far-flung corners of the Human Sphere. He'd seen action against a single Xenomorph discovered on a planet being terraformed in Beta quadrant, and even with their superior firepower his unit had sustained losses.

Later that same tour, he'd stalked and fought a Yautja on a jungle moon ten light years from the Outer Rim.

He was an experienced soldier, carrying scars both physical and psychological. He had killed people, and he had no idea how many. His training made moot the need to count.

He had lost his son.

Now, the greatest loss pressed close, and he couldn't help feeling a momentary panic. Not death—he would accept that with grace, and the idea of his own death had never troubled him—but the idea of losing this battle, and letting down everyone on Charon Station who looked up to him and relied on him for their well-being... That was almost unbearable.

"Prepare final transmissions," he said. Heads turned. No one spoke. Final transmissions were pre-recorded, ready to be loaded with current information and orders, and sent when their situation became untenable. In effect, the final transmissions would pass seniority and control from General Paul Bassett, and their sending and receipt would mark the end of Charon Station.

"Sir, not yet," someone said. "Give the SpaceHawks a chance."

Bassett watched the screens and data streams. A real-time view of the SpaceHawks battle was being relayed through the control sphere, and for a moment he felt something like optimism. Even hope.

The SpaceHawks had gone out fighting. One platoon powered directly out from the station and engaged the Xenomorphs still drifting in from the Rage ship's circular orbit, blasting them apart before they could get close enough to the station to do any damage. Whereas the marines in their combat suits possessed a high level of maneuverability, the Xenomorphs were set in their path. They could not chase the SpaceHawks, nor divert from their trajectory. As such it was relatively easy to set a field of fire and simply wait as the enemy creatures drifted into it.

Killing grounds were created, and scores of Xenomorphs were blown apart, solid, dark beasts becoming spreading clouds of fluid and body parts.

Those already landed all across Charon Station were being pursued and picked off.

The first Marine casualty was met with a sigh across the control hub. Bassett saw it happen, a Xenomorph crawling across a curved surface and then launching itself away from the station, teeth extruding, claws grasping. The soldier's life signs flatlined within seconds of his suit being compromised. A small blessing.

"Watch those angles!" Lieutenant Podmore said over the comms.

The battle spread. For every creature blasted away from the hulls, three more drifted in and took its place. Their deaths were meaningless, causing no reaction from their fellow aliens. Perhaps grief was a human weakness, and although Bassett knew that it was essential to remain impersonal, he also knew that no soldier could function without feeling kinship with his or her comrades.

As more marines began to die, more mistakes were made. The heat of battle grew hotter. Fighting across the welfare unit's hull was suddenly disrupted when a small breach quickly tore and ruptured, the structure ripping open along a line of weakness. Portals blew out, an airlock exploded, and the massive decompression blasted marines and Xenomorphs alike out from the station. Some of them tangled in the few filaments that were still active, and a score of small explosions rippled across the viewing screen.

Once the explosive decompression had settled, the skittering black shapes of Xenomorphs could be seen hauling themselves toward the rent in the hull. They started streaming inside, laser blasts speckling the metal around them. Several caught blasts and exploded across the surface, the acidic mess making the breach even larger.

"Status of the welfare hub?" he asked.

"Seventy percent vented. There are a few sections sealed up and holding out, maybe a hundred people in all, but two blast doors have already failed, and the Xenomorphs are attacking the others."

A SpaceHawk unit aimed themselves inside the broken hull, and several holo screens switched to suit cameras in order to follow their pursuit.

Elsewhere, Xenomorphs continued to self-destruct at various points across the station, and the control hub itself came under sustained attack. The SpaceHawks were defending, but though they were taking out dozens of Xenomorphs, they could do nothing against a spreading stew of molecular acid. Once spilled, it could not be neutralized.

"Sir, there's a new breach in the hangar and docking

unit, and the barracks is being evacuated because of concerted attacks. They're self-destructing at four points around its circumference. Hull integrity down to thirty percent in two places."

"Instruct all civilians to abandon Charon Station," Bassett said. "Tell them to get the hell away, as quickly as possible. Head for preassigned safe havens."

"Yes, sir."

"Lieutenant Podmore, get your SpaceHawks to—"

A massive explosion ripped through the station. Screens flickered, the whole control hub shook, and for a brief, terrifying moment all systems went offline. Darkness fell, holo screens died, and the momentary silence was haunted by gasps and a couple of whispered prayers.

"Report!" Bassett shouted. With no holo screens or data being sent to his suit, he was blind.

"Hangar and docking unit," a voice said. "It's… gone. One of the parked ships, the *Demidov*. Its fuel cell melted down and imploded. Massive damage to all hangars, several other ships destroyed. The structure is coming apart."

"Gun towers!" Bassett said.

Power was restored, and systems powered up again. For a moment he saw fear of the dark on the faces of those around him, and in their eyes he saw his own emotions reflected.

"They're taking out the larger wreckage, but General… it was a big detonation."

Bassett could see that now. Almost a mile away across the other side of the vast Charon Station, the ruins of the large docking and hangar structure were ripping through the rest of the station. Support structures fragmented, hulls crumpled under multiple impacts.

"Did anyone get away?" he asked.

"No, sir."

While computers and automated systems continued their electronic song, the people across Bassett's control sphere watched silently as destruction spread through the heart of Charon Station. The general smelled burning. Acrid, rich, it stung the inside of his nose.

"Hull integrity plummeting!" someone shouted. "There!"

Across the sphere, the wall lining began to melt. Something was coming in.

Bassett eyed his screen and silently signaled a view of the control sphere's exterior. Xenomorphs swarmed across the surface, crawling toward one location. When they reached there, they self-detonated, splashing their corrosive fluids across the hull. In the few seconds he watched, a dozen sacrificed themselves to their cause.

"We only have seconds," Bassett said. "Check your suits. Check your weapons. I'm going to my rooms to make the final transmission."

"We'll give you as long as we can," someone said, and others echoed the sentiment.

Bassett walked back across the platform toward the door to his rooms, and with every step he only wanted to turn and join the fight. He felt as if he was leaving his people behind.

Soon, he knew, they all would be together in death.

In his room, blast doors whispering shut behind him, he accessed the main computer while he checked his com-rifle and ran diagnostics on his suit.

"Purge protocol," he said. He entered his access codes, felt the slight pinprick as his suit checked his blood for genetic identity, and then the computer welcomed him like a calm old friend.

"Good evening, General. I'm ready to send the required signals."

The purge protocol would signal all Colonial Marine

units and bases that the command structure was to be tumbled down one level. A new general would be promoted at the first opportunity, but in the meantime the next tier of command would give all necessary orders in their appropriate locales. It was entirely possible that some of the recipients of the forthcoming signals were already dead.

Perhaps they all were.

Bassett felt an overwhelming sense of loss, and he almost vomited. He held it back. He would need full use of his suit for the next few minutes, and he had no wish to have a puke-spattered visor as his last living view.

"Good. Send on my command." He accessed all system data and took one final look at the situation.

He was not wrong. It was hopeless. Charon Station was coming apart, while life signs indicated that over half of its civilian and Colonial Marine complement were already dead. The SpaceHawks were continuing their fight, but they already knew it was hopeless. Most of them were dead or injured. A few had been sent spinning into space, suits malfunctioned, a cold, lonely death their inevitable fate.

"Will there be any other messages?"

"No," Bassett said. Then he paused, changed his mind. "Yes. A message to Gerard Marshall, on board *Hagen*. Message reads: Good luck, Gerard. Don't make the wrong choice." He fell silent, and the computer waited a few seconds before confirming the message.

"Standing by."

The floor beneath him shook. An image from beyond the blast doors showed him the control sphere venting, people being banged around like feathers in a hurricane. Some managed to secure themselves and open fire as Xenomorphs pulled themselves through the tear in the hull.

"Send messages," Bassett said.

"It's done."

Paul Bassett was no longer commander-in-chief of the Colonial Marines. For however long he had left, he was just a man.

"Initiate VR," he said. "Weaver's World. Ellia's eastern coast."

The world around him—sterile, metallic, stale, and square—flickered from view. He closed his eyes, and when he opened them again he was somewhere else. A beautiful seascape was laid out before him, the beach running for miles left and right. The sea was a deep gray, topped with rolling waves that broke far out across the shallow beach. The sun smeared the horizon, a palette of colors through distant thunderheads. Closer, sand dunes were tipped with grasses that waved in the breeze, swishing left and right as if mimicking the waves.

A different breeze started whistling in. Bassett secured his magnetic boots to the sandy ground and hefted his com-rifle.

The scene before him, carrying memories of family and safety, was suddenly ripped apart as if by a monstrous, spiked, nightmarish sea creature rising for him at last.

1 9

LILIYA

Gamma Quadrant
December 2692 AD

It was strange waking from hypersleep in a cabin filled with other people. As an android, Liliya could have remained awake for the drop, but part of her had welcomed the oblivion of rest. She didn't feel as if she'd properly rested for many, many years.

Hashori was already at the controls, sitting in the main seat extruded from the bridge floor and passing her hands back and forth across the panels before her. A flickering image of two other Yautja floated above the panel—owners of the two ships that had dropped through with them—and the three of them were conversing. Liliya remained motionless, trying to listen to what was being said.

They talked quietly. Secretively. She could not hear.

Around her, the crew of the *Satan's Savior* was waking, along with Yvette and Jiango Tann. They hadn't been under for very long, in comparative terms, but in that time they'd traveled almost seventeen light years. Liliya knew more than most that time lost some of its meaning in such circumstances.

The Tanns stretched in their seats, groaning, yawning. Joints clicked. Jiango smacked his mouth and looked around, asking for a drink. Yvette rubbed her eyes.

The indie crew were immediately alert. Ware unclipped her restraints and pushed away from her seat, floating across to Hoot and Robo. The three of them whispered, then looked around the bridge.

Hashori seemed unconcerned. She must have known that they were awake, yet she continued to converse with her kin in lowered tones.

"So now what?" Ware asked loudly enough for the rest to hear. She looked stern, and uncertain. Losing her ship and one of her crew must have hit her hard.

The holos of the two other Yautja flittered away. Hashori swept her hand across the panel and the viewing screen became clear, a window out onto the darkness of deep space. Long-dead stars speckled them with ancient light. Liliya felt the familiar jolt in her chest at such a sight, and she thought it was because she was becoming more human.

"Rendezvous," Jiango Tann said.

Hashori spoke and Liliya translated.

"Now we meet with more of my kin and make plans."

"More?" Robo asked. "I don't like the three we have."

"Even though they saved our skins?" Yvette asked.

Robo shrugged.

"We're committed," Jiango said. "We've talked about this. Yvette and I have found out all we can about Liliya, and the opportunity to combine our knowledge with others is too important to pass up."

"She just doesn't like being in the hands of Yautja," Yvette said.

"Damn right," Robo said. "Six years ago we killed one

of the fuckers. For all we know it might have been this one's husband. Or wife. Or… whatever."

Hashori sat in her seat and observed the conversation. Her helmet was still removed, and her fanged mouth worked slowly, teeth touching with a delicate click, as if chewing over something. She still wore her full combat kit, and her battle spear was affixed to the ceiling above her wide control panel. She could probably pluck it down without rising from her seat.

It was obvious that she was in control here, and even more obvious that the indies didn't like that fact.

"We're on course," Liliya said. She quizzed Hashori in Yautja, then translated her reply. "Three days until we meet up with them. From there, more decisions to be made."

"Three days in this heap of junk," Hoot said. The ship was far more advanced than *Satan's Savior* and they all knew it.

"I'm going to see," Liliya said, pulling herself out of her seat.

"Going to see what?" Ware asked.

"Him."

Liliya stood before the enclosed suspension pod that contained General Alexander. She knew that sensing someone's presence was a human conceit, a failing in the way their brains were wired, because such a sense did not exist. Yet she felt something drawing her closer to the large pod.

In weightlessness, Alexander's gravity lured her down.

She reached out and touched the pod. Its composite exterior was cool and smooth. Looking around, she moved her hands over its surface, and a virtual control panel appeared on its side. She examined the markings and passed her hand over one section of it.

The pod's lid became opaque, and then fully transparent.

She stared in at the beast he had become. She'd met Alexander many times before, while back on *Macbeth*. She could even recall the moment of his commissioning. It had been almost fourteen decades ago, when the Founders' leader, Wordsworth, implemented a period of android manufacture. That had been after a visit to a small moon, when three crew members had been killed in an accident while attempting to land. Wordsworth had suggested that androids should be used for the most dangerous away missions, and as such a series of worker droids were commissioned and created.

They weren't called generals back then. Purely functional, aesthetically homogenous, more than forty androids had passed through the production line before Wordsworth called a halt.

Back then, Alexander had been called M09.

"Hello, M-zero-nine," Liliya said.

He slept suspended deep in whatever android dreams he enjoyed. She liked to think they were different from hers. She had many more years of life experience than him, and much more of a desire to become human. His drive was to be the best android he could, and since Maloney's murder of Wordsworth, her corruption of the Founders' original intentions, he and others like him sought to be the best soldiers.

General Alexander. Liliya might have laughed, if recent events had not been so terrible. He had even grown bright blond hair, mimicking that ancient general's supposed appearance. Yet his face was still a blank, resembling a human's only in that he had a mouth, nose, and two eyes. Nothing else was there. No emotion or drive, no scars to map his past, no creases folded into his skin by laughter or hate.

In his determination to fulfil his mission, he had become grotesque.

However, Liliya couldn't help but admire his persistence. His desire to complete his Mistress Maloney's orders had driven him across light years of space and through traumatic times, culminating in the need to use parts of his own soldiers to fix the parts of him that were broken. A Xenomorph's clawed arm and hand was spliced into his shoulder. Its heavy leg, tipped in splayed, spiked toes, was melded onto his hip. It was horrific... and yet beautiful, the way this thing had surpassed his programming and made himself more than he had ever been before.

"You knew him?" Jiango Tann asked from behind her, and Liliya berated herself for not hearing his approach.

"Yes. On board *Macbeth*. He wasn't much to look at, then."

"Not much now."

"But have you ever seen anything like him?"

Tann drifted beside her and his boots clamped down. "He's out of it. Just a thing for us to use. He can't hurt you anymore."

"Oh, I'm sure he could," Liliya said. She knew what Alexander would be dreaming—visions of her, in his grasp, as he presented her to Mistress Maloney. "Even asleep, he wants me dead."

"He'll stay asleep."

She glanced at Tann and offered a smile. "I suppose you've come to ask me something."

"Well... Yvette and I thought we might continue working."

"On me." She touched her chest where the hole had been temporarily sealed.

Tann shrugged, embarrassed, avoiding her eyes. She liked that about him. He and his wife wanted to open her up and delve inside, see what made her work. They also regarded her as human.

Which was why she said yes.

It was a long three days on board the Yautja ship. Ostensibly large enough for them all, it seemed as if the Yautja had little need for recreation, dining, or sleeping spaces. Hashori spent the majority of time in her seat at the ship's main control panel, while the others tried to find various means to relieve their boredom.

The indie crew accessed their suit computers and immersed themselves in VR games or battle re-enactments, while the Tanns and Liliya found the most convenient place to continue their experiments. Ironically, the most comfortable place for them to work was in the small welfare bay, close to Alexander's suspension pod.

Liliya submitted herself willingly. The Tanns had brought little equipment with them, but everything they had learnt was still accessible on the datapad Yvette always carried. With so much to learn, it was too easy for them to be working for long periods of time without rest. Liliya didn't require rest, but the elderly humans did.

She would find herself strapped down with her chest open and insides exposed, while Yvette and Jiango slept affixed to the wall, heads leaning against each other.

Several times each day, they convened on the bridge to listen to reports that Hashori seemed only too willing to share. How she was receiving these reports from so far across the Sphere was open to question, but Hashori never responded to any such query. Early on, Liliya thought the Yautja was being helpful. But as time went on, she started to detect something else in the big alien's words, and even in the strange tone her clicking and grinding words sometimes made.

Liliya thought she sounded smug.

"Your planet of Weaver's World is under sustained attack, with many thousands dead. No honor in such a slaughter. It's not hunting, it's murder," the Yautja said. "Many Colonial Marine bases have been destroyed. Many dropholes taken. In accordance with instruction from Elder Kalakta, my Yautja kin are aiding the fight against the Rage whenever and wherever possible."

Relaying news and reports about how the Rage was assaulting the Human Sphere, defeating the Colonial Marines, and decimating populations, Hashori sounded pleased.

Liliya wanted to call her out on it, yet at the same time she saw the danger in that. If she was right, and Hashori had begun to gloat, it might cause fatal tension between her and the indie crew still mourning their lost member. If she accused Hashori of gloating and she was wrong, the Yautja would doubtless take offence at the affront to her honor.

Either option might result in violence.

So Liliya listened to the news, watched the reaction on the human faces around her, then closed her eyes and returned once more to the Tanns' probing experiments. That was how she would best serve humanity. She had fled the Rage for this, and now was not the place to endanger her ability to help. Nor was it her right. If the Yautja were pleased at the human suffering, so be it.

Liliya's purpose had long been the same, and current circumstances could not alter that. She was here to change things forever.

* * *

Four days after capturing Alexander and defeating the Rage at the drophole, the two Yautja ships came in close once more. Flying within a couple of miles of one another, the three ships changed course, and then reduced speed.

Everyone convened on the bridge, with Hashori still in the main seat. She did not tell them what was happening, but there was no need. The holo screen before her displayed three specks indicating their ships, and a million miles ahead were three different colored specks.

Slowly but surely the distance closed, and Liliya felt a thrill of anticipation at the meeting to come.

2 0

ISA PALANT

Gamma Quadrant
December 2692 AD

With four Yautja vessels cloaked and performing orbital patrols, the *Pixie* docked with the ship that supposedly contained five humans, as well as the android who'd fled the Rage. As airlocks equalized, Halley suggested that perhaps it was best if a non-military person made their first contact.

So with Halley and her DevilDogs covering her from all angles, Palant stood before the airlock doors as they slid open. A brief hiss, a breath of cool air, and then the doors at the far end of the *Pixie*'s docking umbilicus also opened. A woman stood there, smiling. Palant smiled back. It was only a few seconds later that she noticed the open wound in the woman's chest, the tubes protruding, and realized that this was the android.

Behind her stood a tall Yautja.

Kalakta! Palant caught her breath.

But of course, it was not. This Yautja was younger, less scarred, and it did not project Kalakta's strange regalness.

"My name's Liliya," the android said.

"Isa Palant." She pointed at the open wound. "That looks... painful."

"It does sting," Liliya admitted. "May I come on board?"

"It's not really my ship, but permission granted."

Liliya walked toward her, held her hand out, and Palant shook it. *This is something important*, she thought, grasping the android's warm hand, feeling her strength, sensing her great age. She exuded it, her eyes glimmering with deep, dark memories. She would know so many stories, and Palant suddenly needed to hear every one of them.

"I think we might be able to help each other," Liliya said.

"I hope so. We had a general, and—"

"Oh, we still have one."

Liliya laughed at Palant's surprised expression, and in that moment the distinctions between real and artificial were forgotten. These were just two women fighting for their futures.

"Welcome aboard the *Pixie*," Palant said. "Why don't we get your people on board, and we can talk."

The tension was palpable from the start.

The two crews mingled. Halley and the DevilDogs met Liliya, the Tanns, and the three indies from the *Satan's Savior*.

Akoko Halley didn't like indies. Though gone rogue, Halley and her remaining crew were still Colonial Marines at heart. As soldiers, they didn't have much time for mercenaries.

Yaquita pulled herself through from the *Pixie*, her lack of legs causing no hindrance in zero gravity, and she and the big Yautja named Hashori held conference on the Yautja ship. While the humans and android spoke, the aliens maintained their distance.

After the greetings, they gathered around the table in the *Pixie*'s rec room, straps and magnetic boots holding them in place. Drink bags were distributed. Palant, Liliya, and the Tanns sat. Halley and her crew marked the doorways, while Ware and the indies held onto wall straps. They'd been allowed to keep their weapons, as a mark of faith. Trust, Palant knew, would take a little longer to find.

They related what had gone before. Palant knew there was much more to tell—she could see it in the Tann couple's haunted eyes, the indie crew's sense of loss, and feel the weight of experience burning behind her own face. But the time for detail would be later, if at all. Everything that mattered was here with them now.

All attention turned to Liliya.

She told her tale, as well—though it took a little while. Part of that was because her tale was so much longer and deeper than anyone else's. Palant suggested she might be the oldest living android in the galaxy, and Liliya smiled, shaking her head, casting doubt.

"There's always a greater story," she said, but Palant doubted it.

Liliya spoke of the Founders and Wordsworth, of the crime she'd committed in his name, her decades spent adrift, their journey from the Human Sphere aboard the ships *Hamlet*, *Othello*, and *Macbeth*. She told the group about Beatrix Maloney and her rise to prominence. Their discovery of the miracle gel that prolonged and preserved life. She related the events of Wordsworth's murder, and the change of their society from forward-thinking Founders to hate-filled Rage.

She talked of *Midsummer* and the wonders they had found there. Suddenly Hashori and Yaquita appeared through the open airlock, as if they had been listening and somehow understanding all along.

"Drukathi," Palant said.

"You know the Faze?" Liliya asked.

"Only as much as Elder Kalakta would tell me, which wasn't much. I'm not sure it concerns us in our current fight. I think they're... beyond us, in many ways."

"We need to know what you know," Jiango Tann said. "Liliya said you have a general?"

"In cryo-sleep, yes," Liliya said. "Sent to hunt me down."

"He's been persistent," Captain Ware said.

"We *had* a general," Palant said. "Yaquita and I learned what we could from him, but we need to know what you know, too. Perhaps combining our knowledge can help— and I already have some ideas."

"As do we," Yvette Tann said. "First, though, a favor?"

"If we can," Halley said. "This is my ship, you're guests now. What is it you want?"

Yvette glanced at her husband, nodded. "Please tell us you have some human food," she said.

They broke bread, still in the rec room. The food came from the *Pixie*'s replicator, but they all agreed it was far better than anything they'd been eating courtesy of the Yautja. Spiced meats and grains followed, and then strong coffee.

Even Hashori and Yaquita ate with them. They growled and grumbled at the strange meal. Some of those assembled even found it in themselves to laugh.

They were heading toward the last known location of *Macbeth*, gleaned from the dead general by Yaquita and her covert interrogations. The ship's computer, Billy, calculated that, traveling at just under the speed of light, they'd reach the Outer Rim drophole in a little less than a day. During that time, they had to prepare a plan of attack.

To Palant the meeting, this strange group of allies, held a weight that every one of them could sense. Eager to know what the other group had gleaned from their captured android, she tingled with the sense of history being made.

She told them about the android Oscar, the Yautja asteroid where they had been taken, and how she and Yaquita had spent many days interrogating and dismantling the general.

"We took his heart. Even after all our cautionary approaches, even though his heart was no longer part of his body, he was close to detonating the charge they all carry with them. Yaquita and I think we could do that. With the right approach, I think we could detonate the heart of *any* general, from a distance. I'm not certain of *what* distance, and… Well, there are still details missing."

"Liliya has the details," Jiango said. He leaned forward, excited, reaching across the table for Palant's hands. He held on tight. "Liliya has something we can use. Tell them!" He nodded toward the android.

"It's why I left the Rage," she said. "I stole the alien tech the generals use to control their troops."

"Where is it?" Palant asked.

"In these veins." Liliya traced a finger down her opposite arm, and Palant followed, seeing the pale white gleam of a vein beneath the android's skin.

"We've been testing it!" Tann said. "It's strange, some form of nanotech I've never seen or heard of before. I think that, with more time, we could understand it."

"We don't *have* more time," Palant said, "but perhaps we don't need to understand it to use it."

"How *do* we use it?" Yvette asked.

Palant looked around at the assembled group. Her datapad floated before her, translating the conversation directly to Yaquita and Hashori. Even they seemed to be holding their breath while listening to her.

"I think I can create a signal that will hijack a general's self-destruct," she said. "Perhaps Liliya here, with the tech she stole, would be able to link herself to a general—*any* general. If so, then I can program the signal into Liliya's heart, and she can transmit it."

"And then we can send the self-destruct signal to *all* of them!" Jiango whispered. "Brilliant. Wonderful!"

Palant held up her hand.

"Don't celebrate yet. It may not be possible, at least not without having physical access to all of the generals. But perhaps from the *Macbeth*…"

An ominous silence fell across the room.

"But would it work?" Halley whispered. "Aboard the *Macbeth*?"

"I really don't know," Palant said. "There are so many variables, so many unknowns." She looked to the Tanns. She'd already recognized their quiet wisdom, and the intellects that hid behind their calm silence. "What do you think?"

"I think the theory is sound," Jiango said.

"I agree," Yvette said. "The greatest unknown is…" She nodded at Liliya.

"Then we have to test it," Liliya said. All heads turned her way. "We have the perfect subject, after all."

"What the fucking hell is that?" Sprenkel said. Halley didn't berate him this time. Probably because she was entertaining exactly the same thought.

Isa Palant certainly was.

"He was a pretty determined android," Captain Ware said.

"Looks like something you might find in a swamp," Bestwick said. "A radioactive swamp. On a dead planet. Only… about a hundred times bigger."

They were on board the Yautja ship now, all of them huddled in the small room containing two cryo-pods. One of the pods was empty, and lay open. The other contained the thing that had once been General Alexander. Liliya stood to one side, staring down at the android–Xenomorph amalgamation. It was as if she was afraid.

Androids don't feel real fear, Palant thought, although she was beginning to see Liliya as something different. Not quite human, because that was impossible. But more than an android. Something unprecedented, perhaps even unique. It might not be her incredible age that set her apart.

"You're sure about this?" Halley asked quietly from her side.

Palant nodded. "We have to make sure it works." She touched Liliya's arm and smiled.

"Don't worry," Liliya said. "I'm growing used to it." She hauled off her jacket and exposed the wound in her chest. Peeling off the cover, she revealed the wet hole in her chest plate, skin pinned aside, skeletal structure wedged apart.

"Jiango, Yvette, you should help me," Palant said. "I know my way around a Yautja's physiology, but…" She trailed off, feeling the weight of the two alien stares. The datapad was still translating. "Sorry," she whispered. She didn't dare glance at them.

Perhaps some of the samples she'd worked on over the years had been their relations.

They showed no emotion. Just stared.

Liliya sat back and opened herself to examination once again. The Tanns had already revealed how much work they'd done on her, and while Palant and Yaquita prepared to probe at her heart, Yvette fetched the samples they'd already taken from her. One such sample was the purified nanotech, the fluid she had stolen from the Rage and injected into her own veins.

Held in a glass container, it looked innocuous.

They went to work. While Palant and Yaquita used her datapad to recall information from their interrogation of the ruined android, Oscar, the Tanns readied the nanotech. Soon, Liliya was paired with the datapad and a program was downloading directly into her heart. They asked her to relay any changes she felt, and especially anything dangerous that her systems might flag. But for a while she simply lay back and accepted the attention.

The Tanns synthesized a small speck of nanotech and imbued it with elements of the same program.

Palant had no idea if this was how it worked. But it was as close as she could be, and Yaquita said or did nothing to suggest that what they were doing might fail. She had shown herself to be a talented scientist, more adaptable than Palant in many ways. Her confidence in what they were doing filled Palant with hope.

Once Liliya confirmed that her programs had accepted the new code, and the nanotech had been programmed, there was just the matter of injecting it into General Alexander.

"Once he's awake, he'll do anything he can to destroy me," Liliya said.

"Can't you neutralize his on-board systems?" Ware asked. "You know… fuck up his brain?"

"The android we worked on was initializing its self-destruct even when we'd removed its heart from its body," Palant said. "I don't think we can assume any level of control once he's awake."

"Then we don't wake him," Hashori said.

"You'd think the humans would have thought of that," Yaquita replied.

Palant pressed her lips together in a tight smile. "We eject the cryo-pod," she said.

"Can we lift the lid and inject him without waking him?" Halley asked.

"It will only take seconds." Palant looked at Yaquita and raised an eyebrow. Yaquita returned the gesture, silent, and Palant found herself worried about what it meant in their language. Maybe it was a come-on.

"The system is automated," Yaquita said. "Once opened, the pod commences the waking procedure, but when closed, the procedure will reverse once again."

"Then he won't wake enough to respond," Palant said. "Get the pod in the airlock, open it, inject him, close it, blast it into space…"

"Ker-boom," Hoot said. Palant eyed him up and down. This group reminded her of the indies back on Love Grove Base. They'd been good people, strong, with normal concerns. She wondered how many loved ones this crew had lost in the ongoing war.

"So let's shake it up," Halley said.

"Yeah," Robo said, flexing her robotic arm. "I wanna see fireworks."

… Mistress, Mistress Maloney, I haven't failed you I'll never fail you, I'm still chasing Liliya and I… trapped, I'm trapped here, down here alone, but that doesn't mean I've failed.

I remember. I was close, so close, and then they came. The Yautja, fighting with the humans. They took me down and still hold me here…

A distance has been traveled. A great distance, and I'm not sure where.

So long as she's still close. I can sense her. I can smell her, and as soon as I'm able...

Palant stood ready with the injector, and as soon as Hashori passed her hand over the control and opened the lid, she leaned in toward the sleeping android.

Up close, and without a layer of wet glass between them, he was even more monstrous.

She ignored the damaged face, pallid skin, and the Xenomorph parts grafted to where his own had been ripped off or burned away. She went for his throat. The injector pressed against his skin and she initiated, pulling away again three seconds later. The glass phial was empty. His throat was still depressed where she'd pressed the point, no longer possessing any elasticity.

The cryo-pod lid couldn't have been open for more than seventeen seconds.

His eyes were moving.

"Close the lid!" she said. "Put him down again, quickly!"

The lid hissed closed, and the Marine and indie crews worked together to shove the big suspension pod into the airlock.

Yaquita touched the controls, and a three-second countdown began.

They've done something, Mistress. I'm still asleep, but something has changed. It's like I've been nudged, my dreams invaded and touched, and whatever I do I can't... pull myself... back up. I'm trying. Believe me, Mistress, I'm trying my hardest and—

But what's this? Something's moving.
Something's scraping.

The pod blasted into space, and driven by the rush of air from the airlock it quickly moved away from the two conjoined ships. Hashori confirmed that the other five Yautja ships were out of any danger zone.

Palant turned to Liliya.

"It's all down to you, now."

"Maybe we should go to the bridge, so we can see," Jiango Tann suggested. Everyone agreed, and all of them—human and Yautja alike—crowded onto the *Pixie*'s bridge. Billy formed a holo screen, and in the distance they saw the suspension pod moving rapidly away. It had developed a gentle spin, and it grew and faded from sight, grew and faded, as it reflected ancient starlight.

"I wonder if he's half-awake?" Halley said.

"I hope so," Liliya said.

Palant frowned. *Was that a hint of brutality?*

"Here we go," Liliya said, and she closed her eyes. In her opened chest, her compact heart made a strange, low sound.

I'm free of their ship, adrift, on my own. They've cast me out.
They must think they have rid of me at last, but they'll see. I'm
not beaten that easily. I'll wait for as long as it takes.

I'll come back.

But—

That's strange.

My heart.

Growing hot.

Almost as if…

* * *

The explosion was a bright flare a hundred miles away, a nuclear bloom that for a brief instant was the brightest object in the sky. Then its fires spread and cooled in the harsh vacuum of space.

General Alexander was gone.

"It worked," Palant breathed. "You did it." She grabbed Liliya's hand and squeezed, and around the bridge there were smiles and pats on the back. A couple of the indies and marines whooped. Even the two Yautja seemed impressed.

"So now to find the *Macbeth*, sneak on board, find how to connect to all the Rage generals, and blast them all to hell," Liliya said.

"Sounds easy," Halley said.

"Yeah," Captain Ware agreed. "And I'm at a loose end. So, which way are we going?"

21

MAJOR SERGEI BUDANOV

Weaver's World
December 2692 AD

Major Budanov had time to cry out once when he saw his gunner fall beneath a Xenomorph, then his fight continued.

Over the past six days, they'd developed a bond. Being shot down, surviving the crash, forging their way into Boston Three and seeing the slaughter perpetrated by the Rage and their beasts, had all contributed to a burgeoning friendship that went beyond private and major. They had seen things together, done things together, that bit deep and drew them close.

Now she was gone, and Budanov lived to fight on. For how long, he didn't know.

He blasted the Xenomorph that had stalked and taken her down, slicing its head in half with a laser burst. She was already dead, but he put a shot into her as well, just to make sure. The dead beast blew apart and slumped down onto her corpse. There'd be nothing left of either of them to scoop into a body bag.

This was the central hub of Boston Three, and he fought

alongside a small contingent of about twenty marines. The city had become one of the main battlegrounds on Weaver's World, much of it already reduced to smoking ruins by the continuing aerial bombardment from the surviving Rage dropships. Since the Yautja had arrived and entered into the fray, their ships had performed random fly-bys, firing on the enemy vessels and moving on.

Three Rage ships remained circling the city, firing down into the flames, and then flying away again, hiding for several hours somewhere out of sight before coming in for another run. Sometimes the Yautja ships were there waiting for them, sometimes not. It was a game of hunted and hunter played out in the skies above a dying city.

Budanov was still in touch with his forces across the planet. Several of their communications satellites had been taken out, but many more remained. Although contact with some locations was spotty, most of Weaver's World was still within reach.

News was dire.

The dead numbered in the hundreds of thousands. Horrific stories reached him of Xenomorphs being dropped into outlying communes, places unprotected by Marines where the only means of defense were a few basic projectile weapons. The result was always the same. Sometimes he received reports intercepted from inhabitants still on the run. More often, the news came from Marine units on seek-and-destroy missions.

Above, the battle in orbit had taken a rapid turn the previous day. The 7th Spaceborne had continued their attacks on descending dropships, as well as the big Rage vessel *Aaron-Percival* in high orbit above the equator. But three of their main destroyers had been boarded by Xenomorphs and taken out within the space of seven hours. The result was that only a handful of frigates and twenty manned fighters remained of their force, and they were implementing a policy of attack-and-flee.

Sometimes the attacks worked, more often they inflicted minimal damage. The 7th Spaceborne were more of an annoyance for the Rage than a real threat.

The battle had changed from repelling an assault to a game of survival.

Budanov would have been the first to admit that without the Yautja's intervention, the battle would have been lost days earlier. As it was, the two old enemies— now allied in the face of a far greater threat—were fighting side by side. In some cases they were holding the Rage at bay.

Much of Boston Three was a burning ruin, but none of those left alive were willing to go down without a fight.

An estimated several thousand civilians had taken shelter in the subway stations and subterranean vehicle parks beneath the city's central hub. The tunnels and underground routes were heavily defended by Marines and civilians who'd taken up arms, along with a contingent of the Yautja.

The real fight, however, was taking place above ground.

"Incoming, three o'clock."

"Large movement at seven o'clock, contact in two minutes."

"Dropship approaching from the east, it'll be over the city in seventy seconds."

"Hold plasma cannon fire until it's over us!" Budanov ordered. "Then blast it when its belly doors are open."

The center of the city was unrecognizable. The large hexagonal plaza itself was a chaos of rubble, craters, dead bodies, huddled defenders, two crashed aircraft, blasted land vehicles, several fountains long-since run dry, countless melted patches where Xenomorphs had been taken out, and three buildings reduced to smoking holes in the ground. Hundreds of Marines and civilian defenders still held out, hiding behind ruins and taking on the endless assaults by Xenomorphs rushing in from other areas of the city.

"Here it comes!" someone shouted.

The dropship rolled in, zigzagging to avoid any ground-to-air fire, micro-laser bursts showering from it as countermeasures in case any Yautja ships were waiting to pounce. This time, there were not.

"Steady…" Budanov said. His voice carried to every Marine combat suit in the city. There weren't that many left. Their forces were reduced to less than a third of their previous numbers.

"It's slowing."

"Steady…" he muttered, readying his own com-rifle.

"Doors opening."

"Two seconds…"

The Xenomorphs, hanging there like giant spiders ready to pounce, emerged from the darkness, illuminated by the blazing fires from below. It was as if daylight would no longer touch them.

"One second…"

The doors were fully open, and the first batch of Xenomorphs dropped away from the Rage ship.

"Fire! Everything you've got!"

From all across the plaza, a barrage of laser, plasma, and nano-shot poured upward, converging on the Rage ship as it drifted rapidly from east to west, disgorging its terrible cargo. The sound was deafening—the pulsing thump of plasma cannons, the sharp crackle of lasers, the hiss and then multiple explosions of nano-shot. The first wave of Xenomorphs were caught in the fire and burst apart, a score of them falling in wet, melting pieces. More were winged, falling away injured, landing, self-destructing or charging, soon to be brought down in the crossfire.

"The ship!" Budanov shouted. "Keep firing on the ship! We'll get those bastards on the ground, it's the ship we want!"

His own com-rifle thumped at his shoulder as he unleashed plasma shots at the dark, open belly of the Rage craft. He pivoted as it swung past almost directly above them. His suit made him aware of the shapes dropping past the gunfire, hunched black things that they had all come to recognize over the past few terrible days. But he ignored them, maintaining fire. Seeing his plasma pulses swallowed by the vessel. Seeing other gunfire impacting and lighting up its insides.

As the ship swung away, a silver streak appeared in the north, closing rapidly.

"Yautja!" someone shouted. Budanov's suit confirmed it.

The Rage ship turned in a wide circle above the city, smoking, losing altitude.

The Yautja vessel unleashed a sustained laser blast, hovering a mile out and maintaining its fire until the Rage ship exploded, showering fire and blazing debris down across the city.

No one cheered. The dead ship's monstrous offspring were launching their attack. Xenomorphs darted left and right, leaping at Marines and civilians. Some of them were taken down by gunfire. Others made it through, pinning their victims down, hacking with taloned fingers and clawed feet, slashing through clothing, flesh, and bone with their wicked tails, caving in skulls with powerful jaws.

Then they'd move on, leaping and slouching, jumping ten yards through the air and slinking deep down in the ruins.

Blood and acid flowed, and the septic stink intensified in the air.

"Regroup!" Budanov said to the marines. Battle-wearied and wounded, many of them had been scorched by acid splashes where their suits had begun to fail. None of them complained. Over the days he'd been there, they had acquitted themselves well.

As the men and women drew together, Budanov spared a glance at his dead gunner.

A Xenomorph dashed at them from behind the burnt-out wreck of a land skimmer. A nano-shot blast enveloped it and it exploded, misting the air with acid and shreds of its hard carapace. Budanov turned so that the splashes speckled his back. His suit's ability to repel the acid was down to seventeen percent. One or two more impacts, and he'd feel the first agonizing burns against his skin.

Part of him would welcome it. It would feed his hate.

"Sir, look, three o'clock!"

From a wide street leading far out through the dying city, a mass of Xenomorphs were advancing against them.

"Where the hell did they come from?" he shouted. His suit's motion detector hadn't spotted them, and he began to wonder at its efficacy in other aspects.

"Crashed ship?" a woman asked. "Doesn't matter. I count fifty at least."

"We're fucked," someone said.

"Then get unfucked!" Budanov said. He climbed a shallow slope of fallen masonry, secured his footing, then unleashed a hail of nano-shot at the advancing enemy.

Others joined him. From closer to the swarm, several civilians emerged from hiding places, shooting at the beasts then fleeing. Too many of them were run down and killed.

"Bastards," Budanov hissed. He fired a plasma burst,

but his com-rifle was overheating. He had to ease back. More nano-shot, effective but not as deadly as plasma, too reliant on accurate shooting and a motionless target.

The Xenomorphs swarmed across the ruins, trampling bodies, never slowing or relenting in their attack.

Not even the sudden flickers of heat-haze movement gave them pause.

Budanov recognized the signs, though. He'd seen them enough over the past few days, and although they rarely fought with the Marines, they were ever-present, their help a major factor in continuing the fight.

Cloaked, the Yautja cut through the advancing creatures as effectively as cannon blasts from a destroyer. A dozen enemy fell in the first wave, slashed apart. Moments later a secondary assault began, the distinctive triple targeting lasers splashing across the Xenomorph troops before blasters opened up, blowing many of the monsters apart. Another wave charged from behind, skittering through their dead and dying brethren, to be met with a fusillade of fire from the defending marines.

As one, the Yautja uncloaked and joined the fray. Having expended the element of surprise, at least a dozen warriors spread across the battlefield, no two quite the same. Some were taller and thinner, a few shorter—though still easily seven feet tall—and of a much stockier build, as if from a different race. A few bore traditional battle spears, others carried what looked like tridents. Spiked throwing weapons, bladed limbs, shoulder blasters, a couple even bore more traditional energy weapons. Massive items easily the size and weight of an average human, which they wielded with ease.

They seemed to dance through the mass of Xenomorphs.

Budanov knew some basic martial arts, but some of

his unit were experts in many facets of hand-to-hand combat, and he always marveled when he watched them training. The power and strength, the economy and grace of each movement, left him in awe. The ancient arts were still practiced—karate, ju jitsu, various tai chi forms—but so were more modern methods, many of them developed over the past few centuries to adapt to new situations and environments. Combat in weightlessness called for a very particular set of talents, and differing gravities imposed unusual and challenging demands on the physiologies of space travelers and soldiers.

The Yautja were something else altogether. It was as if they used gravity as their own plaything, jumping through the air to meet Xenomorphs mid-leap, slashing them apart and using the momentum of their impact to change direction, dropping gracefully to the ground and attacking again. There were no wasted movements. If Xenomorphs were nature's perfect killing machines, then the Yautja were their perfect counterparts.

For the first time, Budanov imagined a true war between humanity and the Yautja. If he were a betting man, he knew who his money would be on. With their high-tech ships and guns, combat suits and computers, humankind had lost the true fighting instinct.

Part of what made the Rage's Xenomorph army so shatteringly successful was their level of imposed control. If these beasts ever evolved their own independent intelligence, they might well be unstoppable.

He shook the thoughts from his head. *Not now!*

"Cover them!" he shouted. As the Xenomorphs scattered, he and the Colonial Marines started picking them off with single, careful shots. Soon there were no attackers left alive.

A brief but heartfelt cheer went up, and Major Budanov

felt a moment of respite in the unrelenting battle. But then he glanced across at his gunner's remains, melted down now beneath the remnants of the monster that had killed her. Such a sight stole away any shred of joy at this momentary victory.

The Yautja began to patrol the battlefield, seemingly ignoring the humans around them. They blasted a few struggling Xenomorphs, remaining at a distance, careful not to move too close to the wounded beasts as their self-destruct function initiated. A couple of them crouched beside bubbling puddles where an enemy had fallen, and he assumed they were looking for mementos. But the dead monsters left nothing.

"Sir! Major!" A shout went up, and a bloodied marine sprinted across the battlefield, barely noticing where his feet were splashing down. He passed by a Yautja without a second glance, and stopped in front of Budanov, breathing heavily. His combat suit was glitching. Half of it across his chest and left shoulder seemed to flex and contract again as its defensive functions malfunctioned.

"Private?" Budanov prompted.

"Sir, down there. In the tunnels. They're in. The Xenos are in, and we're barely holding them off."

"You had to report this face to face?"

"It's fucked down there, Major. Signal relays have been taken out, lighting and power systems are down. It all happened at once, and now they're attacking en masse. It's like they planned it."

"Maybe," Budanov said. He instructed his suit to broadcast to all troops in the city. "Listen up! The subways are under attack. There are thousands of civvies down there. Every second Marine, form up and head down. Units of a dozen, close formation. Keep your comms open and mark your targets. Go to infrared as soon as you're out of the sunlight. Go!"

Exhausted soldiers all across the ruined plaza hustled, and within moments there were a score of units heading to access points that led to the subterranean warren beneath them. Down in the darkness, a new battle was about to begin.

Budanov eyed the Yautja still milling around the battlefield. He wished he could speak their language, understand at least some of those weird clicks and crackles. But then he realized he didn't have to.

He moved quickly across the shattered ground, passing his dead gunner without another glance. He'd be like that soon. If not today, then tomorrow. If not tomorrow, then next month or next year. It was a fate that awaited so many Colonial Marines, and every man and woman knew it, the moment they signed up. With all the benefits of service came the high risk of an early, violent death.

The knowledge made him prouder than ever of the troops he fought alongside. Exhausted and injured, mourning lost buddies and loved ones here and a trillion miles distant, still they were eager to jump into the next fight.

That's why we'll win, he thought with a sudden, unexpected burst of optimism. *Not because we're more intelligent, or have high-tech weaponry, but because we care. We have emotions, and while that can bring us down, it also makes us furious.*

He approached the nearest Yautja. It was a huge specimen, almost nine feet high, helmet heavily scarred. It wore bandoliers bearing glowing blue ammunition, carried a trident, and heavy blades still protruded from the armor on its right forearm. Its blaster followed its shifting gaze, settling on Budanov's face.

"I need your help," he said.

* * *

Major Budanov and his Colonial Marines descended into hell, and the Yautja went with them.

The tunnels beneath the embattled plaza were in chaos. As the private had said, the main lighting systems were down and only emergency lighting glowed, faint strip bulbs powered from localized generators. Panicked citizens ran in all directions, many of them carrying flashlights or following light projected by datapads or personal comm units. The noise was shocking, and echoed everywhere—screams, shouts, heavy footsteps, distant gunfire and explosions, and the occasional sounds of structures warping or collapsing under stress. These tunnels, walkways, and bridges weren't designed for so many people at the same time.

Budanov had been here before, on a downtime visit to the city. The underground was a warren of subway tunnels and stations, elevators, maintenance areas, access points for various basements, storage facilities, and a massive underground reservoir fed from the mountains which provided the city with much of its drinking water.

A person could get lost down here. Many had.

The unit of twenty marines came with him. Their suit systems were paired so they all could access the foremost view—and any other, should the need arise. Onboard computers had already succeeded in differentiating fleeing and panicked civilians from marines, Yautja, and Xenomorphs. He zeroed in on the first group of creatures, and headed that way.

They descended a staircase heaving with civilians, shoving them aside in order to move faster. Two Xenomorphs were close, fifty yards from the base of the staircase and just emerging from one of the subway transit tunnels.

"No plasma down here," Budanov said. "Too many civvies."

Close to the bottom the two Xenomorphs came into view. They scampered across the concourse, each footfall leaving a bloody print behind. Murdering machines, beasts of death and slaughter, they reached for any human they could find. The people scattered in all directions, repulsed from the monsters like opposing magnets.

One man carried a child. He tripped and went down, throwing the toddler ahead of him, turning on his back, arms up and legs kicking in a vain attempt to protect himself. A Xenomorph went for him.

Still descending the staircase, slowed by the frantic flow, Budanov aimed at the beast.

Red lasers flashed. A blaster sounded, a deep boom echoing through the crowded subterranean space. The Xenomorph exploded, erupting in a huge splash of spitting acid and torn body parts.

The fallen man screamed as he was spattered. Other people fell, slapping at burning flesh and only making matters worse.

The second Xenomorph spun around to confront the aggressor, and it went into a crouch as a Yautja stepped from the shadows. People pulled back, fighting to get away from these two circling aliens.

The Yautja's targeting lasers played across the Xenomorph's head, then switched off. It hefted its battle spear instead, holding it low against its forearm and dashing in toward the monster. The Xenomorph lashed out with its tail. The Yautja ducked, but the tail's tip slashed across a woman's throat, virtually decapitating her.

"Mommy!" The shout was high and terrible.

Budanov and three other marines fired at the same time, killing the Xenomorph instantly. It spattered across the ground and started melting down into the rock of the world.

The Yautja roared. Head back, arms held wide, spear scoring the ground as it turned to face the marines at the base of the staircase, its furious call was amplified in the contained environment. Budanov felt a chill, but he did not lower his weapon.

This isn't a fucking game, he thought. *It's not a fucking hunt. This is a massacre.*

Crouching, the Yautja faced him and his unit.

"Hold," Budanov whispered.

Then the warrior beast stood tall again, turned, and ran into the darkness.

"Okay," Budanov said. "Two down. Plenty more to go."

Following the Yautja, the marines ran into darkness.

2 2

BEATRIX MALONEY

Macbeth, *Sol System*
December 2692 AD

As they approached the orbit of Saturn, Beatrix Maloney received news of the fall of Charon Station. She allowed a brief but intense burst of celebration, manifesting externally as a shifting in her gel surround, and a broad, almost toothless smile.

From the start, Charon was one of their prime targets, heavily defended and the central hub of Colonial Marine control. She had never harbored any doubts as to their success, yet it still stood as their greatest victory to date. Maloney had instructed Challar that the base was to be blasted to smithereens. Images of its destruction would be spread far and wide.

Now headless, the greatest military power the Human Sphere had ever known would be flailing in the growing darkness.

It's going better than I could have ever hoped, she thought. Yet there was still that one splinter in her skin, itching and working inward, however hard she tried to ignore it.

Liliya would be absent from her thoughts for periods of hours, and then she'd prick in again.

Alexander hadn't been heard from in some time.

The element of the Faze that had remained on board the *Macbeth* had grown suddenly in size, almost doubling its mass and girth for no apparent reason. The return of a Watcher could cause that, though. If Alexander's Watcher had come home to roost, it could only mean that the android had failed in his task.

If so, Liliya was still free.

Even so, her betrayal had come too late. Only two months into the Rage War, and already they were striking at the heart of the Human Sphere. There was little left to stop them. True, Earth was the most heavily defended planet in the galaxy, and the battle facing them was still great. But with so many successes they held the advantage. The Rage were confident of their eventual triumph.

She was confident.

Once Earth had bowed down before her, then the rebuilding could begin. First they would recreate the Sol System, and then the rest of the Human Sphere, with the Rage as its rulers. Wordsworth had been such a fool, to believe that fleeing his roots would give the Founders the freedom to grow. True freedom meant coming home, and making it their own.

The *Macbeth* and three of its segments were all heading in-system. Her own vessel was traveling relatively slowly, allowing the other ships to circle around and take positions on the sunward side of the planet. That would occur in a little over seventy-two hours. Earth would be anticipating an attack, preparing for it, especially now that Charon Station was gone. Maloney still hoped that some element of surprise would work in their favor.

"Mistress, I have more news," Dana said. "One of the

two ships that attacked Charon Station was destroyed."

Maloney experienced a moment of shock that quickly fell into fury. Her blood surged, and she turned herself away from Dana so that her helper wouldn't be subject to an outburst of rage. None of this was her fault.

"So easily?" Maloney asked at last, when she felt her temper had leveled enough to speak.

"Not easily," Dana said. "It was a battle hard-fought and hard-won. The ship went out in a blaze of glory, and thousands of its soldiers survived, launching a spaceborne assault on the station even as their ship was coming apart. It wasn't an easy demise, and they paid back tenfold."

For an instant, Maloney heard what might have been a tone of defiance in Dana's voice.

She turned and smiled at her helper. Dana's eyes were wide, perhaps expecting a reprimand, and her expression softened.

"Thank you for bringing the news, however difficult," Maloney said. "You've always been a good helper to me. Long may that continue."

"Of course it will," Dana replied.

"Now take me to the bridge."

"Mistress, perhaps you should rest," the shipborn said. "With what's to come…" Letting her voice trail off, she tipped her head down.

Of course, Maloney thought. *Dana is right. She usually is.* She nodded, and subjected herself to her faithful helper's ministrations.

Since Kareth's untimely death only a few days before, the daily rituals had continued uninterrupted, with Dana carrying out his tasks as well as her own. She washed and bathed Maloney's exposed neck and head, performed diagnostics on her platform, then turned her attention to the globe encircling the rest of her withered body.

The gel it contained had never been replaced. Self-sustaining, non-degrading, all it required was a simple cleaning procedure, performed every few weeks. This comprised of drawing it out through a small tap, filtering it, then injecting it back into the globe. Any elements removed from the gel—flakes of skin, shed hairs, the small dregs of bodily waste Maloney still passed through her system—were disposed of. Since Kareth had filtered the gel just before their drop from the Outer Rim, it didn't need to be done now.

Dana cleaned the platform and globe, taking much longer than was needed. It was almost a ritualistic movement, performed lovingly. Maloney knew that Dana and Kareth had been a couple. Such base human instincts and needs had been gone from Maloney's life for many decades, yet she still remembered the draw of affection, the drug of love, and the hot sting of lust.

"What about afterward?" Dana said. Her voice was low and quiet, almost as if she were speaking to herself, but it was a question for Maloney, tentative and troubled.

"After what?" Maloney asked.

"After the war. When it's won, the Rage rules the Sphere, and Xenomorph armies control the major planets. After Weyland-Yutani is gone."

"It won't be gone," Maloney said. "It will simply exist under a new name, with the Rage controlling it."

"So with no more fighting left, what then?"

"You'll always be my helper, Dana. You're like… a daughter to me."

"Thank you, Mistress," the woman said, blushing and glancing away. She was still troubled, however. Something still burned behind her eyes.

"What is it?"

"I didn't mean for me," Dana said. "I meant for all of

us. The Rage. We've lived so long with these days in mind, that when it's all over and we've won, I'm not sure…"

"What your purpose will be?" Maloney could understand Dana's concern and confusion. Shipborn after the fall of Wordsworth and the Founders, all she had ever known was the mission. They were in the heart of it now, and some of what was happening must seem like the end of things to such as she.

With no experience of "before," it was difficult to imagine after.

For a moment, even Maloney struggled. She closed her eyes and pictured herself on Earth, as she had many times before—head of the Global Council, with Rage Elders, shipborn, and new recruits controlling the largest portions of Weyland-Yutani and the military.

She would be in control then, back in their home system, and yet… would they truly be home? The thought had occurred to her, on and off, for years. They had spent so long away from the Human Sphere that the concept of home had become nebulous, much as the concept of time became twisted when dropholes and warp travel were factored in.

"Yes, Mistress," Dana said. "I suppose I'm wondering where this all leads."

"It leads to the Rage becoming settled at last," Maloney said. It was what she had told herself time and again, during her own moments of soul-searching doubt. "There's no saying what Earth is like now, or Mars, or any of the dozens of colonies spread across the Sol System, but this is home. The Founders fled from here because they sought greater freedom, and we've returned to do the same."

"No more traveling," Dana said. It almost sounded as if she would miss it.

"There's no reason to stop traveling," Maloney said. "There'll be whole new worlds for me to rediscover, and for you to explore."

"Then we'll do it together?" Dana responded hopefully. "You and I?"

"I'll always need my helper," Maloney said. "But…"

"But you won't last forever."

It was a phrase Maloney had used many times before, a warning or promise, or perhaps both.

"The change will be greater than that," Dana continued. "They will see us as evil, and as our leader you'll be the subject of so much hate and fear."

"Perhaps. Or maybe we'll be considered saviors."

"Saviors? From what?"

"From a rule humanity has endured for so long that it's almost forgotten what freedom is like. It's part of the reason Wordsworth and his Founders left in the first place. The Company." It came out like a curse. "They've become more than any one single organization should ever be. All-seeing, all-knowing, and that was before I left. Today, I only have an inkling of how much larger Weyland-Yutani has grown. Perhaps for many humans, the Company's fall will be a cause for celebration."

Dana did not reply. She polished Maloney's hover platform, distracted.

"What is it?" Maloney asked.

"We've killed so many," she replied. "Do you really think they will welcome us, those left alive when all this is over?"

Maloney thought of Charon Station and its thousands of dead, and many other places where marines and civilians had been slaughtered, both by the Rage and their unstoppable armies of Xenomorphs. About the agents of the Rage responsible for shattering acts of sabotage, even before *Macbeth* had reached the Outer Rim.

She thought about Weaver's World, where General Mashima was perpetrating a slaughter, just to draw in the Colonial Marine forces. His efforts had worked, to an extent. Now that *Macbeth* had reached the Sol System, she should signal an end of his attack.

Yet she did not. Because she *liked* what they were doing. She enjoyed the power it gave them, the sense of fear it would instill in humanity. She liked the rage.

"It doesn't matter," she said. "We'll be too powerful to care whether they welcome us, or not."

"Too powerful?" Dana said. "Like Weyland-Yutani?"

Instantly the anger returned, and again Maloney had to damp it down. She felt less inclined to do so this time, however, and the effort was even greater.

"Do your cleaning," she said. "Know your place."

Dana bowed down slightly, and silently continued to tend her mistress's gel globe.

As Maloney closed her eye, hoping to rest for a few moments, a chime sang through her chamber.

"Incoming comms," a voice said. "It's from Mars."

"Who is it?"

"He won't identify himself. He demands to speak only to you. Our computers suggest it's probably James Barclay, head of the Thirteen."

Maloney smiled and glanced down at Dana. "The Company wants to speak with me," she said. "It's about time..."

"Shall I pair him through?" the voice asked.

"Not yet. Make him wait for a minute. I'll tell you when." The comms clicked off.

"How do I look?" Maloney asked.

Dana stood and backed away a little, frowning as she assessed her mistress. Then she smiled and nodded.

"Good," Maloney said. "So let's see what he wants." Louder, she said, "Patch him through."

The room dimmed a little as a holo screen formed, the center blurring as a signal paired. Dana stepped away but Maloney objected.

"No, Dana," she insisted. "By my side, as you always are." *And besides*, she thought, *it'll help if he sees a human, as well as what I've become.*

An image appeared on the holo screen. The man wasn't as old as Maloney had expected, considering the fact that he ran the most powerful organization in human history. She supposed he might even have been considered attractive. A consummate politician, he disguised his surprise at her appearance, hiding it behind a stern countenance.

"Barclay," she said, eager to speak first, to take the advantage. "I've been expecting you to contact me. I thought it might have happened while we were still attacking Charon Station, not after it had been destroyed."

"Beatrix Maloney," Barclay said. While in control of his expression, he could not keep the hatred from his voice. Or the fear.

"You don't seem surprised at my appearance."

"Should I? Everything your Rage has done has prepared me to expect a monster."

"That's not nice."

"I'm not in the business of nice."

"Quite. So, what can I do for you? I'll assume this communication is being watched by the rest of the ruling Thirteen, and probably many more people besides. So feel free to—"

"It's just me," Barclay said. "The Thirteen are aware of what I'm doing, but they're not involved in the discussion. I'll be reporting back to them."

"How trusting they are."

"Trust is how we run things here."

"Really?" Maloney laughed. "Next I suppose you'll tell me that you live in a democracy."

"What do you want, Maloney? You've launched these attacks and, I'll admit, caught us quite by surprise."

"What destroyed Charon Station was superior firepower, not surprise."

"You can't win."

"You sound sure of yourself." Maloney was startled by Barclay's pronouncement. She'd thought he might have contacted her to offer some sort of surrender, although likely couched in much more political terms. But not this. It sounded almost like a threat.

"Your forces are spread too thinly," Barclay said. "You're crippled by over-confidence."

"We just wiped out the main Colonial Marine base, one of the most powerful installations in the Human Sphere," Maloney said. "How many dead, I wonder. Two thousand? Three?"

"And you lost a ship," he said. "How many do you have left. Eleven?" That was exactly the number of ships left from the *Macbeth*. It didn't trouble Maloney that Barclay knew that. What troubled her was his apparent lack of fear.

"We're closing on Earth," she said. "Perhaps I'll stop by Mars on the way, take out whichever base you're transmitting from."

"We propose a ceasefire," Barclay said.

"Don't you mean surrender?"

"You may surrender, if you wish." He smiled.

"Your confidence is refreshing. Usually your people die screaming."

"It's not just us anymore. The Yautja are fighting with

us. An alliance, and it's one that you ensured would happen, by attacking them even before you reached the Outer Rim."

"Should that trouble me?" she asked. "So how many are fighting with you… truly. Three hundred? A thousand? For every Yautja that sides with you, a dozen more will continue to follow their own narrow path. There's plenty of fighting in the Sphere for them right now, and plenty of hunting. Soon that will end."

Despite her words, Maloney did her best not to betray her confusion. If she'd expected Barclay to beg for mercy, she had been sorely mistaken. If anything he was projecting a confidence supported by nothing.

"You should have studied the Yautja," Barclay said. "You don't know them at all."

"I know enough," Maloney said, but she was struggling. Barclay had wrong-footed her, and she had to do her best to regain the higher ground.

"Are you offering a surrender?" she asked. "I'm busy, you know. I've no time to spend talking with you unless that's the case."

"Not at all," Barclay said.

"Good," she said. "After all, why would I accept a surrender when we're so close to absolute victory? We're going to annihilate your forces, Barclay, and destroy your defenses. It's time to put your affairs in order. Kiss your loved ones goodbye."

She was about to sever the link when Barclay said one more thing.

"What will you win?" he asked.

"What?" She responded without thinking, hating the surprise and doubt that appeared in her voice.

"When the war is over," he said. "What will you have won?"

"Everything."

Suddenly he looked sad. The mask of confidence slipped away, and he seemed downcast, even lost.

"You have no idea what you're doing."

"I have every idea," Maloney said, her confidence returning. "I've had a long lifetime to plan." She nodded once and the comms link was cut. The holo screen split and retreated into the walls and ceiling.

I have every idea, she told herself again. *Six ships, attacking bases around the system. Four ships, including this one, converging on Earth. Nothing can go wrong.*

"What did he mean?" Dana asked.

"Nothing," Maloney said. "He's lost, that's all. He's feeling every shred of hope slipping away." Before Dana could reply, she continued, "Come on, to the bridge."

Yet as her helper pushed her from the rooms and toward the *Macbeth*'s bridge, Maloney had to wonder.

What did *he mean?*

2 3

AKOKO HALLEY

Gamma Quadrant
December 2692 AD

"I've never seen anything like that," Halley said. "Anyone else?"

It had been agreed that there would be a comms channel left open between the *Pixie* and the Yautja ship on which Liliya, the Tanns, and the Yautja Hashori travelled. They were moving as one group now, a united front, with only a couple of miles between the two ships. Beyond, the five other Yautja vessels had been joined by three more, appearing unannounced as if from nowhere and shadowing their movements.

Yaquita and Hashori said nothing about the new arrivals. Perhaps they were now allies, but Halley couldn't find it in herself to trust.

Together they hovered at station, three miles from the object.

"Not me," Palant said.

"It's weird," Captain Ware said from the other ship. In their short time face to face, Halley had found a pleasing strength in the indie captain and her hard crew. That was very unusual. Perhaps this war was changing her.

"I've seen something similar," Liliya said. "The Faze has been at work here. I think we've found where the *Macbeth* used to be."

"But it's not here now," Halley said. "It must have dropped through and disappeared. Fuck it." She whispered that, not intending for her suit to carry it through to everyone else.

"Don't lose hope so quickly, Major," Ware said. "Hashori is in conference with her friends, and she seems to be accessing some data. Perhaps that will present some options." Halley couldn't tell if she believed her own words.

"Billy?" Halley asked the *Pixie*'s computer. "Any readings from the drophole?"

"Only strange ones," Billy said. "It appears as if it is still open, and programmed to the last drop."

"We can follow them?" Palant asked.

"Could be," Halley said. "Billy?"

"There have been some radical changes made to the drophole configuration, programming, even its structure. I would need some time to assess the results of those changes."

"We don't *have* time," Halley said. "Ware, can you get Liliya to quiz Hashori on what's going on?"

"No need," Captain Ware said. "I think something's—"

Abruptly a Yautja ship streaked past. In seconds it closed the distance, and then it vanished into the obsidian darkness of the hole. One moment there, the next gone. No explosion. No sign that it had ever been present.

"Shit," Halley said, scanning her instruments. "Billy, any readings?"

"No change whatsoever. The hole remains open. It looks like the Yautja ship has dropped successfully."

"Can Hashori confirm that?" Halley asked.

"She seems happy enough over here," Ware said. "From what I can tell, anyway. The tusks tend to distort her smile."

Halley looked around the bridge at her crew, Palant, and Yaquita. The Yautja seemed maddeningly unconcerned.

"Liliya, fill us in on what this might mean," Halley said. "Why do this to the drophole before using it? If the Rage are that advanced, surely they can hack the drophole programming and just use it themselves. We know the Yautja can do that."

"This is something more," Liliya said. "The Faze deconstructs and rebuilds, making the original construct better and more efficient. It will have taken everything the drophole could do and made it more refined, effective, and efficient. I suspect the Rage took the time for the Faze to work on this so that it could extend the hole's limits."

"How much further could it take them?" Halley asked.

"The Yautja who just dropped through could tell you that."

"Thanks. Useful."

"There's another way we can find out," Palant said. "Drop through."

"We don't know what's been done to it," Halley said. "Those things are volatile at the best of times."

"So we sit here and play with ourselves?" Ware asked. "Fuck that."

"I agree," Bestwick said. "With respect, Major."

"Yeah. Right." Halley didn't like having her crew go against her, and at any other time she'd have reprimanded Bestwick, torn her a new one with everyone else listening. But these weren't normal times. Perhaps Bestwick was right.

"We could risk everything," Halley said. "If they left the hole so that it appeared open, but aimed it into the heart of a sun or a black hole, that could be it. Everything we have here—Liliya, the knowledge Palant and Yaquita gained—gone in less than a flash."

"Everything we're doing is a risk," Palant said. "It'll take that to have even a chance at winning."

"Earth," Jiango Tann suggested. "Maybe they've taken the fight straight to the heart of the system."

"That's hundreds of light years!" Halley said.

"Liliya?" Yvette asked.

On the Yautja ship, the android was quiet for a few seconds, as if weighing up possibilities and risks.

She's Rage, Halley thought. *We're listening to everything she says, but maybe she's a double bluff.* She didn't really believe that, though.

"It makes sense," Liliya said. "It's what Maloney would want. Strike at the heart of the Sphere, finish the war quickly."

"Shock and awe," someone said, and Halley thought it might have been Robo.

"What's that?" Jiango asked.

"A phrase they used to use," Robo said. "Seems appropriate."

"So let's drop through on the Rage's asses and shock and awe them," Ware said.

"Right," Bestwick said.

"Right," Halley agreed. "Billy, run another set of diagnostics on the drophole. Everyone else, prepare to drop. Thirty minutes."

As Halley awoke, Sprenkel, Bestwick, and Huyck were already staggering around the suspension suite, holding their heads and groaning. Palant was sitting up in her pod, vomiting into her lap.

Yaquita was absent. She'd remained on the bridge, much to Halley's consternation. Halley had instructed Billy to deny the Yautja access to any of the *Pixie*'s systems. Even so she was keen to get up there and make certain everything was as it should be.

"Huyck," Halley said. She felt like shit.

"Boss?"

"Bridge." He nodded, knowing exactly what she meant. He'd always been the fastest to recover from a drop, a quality no one could explain. Bestwick liked to tell him it was because he only had a small brain.

Bestwick and Sprenkel helped her from the pod and they stood together, boots securing them to the floor. Palant's puke drifted in the air. Environmental whispered on to clear it, but the smell still spread.

"That's charming," Halley said.

"We're not all hardcore," Palant replied. "So where are we?"

"Let's find out."

The four of them went to the bridge together. Huyck was already in the pilot's chair, and Yaquita remained parked where they'd left her on her wheeled platform. Halley had heard rumors that Yautja could remain awake during a drop, but she found the whole concept mind-blowing.

How long did she sit there? she wondered. The ship's chronometer indicated that they'd been suspended for less than eighteen minutes, but for Yaquita the passage of time would have been vastly different. Especially if they'd travelled further than usual.

The Yautja glanced up at their arrival, but didn't say anything, nor did her expression seem to change.

"Holy fuck," Bestwick said.

Halley checked out the displays, then echoed what Bestwick had said.

"We're sure?" Palant asked.

"We're sure," Huyck said. "I'm just checking detailed scans now, but outline indicators confirm that this is Sol System."

"So what's going on?" Halley asked. "Can you trace *Macbeth*? Anything else?"

"Billy's working on it," Huyck said.

"Give me a minute," Billy said, and it was a strange request from the ship's computer—almost an acknowledgement of its own confusion. Maybe even an AI had found such a long drop disconcerting. Or the reality of it all didn't fit with any facts in his programming.

"You okay, Billy?" she asked.

"A minute," the computer said again.

They drifted around the bridge and found their seats, Palant sitting close to Halley. The scientist looked pale, but her eyes were wide with wonder, and she stared out through the viewing ports as if she had never seen space before.

We might be home, Halley thought, although for many Sol was as far from home as anywhere else.

After an uncomfortable silence, Billy announced their location.

"Sol System, outside the orbit of Pluto," it said. "We emerged from drophole Alpha 7. Yautja ships are successfully through, and the one we saw drop before us is patrolling our position on a two-thousand-mile orbit. Evidence of recent combat, but it's several days old. The remains of at least two Colonial Marine ships are spreading away from this location."

"We're really here," Ware said.

"Any sign of *Macbeth*?" Halley asked. A sense of urgency bit in, a feeling that events were speeding away from them. Given a possible opportunity to end this, she hated the idea that they might miss their chance.

"I've picked up some background chatter," Billy said. "Old transmissions, echoed from some of the in-system moons. It appears as if *Macbeth* split into a dozen parts upon arrival."

"End game," Liliya said. "Maloney thinks they've nearly won."

"What does that mean?"

"It means this is their final battle," Liliya said. "She'll want to take out the Colonial Marines, then attack Earth and all of the larger colonies in the system. Once they've been overrun, that's when she wins."

"Patch me in to the Charon Station," Halley said. "I'll alert General Bassett, tell him what we've got here and what we're hoping to do."

"I'm afraid Charon Station has gone," Billy said.

"What?" Halley heard gasps from her crew, and a longer, sad sigh from Palant. "Sprenkel, check that data."

The big man moved to comply, while the rest fell into stunned silence. After a moment Sprenkel looked up, his face ashen.

"Major, according to charts, Charon's position should be a one-eight orbit around the planetary plain," he said, "and it's not there. I'm getting traces of radiation, consistent with a series of nuclear detonations, and several core traces, but Charon's gone."

"Marshall was there," Halley said softly. She'd always hated the Company man. He knew about her old phrail addiction, and held it over her. Yet losing him didn't feel in any way welcome. The Rage's slaughter continued, and destroying Charon Station dealt a massive blow to the Colonial Marines and their Weyland-Yutani controllers.

"What now?" Bestwick asked. "Just what the hell now?"

"Now we go forward with our plan," Palant said. "There's no alternative." She turned to the android. "Liliya, who'll be in charge of those twelve portions of *Macbeth*?"

"Generals," Liliya said. "One for each segment."

"Then that's why we continue, and as fast as we can."

"Maloney will be on the ship's main portion," Liliya continued. "She'll maintain control, so it's her *Macbeth* we have to find and board."

"Yeah, that should be easy," Ware said. "It's not like the system isn't twenty billion miles wide."

"She'll be headed for Earth," Halley said. "That's how we catch up. Billy, plot us a warp course. Liliya, ask Hashori if she can communicate our plans to the other Yautja. I'm assuming they're still here to help. I'm requesting that they cede command over to me."

"I'll ask," she said.

Halley sat back in her captain's chair. "The whole galaxy is on fire," she said.

"Only our small part of it," Jiango said over the comms, "and the galaxy doesn't care."

"What the hell does that mean, old man?" Robo asked.

"It's something they used to say about Earth, back in the days when we'd almost destroyed it, and ourselves, with pollution. People used to talk about the end of the world, but in truth they were really talking about the end of humanity. If we'd died out then—if we hadn't reached the planets, and then the stars, and turned around the damage we'd already done to Earth—humanity would have gone extinct. But the planet wouldn't mind. It would recover, and become a whole new place."

"You're saying it doesn't matter if we win or lose?" Ware asked.

"Not at all," Jiango replied. "I'm saying it's all down to us. The galaxy is indifferent."

"Then let's do our best," Halley said. "Billy, you got that course solution yet?"

"Feeding it into flight nav. Shall I transmit to the Yautja ships as well?"

"Yes, please. Liliya?"

"Hashori is speaking to them now."

Halley listened as the strange Yautja language clicked and rattled through the comms. She glanced back at Yaquita, who was sitting up straight listening, and caught her eye. Yaquita nodded her head almost imperceptibly, and Halley felt a pressure lifting from her. If the Yautja agreed to help them, and act on her command, then perhaps they really *did* have a chance.

But they destroyed Charon Station!

Halley tried to shut away the doubt. There was no room for it in her, not now.

"They agree," Liliya confirmed.

"Good," Halley said. "Let's head out. It's time to come up with a plan."

2 4

GERARD MARSHALL

Drophole Beta 12, beyond Sol System
December 2692 AD

They dropped through Alpha 4, then emerged from Beta 12 five trillion miles away, and cold space was all that awaited them. Beta 12 was an automated drophole, set deep between star systems and rarely used.

There was no one else there.

"This is nice," Lucianne said. "Quiet. A great place to hide out like pussies."

"We're not hiding," Marshall said. He hated cryopods. He'd puked three times already, and even though he'd dressed and joined Lucianne and Rodriguez on the *Hagen*'s small bridge, part of him was still convinced that he was asleep. *This all a terrible dream*, he thought. *If only.*

"So when are you going to tell us what we're doing here?" Rodriguez asked. They knew who he was. Rodriguez displayed at least some deference, remembering that he was one of Weyland-Yutani's ruling Thirteen. But Lucianne's growing hostility was more than evident. He wondered what deep history she had with the Company, and why the background checks hadn't revealed it.

Not that it mattered now.

"Soon," he said, closing his eyes. His stomach rolled. He hated weightlessness only a little less than he disliked suspension. He hated space.

The shadow of Charon's destruction hung over them all, but none had yet chosen to mention it. Perhaps to vocalize it would have made it all too real.

"At least you should tell us where we're going," Lucianne said. "Or we can, you know, drift around at random for a year or two."

"You should be able to pick up a weak beacon," Marshall said. "I'll send frequency to the ship's computer. Home in on that."

"What is it? A planet, or an asteroid?"

"A ship. An old one."

"And what're we doing there?"

Marshall opened his eyes as the shock of what they were doing stabbed in once again. He had dragged these two into it, without giving them any say in the matter. If they went through with his plans—if they actually succeeded—he might be on the *Hagen* with them for a very long time. It wasn't a warp ship, and home was very far away.

They'd probably end up killing him, then eating him to survive.

He laughed, and it turned into a sob.

"Mr. Marshall?" Rodriguez asked, glancing back at him.

"When we're there," he said. "I'll tell you when we're there. But… I need you to both be brave."

Something about that struck a chord with them. Lucianne ceased the wisecracks, and Rodriguez located the faint beacon. Without a word she accelerated in its direction.

Exhausted, Marshall closed his eyes, drifting in and out of a troubled, guilty sleep.

"When you said it was old you weren't fucking with us."

The ship appeared derelict. A heavy trail of radioactivity leaked from a damaged section of hull near its back end. It was spinning slowly, silvery hull blackened from laser fire. Marshall knew it was all part of the charade. It had been decided that sometimes, a heavily defended location wasn't the best place to keep a secret. Sometimes, it was best kept where nobody wanted to go.

"We renamed it *Phoenix*, but there's no name on the hull," he said. "At least four hundred years old. A tug. It used to tow supply pods."

"Right," Lucianne said.

"It's been out here for decades. We check in on it, from time to time."

"Right."

"Swing around to the starboard side, Rodriguez. The radioactivity's targeted, you'll be able to approach without any risk."

"Right. Good. So we're going on board this ruined hulk."

"We are."

"Oh, good," Rodriguez said. "Listen… sir. I think it's time you tell us what the hell we're doing out here."

Marshall nodded slowly. It was only fair. They would have been dead if they'd remained on Charon Station, but he doubted that made these two soldiers feel any better. The opportunity to do something meaningful just might take the sting off.

"I haven't run away from anything," he said, "and neither have you. Truth is, our mission here is more important than you could imagine. We might be the three most important people in the galaxy right now."

"You mean..." Lucianne said, and she looked disgusted. She glanced back at Marshall and looked him up and down. "You can't be serious. We're not here to start the human race again, are we?"

Marshall laughed at that. He couldn't help it, and it came out like an explosion, a release of pressure that had been building over the past days and weeks. He tried to control it but it spewed out as hysteria, and by the time he'd gathered himself enough to speak again, he was crying. The tears continued. It was that more than anything, he believed, that made the two soldiers realize that this wasn't in the least about him.

"*Phoenix* is a control center," he said at last. "From here, we can shut down every drophole in the Sphere."

Lucianne and Rodriguez remained silent for a while, guiding the *Hagen* in the direction of the derelict, matching its spin and roll, edging the docking arm toward the other ship's airlock.

"You mean, turn them off," Lucianne said.

"Yeah," Rodriguez agreed. "Because shutting them down would be insane."

"I mean shut them down," Marshall said. "Don't ask me about the specifics. I'm not a scientist. But you can't just turn them on and off at will. There're set in some sort of sub-space web, on a different plane of reality. All connected, all focused here. I have the codes, and if the need arises—if the Rage take Earth—I can shut them all down."

"But that'll mean..." Lucianne couldn't say *what* it meant. She just frowned, struggling with the concept.

"Yeah, it will cripple us," Marshall said. "But it'll also mean that the Rage ships will be spread across the Sphere, and the ones in Sol System will be stuck there, unable to do any more damage. They'll have won nothing. It's a doomsday scenario."

"It's monstrous," Rodriguez said. "Even ships with warp drives will take years to travel from one place to another."

"The *Hagen* doesn't have warp," Lucianne said. "What will happen to us?"

"We'll be stuck out here," Marshall said. "Maybe two years or more back to the nearest settlement, on the outskirts of the Sol System."

Rodriguez glanced back at him, her expression haunted, but she offered a weak smile. She didn't speak, but that smile said everything. *You're not just out for yourself.*

Marshall considered everything he might be about to give up—the luxuries he owned back on Earth and Mars, the money and power his position afforded him, the women and men who fell at his feet when they knew who he was. Being feted as a powerful man, and being feared.

He would miss none of it.

Nothing about his life mattered.

It was a shattering realization, but something about it made him feel calm. As if his soul had been cleansed.

"Docking," Lucianne said, and the ship shuddered. "We're on."

"Defenses?" Rodriguez asked. "I assume you've got everything you need to get on board this thing?"

"We'll soon find out," Marshall said.

They drifted through the *Hagen* and waited by the airlock. Once given the green light, the door opened. Marshall was the first through.

Much of the *Phoenix* was a ruin. This, too, was a ruse. He led them through compartments made to look burnt out, past smashed bulkheads and melted cable routes, and toward the ship's main hold. The towing vessel wasn't large, relatively speaking, but it had been adapted with a hold big enough to contain everything that was necessary.

In his pocket, on a small data card, he carried all the information he'd need.

At a door that was blasted out of shape, he pressed the card against a control panel. The barrier moved aside with a grinding sound, revealing a smooth silver surface beneath. The real door. Another touch of the card opened this one, and then a blast shield was revealed beyond.

This was where Marshall used a code he'd been made to remember, years before, when the existence and location of this place was revealed to him. He closed his eyes and breathed deeply, suddenly overcome with the certainty that he'd forgotten the sequence, transposed digits, and that he and the other two would be stuck here forever while he tried to remember.

The blast shield slid aside on the first try.

"Whoa," Lucianne said.

Beyond lay a small, packed control room. Just large enough for the three of them. Marshall ushered them inside, then closed the blast shield behind them.

"You know how to work all this?" Rodriguez asked.

"Not much to work," Marshall said. "A lot of the stuff here runs the ship, and there's a big transmitter in the ship's nose. Buried beneath all this tech, though... that's where the hub is."

"Really? In here?" Lucianne said, looking around. "Where?"

"It's small, but it's what we're here for."

Marshall felt a chill, despite his environment-controlled suit. The thought of the power that lay so close to his fingertips, the effect he could have on the whole of the Sphere... The future of humanity balanced on decisions he would make here, in this small hold of a ruined spaceship.

"We need to wait," he said. "We need to watch."

He initiated a power cell and the room lit up, holo screens dropping down, and data started to flow.

"We need to see who wins the war."

2 5

BEATRIX MALONEY

Macbeth, *Sol System*
December 2692 AD

As the small Marine ship unleashed another hail of laser fire against the *Macbeth*, the Watcher drifted onto the bridge. That told Maloney what she needed to know— that Liliya was aboard the attacking vessel.

"Just cripple it!" she ordered. She consulted the Watcher. It cast a display onto the nearest holo screen, a pulsing blue light that confirmed what she had suspected. *So close.* "Disable it, and bring it on board."

"Yes, Mistress."

"Dana, get me down to the docking bay."

What is this? Why has she come back? Maloney felt a thrill of excitement, but also a troubling chill. *Is this her final effort to try and stop me, when everything else she's done has failed?*

If so, it was a vain, pathetic effort.

They'd seen the ship coming from a million miles away, dropping out of warp and approaching the *Macbeth* on an attack vector. All sensors agreed that it was alone.

Although one of the Colonial Marines' fastest, most powerful craft, it was still no match for the Rage vessel.

A brief attack had followed, and been repelled.

"The craft is disabled," Dana said as she pushed Maloney. "It was too easy."

"*Much* too easy," Maloney agreed.

"Maybe we should destroy it."

Maloney caught her breath. Once she knew that Liliya was on board, every instinct had driven her to capture the ship and the android, bring her on board, confront her face to face one more time.

"No," she said.

"But there might be—"

"I said no! Capture the ship and everyone on board. Continue toward Earth. This is far from over."

By the time they reached the docking hold of the *Macbeth*, the Marine ship had been scanned for threats, declared safe, and hauled inside. It was surrounded by thirty Xenomorphs. Their general remained on the bridge, supervising the journey in Maloney's absence, but they were still linked to him, waiting on his every command.

It was a sleek, impressive craft, scored along one side by fire from the *Macbeth*. Clamping arms held it and pulled it close to the deck, and then drones started work on one of its external doors.

"Sensors?" Maloney asked.

"One consciousness on board, non-human."

"Liliya," Maloney said, and she frowned. Was the android really on her own? How had she come to possess such a ship? She had to know, and they had time. *Macbeth* wouldn't reach Earth for another eighteen hours.

The drones broke the door seal and air hissed from the craft, condensing in a small, spreading cloud of moisture. The door fell aside, revealing a dark interior.

"Liliya," Maloney said into the silent hold. "My errant daughter, come home again."

A shadow filled the doorway, then emerged.

Liliya.

The Xenomorphs tensed, hissing, feet scraping the deck, heavy breathing promising violence at any moment. *I should unleash them*, she thought. Seeing her torn to pieces should have been enough.

But Maloney had pride, and she wanted more. She wanted to see Liliya's eyes as she acknowledged that she had lost. She wanted to breathe in her scent as she killed her. The queen was still in her hold, still laying, and Liliya would become one of her final meals.

A fitting end for the greatest traitor.

"Mistress," Liliya said. "I can't say it's good to see you again."

"Bring her," Maloney said. "Search the ship."

The Xenomorphs remained in place as three shipborn pushed through their ranks, guns aimed at the android.

"You could have been so great," Liliya said, and in the large hold her words echoed unanswered.

2 6

ISA PALANT

Macbeth, *Sol System*
December 2692 AD

"I can't believe that worked," Isa Palant said.

"Pure luck," Halley said. "But we won't stay lucky for long. Soon as Yaquita decloaks the ship, we'll be seen."

"Then the clock starts ticking."

"The clock started ticking the minute Liliya left the *Pixie*," Halley said. She stared from the Yautja ship's viewing ports at the *Pixie*, sitting across the docking bay, sad that she'd likely never board that ship again. Slipping aboard the *Macbeth* on a cloaked Yautja ship had been one chance in ten. Actually achieving what they'd come to do, and giving themselves time to escape, was one in a million.

None of them had complained.

In fact, Ware and her indies, as well as the Tanns, had protested at being left out of the initial assault. But there had to be backup, Halley had insisted. They'd split the precious, refined nanotech the Tanns had managed to procure from Liliya, giving them two chances at finding and sabotaging the Rage control hub.

Everything relied on the hub being aboard the *Macbeth*.

Liliya's memory was scarred with worrying blanks, and the more they'd tried to develop a strategy, the more she'd had to admit that she knew less about the Rage's battle plans than she'd believed.

Kept in the quiet and fed bullshit, Ware had said, and Liliya had seemed hurt by the idea. Hurt, as well, that Beatrix Maloney hadn't seen it appropriate to share everything with her.

"Come on, come on," Palant whispered. The Xenomorphs were still out there, spread around the hangar, crouched and motionless. Not asleep, though. Ready.

"They're guarding the *Pixie*," Sprenkel said. "If they were going to leave, they'd have left by now."

"How many are there?" Palant asked through her datapad.

"Twenty-three," Yaquita replied.

"We can take them," Bestwick said.

"And lose any element of surprise."

"We'll lose that the moment Yaquita decloaks so we can leave the ship," Bestwick argued. "We can't just sit here playing with ourselves."

"Maybe you can play with me," Sprenkel said.

"Oh, gross. I'd rather jerk off a Xenomorph."

"I don't spurt acid."

"Shut it, you two," Halley said. "We can't sit here. That much is true. Palant, ask Yaquita to decloak on our signal."

Yaquita spoke. "My ship's minor laser will take out some of them."

"Good," Halley said. "I hope she's a good shot."

They readied themselves in the area around the external door. Suited up, heavily armed, ready for their final fight, Halley and her Colonial Marines—Huyck, Sprenkel, and Bestwick—filled Palant with a surprising sense of confidence. They'd already been through so much together that the very idea of failing here seemed so unfair.

But the universe wasn't fair or unfair. It was indifferent.

Palant caught Yaquita watching them, and nodded. The Yautja nodded back, then spoke into her control panel. Nearby in space, several Yautja ships would be decloaking and launching a sustained attack on the *Macbeth*. Sustained, yet not quite heavy enough to destroy the Rage ship.

The distraction had begun.

"Here we go," Palant said, and the door before them melted away. The ship decloaked, and as Halley and the others stepped out onto the deck, the Xenomorphs saw the newly revealed intruder.

They charged.

A volley of laser fire from the Yautja ship took down the first wave of attackers, spilling hissing body parts across the deck. Halley and the marines opened up, carefully picking their targets, moving quickly away from the ship with Palant in their midst. She had refused a weapon, carrying the precious vial of nanotech in one hand, the datapad in the other. It was their only communication to Yaquita, and thus the outside.

They passed close to the *Pixie* as they raced toward a set of doors. A shape appeared in the Marine ship's doorway.

"Bestwick!" Palant shouted, and the soldier turned and fired. Direct hit. The Xenomorph came apart and disappeared back inside the *Pixie*, acidic blood instantly eating into the hull.

The laser fire from Yaquita's ship ceased, and the marines picked off the last of several charging Xenomorphs. The fight had been fast and furious, and alarms would be sounding all across the *Macbeth*. They didn't have much time.

"Keep this channel open," Palant said, and she heard

Yaquita's reply. If things went bad, the Yautja was ready to detonate her own ship in order to destroy the *Macbeth*. Even if she did, that would be a useless act if the generals were left alive.

They dashed from the hangar and into a network of hallways and passages, strange places that appeared more biological than constructed. Palant guessed that she was looking at the Faze's handiwork. She could have spent a year, simply examining one small part of this ship, but her purpose now wasn't scientific endeavor and examination, but destruction. Somehow she had changed from a scientist to a warrior, and she wasn't even sure when that had happened.

"Watch the corners," Halley said. "Mark your targets."

They followed a basic schematic projected onto their visors, a rough map provided by Liliya. She knew that the *Macbeth* had broken down into a dozen parts, and she'd suspected that this main vessel still retained some of the layout she remembered. But there was also the possibility that things had changed—levels flipping, hallways and passages turning. They had to trust what she'd told them, but they also had to follow their instincts.

The passage ahead jigged left, and as they approached shadows were dancing there. Motion detectors came alive. Xenomorphs rounded the corner, and the marines opened up. Plasma bursts smashed the creatures apart and set the walls and ceiling aflame, suits darkening and hardening against the assault.

Palant hunkered down, trying to regulate her breathing and control her fear. Since helping to formulate their plan she'd had little time to consider her likely death. Now that it was much closer—perhaps only seconds away—it loomed large.

Yet she was strangely calm. Dying didn't trouble her, but

the possibility that they might not achieve their aim did.

Moving on, they stepped carefully through an area still burning and sizzling from plasma charge and dead Xenomorphs. Suddenly the *Macbeth* shuddered as Yautja ships attacked from outside, and she thought of the Tanns and the indies on one of those ships, standing away from the action because they were the backup.

Palant hoped they were never needed.

Reaching a vertical shaft, they dropped down using scrambling wires from their suit belts. The route on their visors suddenly turned red as the ship's layout no longer allied with Liliya's memory of it.

"We're almost there," Palant said into her datapad. It was only a small lie, and she hoped it would give Liliya some small comfort. One way or another, that oldest of androids was soon going to meet her doom.

Palant remembered her face as they'd parted. Liliya had looked scared, nervous, and uncertain. She had looked human.

"Movement on all sides," Sprenkel announced.

"I see it," Halley said. "Palant, get in the middle, with us all around you. This is going to be a fight."

Converging on them from four directions, darkened hallways suddenly became darker with rushing shadows. Xenomorphs, monstrous attackers with no thought for their own safety or survival. Laser and nano-shot took them apart, plasma bursts smashed and melted the structure around them, and dozens of the creatures died screaming. But there were always more, and as the Marines' ammunition began to suffer and their com-rifles grew hot with overuse, the beasts pushed closer.

Palant plucked a sidearm from Halley's hip, and started firing.

Nothing happened.

Safety!

She almost laughed, wondered what "safe" meant, then started shooting. She picked her target, squeezed, then moved on without waiting to see the result. Turning a quarter circle every time, she shot down each of the four passageways, adding her effort to every direction. The noise was deafening. The stink was foul, even through the suit masks—burning, acidic, hot metal and air cooked from electrical discharges.

"If we die here, the others might not even know," Palant said. Once uttered, it was a very real possibility. Ware and the Tanns had been told to hold off at a distance, and only attempt landing on the *Macbeth* if Palant, Halley, and the Marines failed in their task. They'd agreed on a code word, but holding off on broadcasting that word might mean wasting the opportunity entirely.

It was a long shot anyway, even if they did reach their destination. No one knew if the plan would work. It felt cobbled together, too rushed to be effective, too obscure to have any chance of success.

From one second to the next, Palant might be slashed, bitten, gutted, killed by one of these monsters. That would spell the end.

"Call them in," Halley said.

"You're sure?"

"Two groups trying to get there stand a better chance than one," the Major said. "Call them in."

Palant didn't hesitate. She spoke into her datapad, "Wave two. Wave two." Then she started shooting again.

"Everyone, plasma on three," Halley said.

"We'll be cooked alive!" Sprenkel shouted.

"Better that than—"

A Xenomorph broke through the hail of fire, darted closer, lashed out with its tail as Palant pumped three shots into it, and Sprenkel's decapitated head bounced from the ceiling, body slumping forward spurting blood from his tattered neck. Alive one moment, dead the next. Snuffed out.

"Plasma!" Halley screamed, and Palant had never heard the Major sound so out of control.

The air around them lit up, and her suit couldn't handle the sudden burst of heat or glare of fire.

Screaming herself, Palant fell beside Sprenkel's body.

She fully expected to die.

2 7

LILIYA

Macbeth, *Sol System*
December 2692 AD

Just one word, Liliya thought. *That's all I'm waiting for. Just one word.*

She wore a receiving speck in her ear, minute and undetectable, and tuned into the Colonial Marine and indie suits. All she needed to hear from Palant—or from the Tanns if Palant was killed—was the word, "Ready!" Then she'd know that the control hub for all Rage generals would be available to her, linked through that strange alien tech she carried in her blood.

Hopefully.

They would have used the purified nanotech to allow her access. It had worked with Alexander, her order sent for his self-destruct. There was no reason it would not work for all of them. With a signal boosted by the *Pixie*'s computer, and powered by a sudden draining of the *Pixie*'s warp drive, her message would be carried instantaneously to every single general across the sphere.

She remembered the feeling in her own heart when she

had destroyed Alexander... the heat, the pain... and she anticipated worse this time. Much worse. If she wasn't killed when the *Pixie*'s warp drive melted down, her own imploding heart would do the job.

She was at peace with the idea of her own demise. Yet she did not view it like an android. She was going to *die*, not cease to function. All her memories, good and bad, would bleed away to nothing as soon as her mind failed. Unstored. Unsaved. She was facing her own extinction as a human being, and in these loaded final moments, that made her glad.

Then she realized where they were taking her, and fear seeded inside her once again.

The main hold was heavily reinforced, and she had walked this route a thousand times before, always aware of what was inside yet never inclined to see it. She'd looked once, many years ago when the queen was still settling in. Since then, just knowing what they carried was enough to give her the jitters.

Now they were leading her there, and her end was too close. If they killed her quickly—if Maloney didn't take the time to gloat, as Liliya had hoped would happen— then nothing that Palant and the Tanns did would matter.

The ship shuddered.

"They'll destroy you in the end," Liliya said. "That's the Yautja out there, at least five ships, with more on the way."

"It doesn't matter," Maloney said.

"Really?"

The Rage leader was ahead of Liliya, being pushed by her slave Dana, the poor shipborn who regarded herself as a helper. Now, Maloney commanded her to stop.

"We'll snuff them out," Maloney said. "You know some of what this ship is capable of, Liliya, but not all. Now, let's go and see the old girl, shall we?"

Liliya thought about fighting. She could probably take down two of the shipborn who were standing guard, but there were two more following further behind, and behind them were a dozen Xenomorphs, hissing and growling softly as they awaited orders from their Mistress. Getting herself killed would be disastrous. So many people were risking their lives, and Liliya had a duty to keep herself alive for as long as possible.

Whatever tortures came, whatever pains, she had to remain alive.

"You think your friends on board will rescue you?" Maloney asked. "The Yautja craft that sneaked into the hangar with your ship has already been put out of action. There was a Yautja bitch on board, an old cripple. I allowed the Xenomorphs to take her. They stormed the ship and took her apart inside. She put up quite a fight, by all accounts. As for your friends, they didn't get far from the hangar. Even now they're…" She tilted her head, listening. "Ah, good. They are as good as dead."

Liliya tried to keep her face neutral. If Palant and the marines really were killed, the Tanns and indies would attempt to board the ship. It was becoming more and more hopeless.

"You're only a shadow of your old self," she said. "You could have been so great."

"I *am* great!" Maloney said. "And soon I will be *greater*! Haven't you seen what we've already accomplished? What you could have been a part of?"

"Murder? Slaughter?" Liliya looked at Dana. "You must be so proud."

"Open," Maloney said. The wide doors opened onto an airlock, a barrier between the ship's atmosphere and the danker, damper air inside the hold. A gun pushed harshly against Liliya's back and she was sent a few steps closer to her doom.

"This is a first for both of us," Maloney said. "No human has been in the queen's presence for many years, except as food."

"Isn't that why I'm being brought in?"

Maloney shrugged.

"She'll probably choke on me," Liliya said, and she started laughing. Humor was one of the facets of humanity that troubled her still, but she fully understood irony, and she realized the irony in this situation. *Lived as an android, died as a human, fodder for a beast.*

If she kept Maloney talking, it might not need to be her epitaph. She preferred something simpler.

Lived as an android, died as a human.

"I shouldn't be down here," Maloney said. "I should be on the bridge overseeing the final battles—but the Rage know what to do. The generals are progressing the war. I'm almost in the way, now."

"Your time will come," Liliya said.

Maloney turned on her platform and looked at her. The gel surrounding her body seemed to pulse, strange currents surging like hidden emotions.

"My time is already here," Maloney said. "Yours has long gone. Open."

The inner doors opened. Dana gasped, as did the shipborn guards. Maloney only smiled and floated forward, urging Liliya to follow.

The android knew that she had no choice. She waited for the word—*Ready! Ready!*—but in waiting she had to do what Maloney wished. Resistance might bring about a quicker end. Allowing Maloney's ego its room might just be enough to destroy her.

Liliya followed her into the lair of the Xenomorph queen. The doors closed behind them all, and everything changed. The guards followed at a distance, moving almost silently across the grotesque landscape.

The entire hold had been transformed, a more striking change than any the Faze had made. There were few straight edges in sight, and no original deck or bulkheads visible. The Xenomorphs had made this place a home for their queen, coating all surfaces with their strange extrusions, protecting the eggs in several distinct nursery areas, and guarding their domain.

It wasn't only the physical changes that struck Liliya.

The air was heavier, more dense, humid and warm, and it smelled of something acidic and rank. The hold was silent but for the queen's constant, heavy breathing, and the fluid sounds of her birthing sac as it pulsed with new eggs. Staring across the wide area, Liliya saw the queen deposit another one with a delicate, moist kiss from her opaque abdomen. What affected Liliya the most, though, was the *feel* of the place. It was as if they were no longer on board the *Macbeth*, or anywhere human. This place was totally *other*, never meant to be seen by men, or understood by them. Here the Xenomorphs ruled.

"She's quite beautiful," Maloney said.

Liliya could not disagree. The queen was huge, dark, all sharp edges and teeth, both beautiful and terrifying.

"So feed me to her and get it over with," Liliya said.

"I've never been so close," Maloney said, her ancient voice filled with wonder.

"I wonder what she sees when she looks at you?" Liliya mused. "A mad old woman kept alive too far beyond her years."

"My years are far from over. I have a future, Liliya, and you could have been part of it."

"I wouldn't want to."

"You stole from me. Sought to betray me. And I

wonder…" Maloney turned her platform, putting her back to the Xenomorph queen so she could focus on her prisoner. "I wonder why you came back."

"To stop you. To defeat you."

"Whatever you think you can do, it'll fail. The Rage are too strong."

Liliya looked past Maloney at the monstrous queen, tethered and chained for so many years, still laying eggs, still surviving. She wondered whether the beast craved freedom, or had forgotten what it was like to be truly free.

"I'm the general of my ship, you know," Maloney said. "One thought from me and every Xenomorph in here will be driven to tear you apart."

That surprised Liliya. There had been serious doubts whether or not humans could use the alien tech at all. A decision must have been made. Either it had come after she fled, or it had been kept from her all along.

Whichever it was, it didn't matter. One word, that was all she needed to hear. One word, and then she and Maloney would die together—a poetic end, she felt— along with every Rage general, their ships obliterated.

"What are you waiting for?" Liliya asked.

"I'm waiting to defeat you," Maloney said, and she smiled. "An old woman's ego, perhaps, but I want you to know that you've failed before you die."

"That presents an unnecessary risk."

"Does it?"

"Of course. Kill me now, and you eliminate the chance that I'll defeat you. Wait, and every second is another second of danger for you."

"As I said, an old woman's ego."

One word, Liliya thought. *One word.*

"But perhaps you're right."

Maloney backed away from Liliya. She stopped smiling.

The Xenomorph queen hissed, her breath condensing in the warm, heavy atmosphere, steam billowing around her head.

Maloney blinked, and all around her, Xenomorph soldiers obeyed their general's command.

2 8

JIANGO TANN

Macbeth, *Sol System*
December 2692 AD

Without Liliya or Palant, there was no one to translate what Hashori was saying, but the holo screen display made translation unnecessary. The ship Yaquita had flown onto *Macbeth* had been boarded, and Yaquita was dead.

Hashori performed a brief movement with her hands, uttered some angry-sounding words, and when the ritual was over she continued flying the ship.

Ware, Robo, and Hoot were suited and armed, strapped into their seats and raring to go. Eager for a fight.

Jiango and Yvette were similarly suited, but they were nowhere near ready for a fight.

Hashori paired one of the ship's holo screens with Ware's suit, and a projection above the control panel showed data that they could understand, alongside the indecipherable Yautja language.

"Fifteen seconds," Jiango said. "How did anyone think this would work?"

"It *has* to work," Ware said. "And if it doesn't…"

"Yeah, right," Yvette said. "We won't even know about it."

"Stardust to stardust," Robo said. It was strangely poetic from the gruff woman's mouth.

"Ten seconds."

They were rolling in toward the *Macbeth*'s stern fully cloaked, all weapon systems disarmed, drive turned off, using the force applied by a carefully launched nuke to spin them in toward the Rage craft. If they were somehow seen, then all indications would be that the ship was dead. From what they'd seen of Yaquita's approach and landing inside the docking bay, however, the Rage couldn't perceive a cloaked ship.

But what if they learn? Jiango thought. *Maybe missing the first ship means the* Macbeth's *computers will determine what they did wrong. They might be watching us now, zeroing in with their weapons and ready to blast us to dust.*

The fact that he'd never even feel the impact offered no comfort. He held his wife's hand and they both squeezed.

The ships that had come with them continued to engage the *Macbeth*, directing their assault against the ship's bow. In doing so, they sought to distract the Rage from the boarding.

One mile, the display read. Too close for a nuke, now. Too close for the Rage ship to take them out without risking its own damage.

Closer, closer…

Suddenly Hashori became animated, talking rapidly and sounding excited.

"What is it?" Ware asked.

"No idea," Jiango said. "I told you, I don't speak their language!"

"Half a mile," Yvette said. "Whatever's happening, it better happen quickly."

"Oh, my God," Hoot said. "Look! Not at the holo screen, but out there. Look!"

It appeared that the cavalry had arrived.

Three more Yautja craft had decloaked close to the *Macbeth*. Confused, Jiango checked the displays.

"More of them?" Yvette asked.

Hashori spoke again, perhaps frustrated that they couldn't understand her. Then she calmed herself a little, and tilted her head.

"Elder… Kalakta," she said, speaking slowly and with some difficulty.

"Who?" Ware asked.

"A Yautja Elder," Jiango said. "He's the one Isa met months ago, when it was believed the Yautja were launching an invasion. The one who agreed to the treaty."

"Well, it looks like he's come to join the party," Robo said. "Docking in fifteen. Let's hustle!"

The first of the newly arrived Yautja ships docked at an airlock, and the second and third ship were settled alongside, linked ship to ship and forming a bridge into the *Macbeth*.

Hashori brought their ship around and nudged against the outermost craft. She worked quickly, efficiently, and as soon as they were stable she snatched up her battle spear and pulled herself toward the bridge's door.

"Kalakta!" she said again, and Jiango could see the excitement ripple through her. Her eyes gleamed, she seemed taller than before, stronger, and he knew that he was witnessing a Yautja's pre-battle state.

"Are you ready for this?" he asked his wife.

"No," Yvette said. "I'm afraid, and I don't want to die just yet. There's so much more time I want to spend with you."

He pressed his head against hers, unable to kiss her because of their suit masks.

"We'll live or die together," he said.

"Some small comfort," she said, and she shot him a look. "Come on, old man, let's go and save the galaxy."

Ware, Robo, and Hoot headed toward the airlock. Jiango and Yvette followed, and as they reached the door it hissed open, whistling briefly with the equalizing pressure. Hashori was through first, then the indies, and Jiango and Yvette brought up the rear.

They crossed into the next ship, then through to the next, leapfrogging through the three other Yautja craft. Each vessel looked and smelled different, but there was no time to pause and figure out why.

As Jiango and Yvette approached the hacked airlock leading into the *Macbeth*, a huge explosion erupted behind them.

He felt a tug, and then Yvette was holding onto his legs. Ware grabbed his arms as decompression sought to suck them out into deep space.

One of the Yautja ships had been taken out by a gun tower.

Ware was screaming at him, but he couldn't hear. Atmosphere roared past, and he felt the air sucked from his lungs, suit compressing around him. He'd survive for a while, he knew, even if he let go and was pumped out into space. If they missed being pulverized by debris from the battle, he and Yvette might drift for a day or two, with enough oxygen for them to survive. He'd heard tales of spacefarers starving to death before their suits gave out.

He wouldn't go that way. One quick shot through Yvette's eye, another through his own, they'd meet oblivion together.

Huge hands hauled them in.

A Yautja was there, taller than any he'd yet seen, its hands wider than his head. It roared something, and

Robo slapped at a control panel on the airlock's interior. The doors powered shut and air hissed as atmosphere was replaced.

Beyond the doors another silent explosion boomed, and the ships were blasted away from the *Macbeth*.

"Shit!" Hoot shouted. "That was closer than close!"

Jiango finally caught his breath and looked up. The airlock's inner door was already open, and from beyond he heard the sounds of combat. Shadows danced, Xenomorphs screamed. Yautja roared. They were into the battle, with no time to consider their survival.

"It's down to you two!" Ware said, grabbing the back of Jiango's neck and pulling him close. "We're all here to protect you and get you to the hub. They're here for that, too." She gestured back over her shoulder at the fighting beyond the doors.

"How many?" Jiango asked.

"At least a dozen of them," Ware said. "I've never seen anything so…"

"Powerful."

"Fucking terrifying. I'm just glad they're on our side. Come on. Palant and her team are still moving inward, so we'll take the next level."

"Are they all okay?"

"No," Ware said. "They lost Sprenkel, and Bestwick's badly burned."

"Oh, no," Yvette said.

"That's war," Ware said. "Let's go."

Like a massive termite's nest, the *Macbeth* was a warren of tunnels and chambers, and its insects were running, crawling, scampering everywhere.

The Yautja and indies stood side by side to fight the

dreaded enemy. Yautja targeting lasers flickered here and there, spears of light arcing across shining black carapaces, finding their targets, blasting them to pieces, and then moving on. Wielding tridents and battle spears, bladed limbs and throwing stars, crossbows and maces, the warriors surged forward to meet their enemies head-on. With each kill the Yautja let out distinctive roars of triumph, until Jiango came to recognize different voices, and different kills.

And there was Kalakta.

Throughout the chaos—moving across the docked ships, the sudden explosion and decompression, and the sustained Xenomorph assault—Jiango witnessed the creatures' reverence for one of their party. Tall, regal, and patently older than the other Yautja, still he retained a grace in battle that was almost beautiful to watch. The other warriors didn't huddle around him to protect him, because their honor and sense of power wouldn't allow them to denigrate him so. But they glanced at him now and then, even while fighting, as if keen to impress him with each kill.

Elder Kalakta made many kills of his own.

Ware, Hoot, and Robo kept close together, fighting in a loose unit that contained Jiango and Yvette at its center. They were formidable. Any doubts he might have had concerning their effectiveness as a fighting unit—old preconceptions, comparing Colonial Marines to indies—were blown away with the first blasts from their varied weaponry.

Robo wielded a huge, old projectile weapon, its ammunition explosive-tipped and devastating in its destructive power. Her robotic arm hefted the gun with ease and consummate skill. Hoot used smaller, more modern weapons, holding laser pistols in each hand and firing both in concert, often in different directions. Jiango thought it probably wasn't just the suit that enabled him to draw down on two targets at a time.

Captain Ware used a Marine com-rifle, with adaptations that allowed it to fire nano-shot and laser blasts concurrently. A blast would halt an enemy, then nano-shot attached and exploded. It left no possibility of error. If Ware fired at a Xenomorph, that creature died.

The passageway became a killing ground. So many of the beasts went down that quickly the air was filled with acrid smoke and steam, agitated by the chaos, forcing their suits to switch to infrared and heat-reception vision. Jiango felt movement in the floor, and at first he thought it was the results of the continuing Yautja attacks from their ships.

Then Ware revealed the truth.

"Floor's melting!" she shouted. "We need to move away, or we'll become Xeno soup!"

The Yautja seemed to have recognized the problem, as well. They moved forward against the throng, kicking through fallen Xenomorphs piled almost to their knees, the dead creatures self-destructing and melting down into a rancid mess that was eating rapidly through the decking.

A Yautja went down. Three Xenos dropped on it from above, synchronizing their attack. Two took a shoulder each, the third clasped around its head and neck and then smashed its inner jaw through the helmet. The dying warrior fought on, blaster aiming upward and searing a blazing hole through its own skull as it took out two of its attackers. It fell without another sound.

Its companions fought on. Ware and her indies followed close behind the Yautja, recognizing the safest place, the Tanns protected between them.

More Xenomorphs dropped from above, following the success of their cousins on the fallen Yautja. Elder Kalakta and three others concentrated ahead, blasting, hacking, and slashing a clear path along the passageway.

"This'll take forever!" Jiango said. "Ware, we don't have long, we need to speed things up!"

"I hear you," Ware said. "Keep close. I've got an idea." She moved forward until she was close to Kalakta. She caught the Elder's attention and the two of them seemed to converse, using a basic sign language that Jiango struggled to catch.

"What's happening?" he asked as Ware returned to their group.

"I just hope he understood," she said.

"Understood what?"

"We're changing levels," Ware said. "Stay close. Hoot, Robo, get your mag charges ready, we're going to pair all three." The indies each took a small object from their belts. They paused as their suits performed some function on the explosives, then in an almost balletic movement they lobbed the objects way down the corridor, past the Yautja and into the seething mass of Xenomorphs.

"Five seconds," Ware said. Kalakta glanced back and Ware waved at the Yautja Elder. His companions unleashed a vicious fusillade of blaster fire along the passageway, then the Yautja, indies, and Jiango and Yvette crouched down low to the floor.

The perfectly synchronized explosions punched up through the floor, thudding into Jiango's chest, winding him. His suit absorbed much of the impact and noise, and moments later Robo and Hoot pulled him and Yvette to their feet.

"Let's go!" Ware shouted.

The Yautja led the way. The whole passageway ahead of them had been blown apart, the floor sloping down to the ship's next level, and they blasted and fired into the hole before starting their descent.

The large room below contained only dead and dying Xenomorphs.

"We don't have long," Ware said. "This way."

Consulting the rough schematic supplied by Liliya and programmed into all their suits, the strange group of Yautja and humans moved deeper into the ship.

2 9

AKOKO HALLEY

Macbeth, *Sol System*
December 2692 AD

All her people were dying.

Sprenkel had gone out cleanly, probably not even registering the fact that his head had been parted from his body. *Lucky bastard.* Bestwick was dying harder. Their plasma deluge had wiped out many of the attacking Xenomorphs, but it had also half-cooked them all, their suits absorbing some of the effect but the plasma fire sticking, melting, burning. Bestwick's suit had taken the bulk of the impact.

Halley cursed with every breath, and punctuated each curse with a silent vow to carry on.

"It's not far!" Palant said. "We're almost there!"

There won't be any of us alive to get there, Halley thought, but now wasn't the time for doubt. Their suit sensors showed Ware and the others pinned down four hundred yards away and three levels up, and much of the Xenomorph movement centered on them. Bad for Ware and her companions, good for Halley's team.

Huyck held Bestwick, gripping beneath her arms. He was almost carrying her, one-handed, com-rifle cradled in his other arm and aimed ahead. Their suits projected a schematic of Liliya's plan on their visors, and if she'd been accurate, then the room housing the control hub was only fifty yards ahead of them.

As much as she tried to push them away, doubts plagued Halley. In the heat of battle, instincts took over, but they were tempered with her training. Cool, calm, her nickname of Snow Dog came to the fore again. Her heart rate remained steady. Her reactions were cool and sharp, well thought out and measured. But a sense of doom surrounded her. With every second that passed she feared failure, expecting death to circle around and take them down. It would all come to a head in the next few minutes, one way or another.

"Movement, fifteen yards," Huyck whispered.

"I see it. Down." They hadn't had a contact for three minutes, and this close to the control hub, Halley chose cover over conflict. They crouched down and ducked into an alcove. Huyck tried to quiet Bestwick. Her suit was feeding her heavy doses of painkiller, virtually numbing all her pain receptors, yet she was still panting with shock.

She'd be dead in minutes.

Their movement sensors showed a dozen shapes moving quickly toward them from back the way they'd come.

"Palant, you and me—" Halley began, but then Bestwick groaned and rolled into the passageway.

"Go!" she said.

"Bestwick."

"Fuck's sake, boss, go!" She staggered back along the hallway, and seconds later she opened fire, laser flashes matching the squeal of dying Xenomorphs.

Halley glanced at Huyck and saw his grief, and his

pride. Bestwick must have pleaded with him, and she couldn't berate him for his decision. He'd given her the brave death any Marine would prefer.

They would not waste it.

"Run!" Halley said. She, Huyck, and Palant sprinted, not looking back. They could hear the blasts of Bestwick's weapon, the screams of dying enemies, the heavy impacts of sharp claws on walls and decking. She wouldn't last for long, but if they hurried, she might last long enough.

"Ware, we're almost there!" Halley shouted into her comm. "We need you to provide as much distraction as you can."

"Roger that," Ware said. "We've got some friends fighting with us. Kalakta."

"He's here?" Palant asked.

"Yeah, I hear you and he are friends."

Palant did not respond. Halley understood what a momentous occasion this was, with Yautja fighting alongside humans to defeat a common foe. They'd probably have songs sung about them, whatever the outcome.

Though with no survivors, there wouldn't be anyone to write the songs.

"Let's get all huggy when this is done with," Halley said. "Ware... give 'em everything you've got."

"Here comes hell," Ware said. "Good luck, you guys."

It sounded like more than a signing off. It sounded like goodbye.

A few seconds later, Halley's suit registered a massive burst of plasma fire from Ware's location, sustained explosions that rippled through the ship and vibrated beneath their feet.

"This is our chance," Halley said. "We get to the hub, get in, check that we're alone, then me and Huyck stand guard while you do your thing."

"Yeah," Palant said breathlessly.

More gunfire erupted behind them, then a long, loud scream from Bestwick. Not pain, but defiance.

"Down!" Huyck shouted. He grabbed Palant and threw her to the floor, falling beside her just as a massive explosion shook the passageway. Structures groaned under pressure around them. Halley was up again instantly, trying to shed Bestwick from her mind. She'd died to give them every chance she could, and now they had to grab that chance and wring its neck.

She grabbed Palant and dragged her along, checking movement on her visor, and using her own eyes to pierce the gloom ahead. Tech was great, but it could glitch. She trusted her own eyes more than any computer program.

"This is it," she said, pausing before a small, innocuous door. It was locked shut. A single blast from Palant's sidearm broke the lock, and the door whispered into the wall.

"Huyck, tail," she said, heading into the room. It was small, square, dark, and at its center was a raised platform. On that platform sat something the likes of which Halley had never seen before.

"Okay, so what the fuck is that?" Huyck said.

"Faze," Palant breathed. "Or… maybe part of it. Which means…"

Halley circled the thing, gun aimed. About the size of a human head, and of similar shape, it floated gently above the platform's surface, turning slowly like the smallest world still spinning after its creation. It was a pale blue color… and then dark green… or perhaps pink, those colors not fading in and out, but suggested to Halley's mind each time she blinked, or frowned, or glanced away.

"I don't like it," Halley said.

"It doesn't matter," Palant said. "Maybe *none* of this matters."

"What do you mean?"

"Drukathi," the scientist said. She shook her head, the small phial of nanotech clasped between thumb and forefinger of her left hand. "Yaquita found them in the mind of the android Oscar, and recognized them. Elder Kalakta told me something about them. But this… if the Faze is the hub for controlling the generals, none of what we're doing here might matter. We have no choice. No free will. Everything is the will of the Drukathi."

"But what does that *mean*?" Halley demanded. For a scientist, Palant was speaking in obscure theological riddles.

"We can only do what we can do," Palant said. She circled the floating object.

"So do your thing and let's get the fuck out of here," Huyck said. "I don't like this."

"Nor me," Halley said. "Huyck and I will watch the door." She nodded to Huyck and they retreated to the entrance.

"Boss?"

"Yeah. Weird. Stay sharp."

The passageway outside echoed to the sounds of distant battle. The room behind them was silent.

"Here goes nothing," Palant whispered. Halley looked back in time to see the woman injecting the contents of the phial into that weird, troubling being

She stood back when it was done, and looked to Halley.

"Well?" Halley asked. "We good?"

"One way to find out," Palant said. She closed her eyes, whispered a name to her suit, and spoke loudly and clearly.

"Ready."

3 0

LILIYA

Macbeth, *Sol System*
December 2692 AD

Liliya felt it happening.

As the Xenomorphs closed on her, she sensed the strange, arcane link being established. Her mind opened up to wider potential. Her heart throbbed, heavy and hard, taking her breath away. With Alexander it had been different—the sense of a route from her mind to another, along one long, narrow pathway through which she could reach, and nudge.

This was *limitless*.

Ready, she heard in her inner ear, and in Palant's voice she heard the ghost of doubt.

"There is no doubt," Liliya said.

Maloney's eyes widened, perhaps in fear. Even as the first Xenomorph drew close to her, Liliya started exerting her influence. Her heart pulsed, hotter and hotter. A thought formed deep in her mind—*Destruct… destruct…*—and she pushed it *hard*, shoving, sending it down a billion pathways, a trillion routes.

On the *Pixie*, the automated transmission booster swung into action. Its transmitter started drawing power from the ship's drive. Within milliseconds the warp drive melted down, that strange multi-dimensional knot of nuclear matter and tied dimensions imploding and exploding, releasing a vast wash of energy that caught Liliya's message and blasted it into planes beneath and around space.

"What are you doing?" Maloney demanded. Her eyes were wide, and Liliya could see her gel containment spiraling, whisking, bubbling as her own augmented heart began to boil. She screamed. It was a weak sound, because Maloney should have been dead decades ago. In her final seconds, perhaps her darkened soul began to understand that.

"There... is... no... doubt," Liliya said again. The prompt she sent felt strong and undeniable, because it came from her own heart and what the Tanns had made of it, and her heart was strong. Modeled on the object they had taken from the android Oscar, the alterations had only been minor. She shouldn't have been surprised that even a heart as old as hers, one filled with passion and certainty, contained so much potential power.

Maloney was screeching, a high-pitched sound. Behind her, the Xenomorph queen turned her head and stared at Liliya, perhaps sensing her own imminent demise. Perhaps welcoming it.

Born as an android, died as a human being, she thought. She sensed the *Pixie* beginning to burn, still sending the signal from her superheated heart. She felt the shred of the Faze used as the control hub for all the Rage generals.

Destruct, she pushed. *Destruct*.

For her final moment of existence, Liliya knew the Faze.

3 1

GERARD MARSHALL

Drophole Beta 12, beyond Sol System
December 2692 AD

Forgive me for what I have to do, Gerard Marshall thought.
He wasn't sure who he was asking. He believed in no
gods, and the Thirteen were lost to him now.

Evidence of the Rage's victory had pulsed through
drophole Beta 12, and he had immediately cut off the ship
from further communications. No one could know they
were there. This had always appeared a dead ship, and
that appearance had to remain, for as long as it took to do
what needed to be done.

He'd expected resistance from Lucianne and
Rodriguez. He'd even prepared himself for that, slipping
a sidearm into his belt when they weren't looking. They
were soldiers, true, but he knew how they regarded him.
One of the Thirteen. A corrupt man given power, and
using that power to make others do his bidding.

I'm not even sure who I am anymore, he thought as he
stared at the holo screen one more time. Perhaps facing
what he was about to do winnowed him down to his

basic self. Not the greedy man who regarded Weyland-Yutani as the be-all, the end-all. Not the power-hungry member of the Council, who would do anything to guard and protect his position.

A human being. Sad that he had never loved, Marshall felt regret piling in around him. But regret was for the weak, and he was not weak. He could not be weak. What he had to do required strength of mind and true conviction, and as he turned away from the screen he saw the two marines staring at him wide-eyed.

"We'll help," Lucianne said. Rodriguez nodded.

"You just decided that?" Marshall asked.

"Yeah."

"And if you'd decided the other way? That what we're doing here is wrong?"

"You'd be dead by now."

Marshall smiled. Then laughed. In the end, the fate of five hundred years of progress, across the Human Sphere, rested in the hands of two Colonial Marines. That didn't excuse him from taking responsibility for the decision, though.

"Maybe it'll be… for the best," Lucianne said.

"Really?" Marshall asked.

Neither of them replied.

He glanced back at the holo screen one more time. The nuke signatures still bloomed all across Sol System. Ten at least, perhaps more, and none of them resembled the traces of any human nukes. These were Rage weapons, massive and deadly. Two appeared among Jupiter's moons, one a billion miles north of Neptune's orbital plane, three scattered through the asteroid belt, others huddled around Mars and the settlements and bases there.

There were four traces close to Earth.

"Keep watch," Marshall said. "Any more signatures, anything else that might indicate what's happened, let me know. I'm starting the procedure."

Lucianne and Rodriguez nodded and remained by the derelict ship's comms station.

At the center of the room, Marshall braced himself against the control station. In the short time they'd been waiting there, he'd stared at this small unit and wondered that something so innocuous could contain so much power. The Thirteen had always recognized that a failsafe for the dropholes was required. Such a vast network was essential for human growth, but it was also a gift to any invading force.

Many considered Weyland-Yutani arrogant and power-crazed, blinded to reality by their constant craving for more knowledge, more power. Yet though there were elements of that in the Thirteen's structure, there were also wise women and men who ran the Company. They knew that human history had to be taken into consideration when projecting forward into the future, and history was filled with tales of invasion and conquest.

In the overall scheme of history, they had only been traveling into space for a short span of time, and warp travel had been possible for an even shorter period. Over several centuries they had still only expanded into a tiny percentage of the galaxy's vast space, and of the area covered they had explored perhaps one percent of one percent of its countless worlds.

Even in that short time they had encountered the deadly Xenomorphs and Yautja, the enigmatic Arcturians, and other forms of non-sentient species. What the future held, no one knew. It had to be assumed that eventually their continuous expansion would bring them into contact with a race that might seek to subdue, dominate, or even destroy humanity.

That was the reason for the *Phoenix*.

It was a great irony that the crisis that had caused him

to come here at last had originated with humankind.

Marshall accessed the main control hub. He entered the first of a series of activation codes, and the device started to hum. He felt like a god, playing his fingers across the Human Sphere and touching on perhaps their greatest creations, the dropholes that folded space and time. At the same time he felt like a demon, toying with the lives of billions.

"Anything more?" he asked.

"Nothing," Lucianne said.

"Keep listening."

"No, she means nothing," Rodriguez said. "No chatter, no errant signals. The whole of Sol System has gone quiet. No one's transmitting. It's just… gone."

Marshall only paused for a moment. Then he continued entering a series of codes. Some were retained in his suit. One was written on a piece of obsidian he wore around his neck, a decorative pendant on which sixteen letters, numbers, and symbols were encoded.

The final series of digits was one he simply remembered. He entered all but the last three digits.

"Anything?" When the soldiers didn't reply he looked back at them, and they both started at him with wide, frightened eyes.

"It's all gone quiet," Lucianne whispered.

"We have to stop this now," Marshall said. "You know that. You understand. Whatever they've done, we can't let them spread everywhere." He was trying to convince himself as much as them. They nodded in agreement. He felt himself nodding in response.

Gerard Marshall entered the final three digits that would enable him to send human endeavors back four centuries. He whispered the numbers as he programmed them in.

"Four… two… six."

The control hub glowed a deep red, and a virtual button appeared beneath his hand.

Without giving himself time for fear or doubt, or even a moment more to contemplate what this would mean for so many people, he pressed the button.

The hub whispered, then fell silent. It was as if nothing had changed.

In truth, everything had.

3 2

SURVIVORS

Macbeth, *Sol System*
December 2692 AD

Behind the chaos of war, while the Yautja warriors took on Xenomorphs hand to hand, and the indies expended their depleted ammunition into the hordes of attacking monsters, Jiango Tann heard Isa Palant speak.

"Ready!"

He turned to his wife and took her hand. For their final seconds of life they looked into each other's eyes, with no need to speak, only to smile. They'd had a long, loving life together, losing a son, gaining deeper love. Compared to many people they were very, very lucky.

The explosion punched air from his lungs and shattered his senses, and the last thing Jiango Tann thought was, *I'm still holding her hand.*

Isa Palant expected to die. The strange creature, the Faze, seemed to pulse and glow, and she knew that Liliya was playing her part. Then came the explosion. She closed her eyes to welcome oblivion, and in the split second before the world started to spin she realized that just as she'd closed them, the Faze had vanished.

Something hit her, hard. She grunted. Battered from every side, she curled into a ball to try to protect herself, hands laced behind her head. The combat suit hardened to absorb some of the impacts, but it couldn't take them all.

I'm not dead yet, she thought. Confused. Concerned. If their plan had worked, Liliya would have destructed, along with the rest of the generals, and that should have destroyed *Macbeth*, blasting it to shreds, to atoms. *Or maybe I am dead.*

She opened her eyes just as a bulkhead rushed to meet her. Grabbing on, she swung around and slammed into the wall, back first. Across the small room, Halley and Huyck were hanging onto each other, arms hooked through pipes running down the wall.

Between them on the low platform, the Faze had vanished. There was no sign that it had ever been there at all.

"Saved itself," Palant whispered, and that made her think of the Drukathi.

"What's happened?" Huyck asked.

"We're alive, that's what," Halley said. The Major accessed suit sensors and projected them onto all three suits.

"Fucking hell," Huyck said.

Palant could only echo his sentiment.

The *Macbeth* was gone. Their suit holos showed a schematic of the ship, and it was perhaps one-sixth the size that it had been before. Much of what remained had changed. The ship was missing its bow and large central holds, and all that remained was the rear two hundred yards.

"It ejected its drive core," Halley said.

"Or maybe the Faze did that to save itself," Palant said.

"Ware!" Halley called. "Tann! Anyone?"

Static.

"If we survived, stands to reason some of the nasties did, too," Huyck said.

"So it's not over yet," Halley said. "Check your weapons. We've got to get off this floating coffin."

"On what?" Huyck asked.

"Check your suit screen."

Palant checked as well. Flickering in and out of focus as the *Macbeth*'s detached stern spun away from the radiation-hot cloud of the main ship's destruction, three splinters seemed to be following them.

"Wreckage?" Palant asked.

"Yautja ships," Halley said. "Come on. Let's see if anyone else is left."

As Huyck pushed off from the wall and approached the exit, Halley and Palant aimed their weapons. Huyck nodded a slow countdown from three, then activated the door.

The darkness beyond was immediately filled with movement. Hashori appeared in the doorway, wounded in a dozen places and minus her battle helmet, spear deformed and melted from contact with Xenomorph blood.

Palant's datapad crackled as it translated her words.

"More humans survived," she said. "They're harder than we think."

"You better fucking believe it," Halley said.

Behind Hashori, Palant saw the Tanns and two of the indies.

"Hoot?" she asked.

"Hoot's dead," Ware said as she shoved past Hashori to enter the room. "Killed in the blast. Two of the Yautja bought it, too, and the hallways are still crawling with Xenomorphs. They seem... confused. But no less dangerous. Looks like the android did it."

"Looks like she did," Palant said. She felt a twinge of sadness, knowing that Liliya had gone, and a measure of respect for her sacrifice.

"There are more Yautja incoming," Halley said.

"Good," Robo said. "I wanna get off this piece of shit."

"Me too," Halley said, "but we've got some cleaning up to do first."

"Hang on," Palant said. "We need to know for sure. Hashori, can you ask one of the ships what's happened?"

While Hashori communicated with the Yautja ships circling the ruined *Macbeth*, the humans huddled into the room, silent and shocked. The possibility that they'd truly succeeded was tantalizing, but without confirmation, none of them felt like celebrating.

Hashori spoke.

"*Macbeth* exploded and ejected the stern section we're on now," Hashori said. "It contains the ship's warp drive, and little else."

"Good," Halley said. "That means—"

"More news from elsewhere," Hashori interrupted. "Massive explosions across the system. Other Rage ships being destroyed. The generals have self-destructed."

Despite everything—the violence, the losses, the dead friends and slaughtered settlements—Palant broke into a smile. Her expression was mirrored all across the room. Even Hashori's face changed a little, eyes closing and mouth hanging slack.

"She really did it," Halley said.

"So what about us?" Jiango Tann asked.

"What do you mean?" Robo said. "We're heroes! I'll start writing the songs right now."

"No way," Ware said. "I've heard your singing."

"We haven't finished yet," Halley said. She looked to

Palant, then back at the Tanns. "You know what I mean."

"You mean the Company," Palant said. "They'd like nothing more than to get their hands on what's left of this ship. The warp drive, developed by the Faze. The surviving Xenomorphs. Who knows what else."

"Yeah," Halley said.

"Let's take off and nuke it to fuck," Huyck said.

"I'm not sure that's our choice," Palant said, looking to Hashori. The datapad had been translating their conversation for the Yautja, and now she tilted her head and spoke.

"The Yautja will retain *Macbeth*'s remains," she said.

"No," Halley said. She didn't raise her gun, and neither did anyone else, but there was a ripple of something passing through the room. A tension, a potential. Palant didn't like it one bit.

"We can't stop them," she said. "Even if we wanted to. Akoko, do you really want to carry on fighting?"

Halley sighed heavily.

"What about you?" Yvette Tann asked.

"I'm going with her," Palant said, looking to Hashori. "I think... I hope... there'll be room for you two, if you'd like to come."

"Come where?" Jiango asked.

"I don't know," Palant said. "That's what makes it exciting."

"There'll be Xenomorphs left behind," Palant said. "All across the Human Sphere, even if the Rage is dead and gone, their soldiers will still be there."

"Leaderless now," Huyck said.

"Just sitting there, waiting to be found," Ware said.

"That'll keep the Company occupied for years to come," Jiango said.

Palant sighed. "I don't like the sound of that."

"Me neither," Halley said. "But... me and Huyck, we're Marines. We'd best go back and face the music."

"After all you've done?" Jiango asked.

"I was a Marine once," Ware said, surprising them all. "Doesn't mean you have to stay one. Me and Robo, we've lost two crew. And our ship, as it happens."

Halley raised an eyebrow and looked at Huyck. He shrugged. Maybe the time wasn't yet right for such a decision, but the offer was there.

"Let's talk," the Snow Dog said to Ware, and she smiled.

"So what about the Faze?" Jiango asked.

"The Faze has gone," Palant said, looking at the empty pedestal at the room's center. "Maybe it did what it intended. Maybe we'll see it again. Either way, I'm not sure we can do anything about it."

Hashori took command of a Yautja ship, and reported the unthinkable. Soon after, the Tanns and Palant sat close together, trying to comprehend the enormity of what had happened. The implications were more staggering than they ever could have imagined. The dropholes had deactivated. All across the Human Sphere, those vast structures hung dead in space, like the corpses of living beings. And like corpses, their demise could never be reversed. Palant thought of those people on Weaver's World, assaulted and massacred by the Rage, now left to fight whatever remaining Xenomorphs still haunted their planet. Perhaps it would take months, or even years. They were alone.

She thought about the Titan ships, even now building new dropholes at the far reaches of the Human Sphere, and how they were trapped five hundred light years from home. They would never return. Perhaps those brave pioneers would die out there, or maybe they would settle on a planet or asteroid, start again.

Human civilization had gone from a single, widespread entity to many smaller pieces, parts of the same whole that had nevertheless been ripped asunder. Some would survive, and perhaps grow in new, distinct ways. Others would die.

All the while, the Xenomorphs would be waiting. Leaderless again, directionless, they were still as deadly as ever before.

"So many people," Tann said. "So far away."

"Humanity's been pushed back centuries," Palant said.

"No," Yvette said, smiling. "I don't think so. That sounds so negative. I think, in truth, humanity has been given a fresh start."

Hashori said something from her seat, and Palant's datapad crackled as it translated. She already knew what it would say. She was becoming very good at understanding Yautja, and in time she believed she could become fluent. She had plenty of time.

"The dropholes might be gone," Hashori said, "but the Yautja have some of their own, as well as many other secrets."

"And you'd show us?" Palant asked.

"Perhaps." Hashori stared from the viewing port for some time before speaking again. "Every Yautja makes one pilgrimage to our home world during their adult life. Perhaps my time is now."

"How far?" Palant asked. "How long?"

"Far. Long." Hashori uttered something that might have been a laugh. For now, she said no more. Palant hoped that, given time, she and the Tanns would come to understand some of those secrets.

ACKNOWLEDGEMENTS

Thanks to everyone at Titan who has helped me through The Rage War, especially Steve Saffel, Natalie Laverick, Lydia Gittins, Katharine Carroll, and Chris Young.

ABOUT THE AUTHOR

TIM LEBBON is a *New York Times*-bestselling writer from South Wales. He's had more than thirty novels published to date, as well as hundreds of novellas and short stories. His latest novel is the thriller *The Family Man*, and other recent releases include *The Hunt*, *The Silence*, *Coldbrook*, *Alien: Out of the Shadows*, and *The Rage War* trilogy.

He has won four British Fantasy Awards, a Bram Stoker Award, and a Scribe Award, and has been a finalist for World Fantasy, International Horror Guild, and Shirley Jackson awards. Future novels include the *Relics* trilogy from Titan Books.

A movie of his story *Pay the Ghost*, starring Nicolas Cage, was released in 2015, and several other projects are in development for television and the big screen.

Find out more about Tim at his website
www.timlebbon.net